BISON
BOOKS

The Scent of Distant Family

A NOVEL

sid sibo

University of Nebraska Press
Lincoln

The University of Nebraska Press is part of a land-grant institution with campuses and programs on the past, present, and
future homelands of the Pawnee, Ponca, Otoe-Missouria, Omaha,
Dakota, Lakota, Kaw, Cheyenne, and Arapaho Peoples, as well as
those of the relocated Ho-Chunk, Sac and Fox, and Iowa Peoples.

Library of Congress Cataloging-in-Publication Data
Names: sibo, sid, author.
Title: The scent of distant family: a novel / sid sibo.
Description: Lincoln: University of Nebraska Press, 2024.
Identifiers: LCCN 2024002481
ISBN 9781496240279 (paperback)
ISBN 9781496241252 (epub)
ISBN 9781496241269 (pdf)
Subjects: BISAC: FICTION / Animals | FICTION / Westerns |
LCGFT: Novels.
Classification: LCC PS3619.I26 S34 2024 | DDC 813/.6—dc23/
eng/20240212
LC record available at https://lccn.loc.gov/2024002481

Designed and set in Arno Pro by K. Andresen

*Dedicated to my parents
and to all the animal family,
past-present-future*

The Scent of Distant Family

Nikki

Nik Delaney checks the phone number again as she steps away from Charlie's exam room and back to the clinic's waiting area. She used to ignore any numbers not in her contacts list, but now any call could be the one. She leans against the wall to steady her legs. The phone is pressed hard against her ear, her free hand over her other ear trying to mitigate the clinic's whirring lights and noisy machines. She didn't choose to be the family matriarch. Mothers protect their families, and she is failing. Someone pushing a yellow mop bucket on wheels just misses her feet, and she closes her eyes. Mothers keep families together. The recorded phone voice reports another Zolo sighting. She had assured the nervous shelter dog his adopter would keep him safe.

She isn't used to being wrong. But this time, she'd been so wrong. Hope beats her up, but it keeps her heart beating. Fast.

She leans toward the receptionist, interrupting someone else trying to check in. "Stacy—I'm sorry. I have to do something, but I'll get someone over here to collect Dad. About an hour, right?"

The receptionist has time for half a nod. Nik wheels and gallops down the hall, her winter boots heavy and awkward, people staring. As she pushes against the too-slow automatic doors, she remembers—no car. She and her dad rode the commuter bus up from Moon Valley. More cussing and more finger tapping on the phone even as her long legs, in bright patterned leggings, carry her across the parking lot toward the street. Her nephew, Finn, is home from college with his girlfriend. They were supposed to get together after Charlie's appointment. Staring at the phone doesn't make a text appear. They were backcountry skiing so are probably still out of service.

Exasperated, she calls her brother instead. When Phelan fails to answer, she doesn't bother with a message. He's five blocks away.

She skids across hard ice and mounds of crusty plowed snow, her breath sharp and frigid in the back of her throat. Half the parked cars gleam in the diffuse light, and the rest slink against the curb under frozen dirt coatings. She tries not to touch any, despite the treacherous footing—a car alarm would send her heart into convulsions. When she reaches the lot where her brother's Range Rover reflects a brilliant silver, like the oh-so-distinguished hair now on his temples, she pauses, leaning against the fence to civilize her breathing. Her amped legs, however, do not let her rest.

She pushes through the glass front door, bare hands smudging the crisp letters of the International Resort Development Corporation, and in four long strides, she faces his closed inner office. A raised voice carries through and echoes off the ridges carved into his door's redwood landscape. Not *his* raised voice. So—Phelan will appreciate the interruption. She's already leaning on the handle as she knocks, curt and loud.

"Sorry to barge in." Nik glances at the person who's voice she'd heard, but she sees nothing, her whole attention on the mission. "I need to borrow your car. And I need you to be at the hospital in a half-hour to pick Dad up. You can't be late. You know how he'll get."

Phelan's eyes cut toward his client. Now Nik is conscious that the raised voice was a woman's. A large-boned young woman in heavy canvas coveralls. Unusual. Not someone her brother, in his mint-green button-down and corduroy casual suit jacket, should have any trouble handling.

"Nik, what are you talking about?" Phelan angles his body so he doesn't dismiss either of the women but also doesn't include them in the same conversation.

"Bart totaled my car last night, so I brought Dad up on the bus. But I just got an urgent call from a guy over to Yahanna who's sure he's seen Zolo. I've got to go check it out." Her voice starts strong but fades at the end. Committed but unsure.

Phelan holds one finger up toward the other woman. He doesn't introduce her. He runs his finger down his appointments for the day, and he's shaking his head. "Nik, I can't make the bus back to Dad's. I've got a late meeting today. Can you rent a car? I'll run you out to the airport to get one." Again he glances at his waiting client.

"A half-hour in the wrong direction." Her face heats up, the run here leaving her too steamed for the suffocating room. "Reschedule." The power is back in her voice, and though Phelan is older and used to getting his way with his lucrative career, she pushes the single-word command through her chapped lips without considering it negotiable.

When the silent creature in canvas speaks up to negotiate, Nik startles like a doe on the side of a highway.

"Phelan—can I butt in?" Voice calm now, she leans toward his appointment book. "Since we've agreed to meet again first thing tomorrow," she smiles a slow smile, picking up a pen and writing her name above the first appointment, "I could maybe help out?"

Nik can't deal with slow right now, not even in a smile. "I need a car. I need to spend some time looking around Yahanna. I don't have any idea how long it will take."

"I have a truck, if that works. I live outside Yahanna. Hell, drop me at home while you look, I don't care. So long as I get back here for our meeting," she turns to Phelan, "at eight o'clock tomorrow."

Nik would have been taken aback, in the days when she only answered calls from numbers she knew. Today, though, she hesitates less than a second. "Okay. Finn and Kiran should be able to pick Dad up and bring him over to the condo. I'll send him a message."

"Finn's in town? I didn't realize." Phelan pauses, but something flashes across his eyes. Maybe he catches her urgency. "Where will you stay? Nothing'll be open over there in February."

The woman in the wheat-colored coat responds, faster now.

"I own a dude ranch, remember? She can stay in her choice of rooms. And I have food too. To fuel whatever search is underway." She tips a flat-brimmed, low-crowned western hat onto her forehead and sweeps an arm toward the door. "Name's Jaye. Truck's open."

Charlie

Once upon this ground now called Wyoming—

In his head, Charlie starts the story like he always did when Finn was a little kid and they sat together in the pediatrician's office, staring at swirling patterns in a linoleum floor, racing each other to find images of fantastic creatures who lived here long ago. He pays no attention to sounds from the corridor, door left slightly open when Nikki and the nurse deposited him here, nor to the fluorescent lights buzzing overhead.

—saber-toothed cats weighing twenty-five pounds preyed on the twelve-inch-tall "dawn horse." Can anyone imagine, actually, fifty-five million years ago? The Eocene. He pictures Finn's dark face lit from inside with excitement, mouth open in wonder, teeth bright like newborn Charolais calves.

Charlie always found a cat, and today is no exception. Long dagger teeth lead him upward to the round eyes and short ears he still loves. White paper on the exam table rustles, loud, under him. What he wants to hear, though, are the voices of all those mother elk outside the clinic window. Double-paned glass, a pain in the ear. In his memory, he can hear them. Comparing notes, like mothers everywhere.

When Finn got to junior high, he informed Charlie that dingoes arrived in Australia only three to five thousand years ago. Wild dogs actually began here on the North American continent back when saber-toothed cats were chasing Eohippus around. Charlie prefers cats, but his daughter loves dogs, and Finn takes after her, even though he's not her kid. Finn felt bad for the scared white-and-black hound at the shelter, convinced Nikki to foster him. In their snowy yard, the hound wouldn't play, not until Charlie played his fiddle, and the dog sang along, and Nikki laughed and a tail wagged and life was good. For a little while.

Charlie doubts his nurse knows when horses disappeared from North America or that the largest saber-toothed cat could take down young woolly mammoths, many times bigger. These aren't the kinds of questions anyone here bothers to ask him. Their damn tests find what they want to find. He'll challenge any of these doctors to an evolution pop quiz. The things having a curious grandkid can teach a guy.

He perches on the edge of the exam table. His feet tap, not happy with their location on the treaded footrest. His pale, waffled long johns are bunched up, and he shifts. He can't remember the name of Nikki's hound. Everything changes. The best parts about coming to the clinic are the elk outside the silent window, their blond butts a shade away from pissed-on snow. He squints to sort the young ones from the adults, the antlered ones from the mothers.

Charlie's eyes aren't what they used to be. Used to be he could see the tiny mole in the small of his wife's back. Maggie loves imitating the elk mothers' soft birdcalls. He loves hearing that sound—sounds like: *family*—and watching calves bump into their mothers when their legs get ahead of them. He hasn't been to a high summer meadow, full of calves and wildflowers, for a while now. He didn't know, when he was there last, that it was going to be the last time. Last time they came to Teewinot, Nikki parked where they could listen to the elk cows chatting. Little birdcalls coming from an animal the size of a modern horse.

"Hi Gramps—have the doctors forgotten about you in here?"

Charlie's back straightens. Why is Finn here? He feels awkward with the cotton gown draped over his shoulders and his only grandson at the door. Things started going backward at some point, but he never heard that point slip up on him.

Finn doesn't wait for an answer. "Aunt Nik had to leave for a while. When we get done here, you can come to Dad's with me. We can pop some corn. Sound like a deal?"

Popcorn blows like drifts, and saber-toothed cat tracks disappear, erased by a high desert wind.

"Buttered?" Charlie looks up, hopeful. Finn likes buttered popcorn, though Nikki tries to convince everyone to eat it dry. Buttered popcorn is the color of pissed-on snow, where tender elk sing to jostling calves, almost adults already.

Zolo

The opened gate disappears behind him, and his legs stretch over snow, over sagebrush. Hundreds of green velvet hands stroke his sides, and steel stems spur his flanks, urging speed. His passage frees the plant's scent, and it rises with him into the air like a flying dream. His ears pulse up and down with every leaping stride, dark raven wings. He can do anything. He is free.

Without noticing at first, he races westward. The direction the open gate faced. But he registers, as he runs, absence of houses, absence of loud stinking highway. As he runs, something else. He isn't running *away*. To the west, thick mountains mass, something pulls him. Someone. To the west, he points an eager nose.

Juniper flashes past his cheeks, flat lizard-scaled leaves spreading rich stink of cat. His mouth opens and tongue surges. Wide sage plains split with narrow waterway's slash. He descends, weight shifting to haunches, bent hocks. Even in tight closed buds, sugared–soda pop smell of cottonwood leaves can't hide from his nose. He remembers little kids—sticky source of dropped morsels, like berry bushes.

Ice holds water in creek bottom, but Zolo smells motion, slight lift of water's live heat under solid skin. He skids across, claws scrabbling as speed sends him into spin. He chases his tail, dark blotches against background white like cottonwood trunk against snowy bank. Joy fills him, buoyant; it spills him, legs in air, smooth white coat sliding across white smooth ice.

He flips upright, front end low on elbows, nose over toes. Hidden water wants to play. Plays hidden music. His tail waves, left, right. Waving water touches ice, then troughs roll low, as if mouse scuttles over twigs, under grass. His eyes follow motion. Muscles gather, electric, he leaps. Again his ears spread, holding him in sky until strong earth calls. Legs straight, body arched, he plummets.

Ice rocks legs shoulders hips backbone skull. Rock hard conviction points him west again. Mass of mountains, gravitational. He lifts his nose, and world floats around him, waves of toothy cats, ancestral dogs. A fiddle calls, plaintive, through bare bitterbrush twigs, and live heat of noodles in mushroom broth, buttered toast, wafts into memory. His stomach growls. He climbs back onto cream-covered prairie. Velvet hands wave him forward. In a ground-eating lope, he moves—hungry—through the world's gathered smells.

Jaye

Spontaneity, she thinks: not the trademark of western ranchers. Jaye often changes up stereotypes, but not on purpose. She thwarts expectations, but only because other people's habits are not her own. Inviting a lovely lady into her truck would not seem out of character to those who know her.

She doesn't have a clue what to say to Phelan's sister, however, so she drives the old Dodge like it takes her full attention—pulling the steering wheel hand over hand, triple-checking mirrors. She can let Nik start the conversation. Horses have taught her this much. Don't show nervousness, or you'll face eleven hundred–pounds of nervous reflection trying to run you over. She rests one hand on the round top of the floor stick shift, rough from puppy teeth. Considers the traffic. Tries not to consider what to make of Nik Delaney in her truck. As her ex would say, that's one well-put-together woman.

Nik's feet look trapped on the Dodge's cluttered floorboards, and her legs jiggle in place as if she's running past the southward sprawl of the town's car dealerships and brew pubs. Not sounding any too confident herself, she finally starts the conversation. "So, Jaye of the unlocked truck, do you go by one name, like Bono? In the wide world of Yahanna, probably not a lot of Jayes around."

In Jaye's opinion, the curiosity sounds forced. "Nope, out of 380 people, I'm it." Nik's dismissiveness about Yahanna, on the other hand, seems genuine. Through the not-so-tight seal of a rattling window, Jaye smells diesel and fermented rye mash. She maneuvers among tourist traffic, drivers who flick on their blinkers only after braking for turns. Her pickup lurches and jerks, like her thoughts, but it carries enough dents and dings that drivers of sporty rentals grant her a respectful distance.

Her anxious passenger pushes on. "Born and raised Yahannian?"

Her ears hear scorn, her fingers tap on the wheel. "Fourth generation Moon Valley. Folks got divorced and sold out. I moved over the mountains two years ago." Jaye's eyes flicker toward Nik but return to the highway. Traffic thins, and the lanes drop to one in either direction.

Nik pushes her hair behind her ears. "Moon Valley's where we come from. Who do you belong to?"

"Myself."

Nik's legs jiggle harder. "Sorry. I always hate that question, even though both my parents were raised in the valley."

Jaye knows what she means. She feeds her a crumb. "Hawkins. Crescent M Ranch, under the Pinnacles."

"Did I go to school with an older brother?"

Jaye snorts. "No doubt. There's four of 'em." Unlike most of Moon Valley, her family isn't Mormon, but they had kids as if they were.

"And you're all in Yahanna now? Still ranching?" Nik's jiggling legs shuffle the pile of dirty mail into static behind the conversation, words that seem more about maintaining personal distance than bringing people together.

Jaye's eyes are drawn to a classic herd of Herefords in cross-fenced pastures. The ranch they're passing is part of a conservation trust. Most commercial ventures can be managed in higher density than cattle, but other commerce in Teewinot appreciates the western look of a ranch at the town's borders. Jaye wonders about the Delaney family, but the siblings are enough older than she is that she can't place a connection. Her own family seems happy to have gotten away from the valley and all the work ranching entailed. "Nope. Just me."

Development diminishes, like Nik's questions, as the pavement rolls. Still unsure, Jaye lets her lead the conversation. If she were more strategic, she could pry for useful information. Nik's legs agitate the air. Her pursed lips are darkened with some no doubt cleverly named color, in deep contrast against her winter-white face.

The Dodge swings through the roundabout, and they aim toward the Astorian River's mountain headwaters, passing several bighorn sheep resting on high sandstone outcrops. She can be every bit as hardheaded as a wild ram. Among the wildly wealthy, like Phelan's usual clients, however, she fears a more subtle kind of game. Nik might provide some clues about what lies ahead.

Nik's heels finally lower to the floorboards. She exhales. "So what brought 'Just You' to Phelan's office this morning?"

"Hell if I know." The swing to animosity is vestigial, a reaction to the earlier argument. "The man calls me 'on behalf of a client' with something to discuss. I get all the way over here, and his schedule's changed."

Nik shakes her head, tries to smooth things over. "Cell service in the canyons. Probably his secretary couldn't get through to let you know."

Jaye stays silent.

She persists. "Did he mention what the client's interest is?"

Jaye would like to hear what Nik needs to find in Yahanna. But her own dilemma seeps out her pores, like oil from an Oklahoma hillside. "He said the client's excited about new business ideas I'm trying to put in play." She hopes her eagerness isn't audible.

"Like, someone wants to invest?"

Jaye nods, while her focus stays on the canyon's icy curves.

"Well, that's kinda backward, isn't it? Entrepreneurs usually have to beat the streets."

Jaye shoots her a glance. "You have your own business?"

"I was a wildlife biologist, and nonprofits court money endlessly."

"Begging's not my thing." Her canvas coveralls scratch a disquieting noise against the seat back.

Though the truck continues, the discussion stalls. Maybe Nik feels bad about meddling. Or her own concerns couldn't be pushed away any longer. Snow in the shadowed canyon layers upward, leaving the highway a narrow, winding tunnel along the occasionally visible river, its backward ice clinging to the shallow bottom while moving water runs above it, between wide white edges.

Nik shivers.

Jaye notices and swerves the truck into a narrow pull-out. She twists out of her heavy coat and reaches for the knob to turn the fan up on the truck's heat. "Sorry. Left home right after I fed the horses. Overdressed for an office visit."

Nik scrunches into her seat, pulling her legs up to her chest, letting her backbone round against the soft seat cover.

Jaye has no trouble translating her unspoken response. "Overdressed only in the temperature sense of the word, I know." From the dashboard vents, heat coaxes the smell of alfalfa out of her discarded coat. "Do I get to ask the questions now?" Her face turns toward the driver's side window. She notes a moose furrow plowed down the steep slope to the river.

"It wasn't an interrogation." Nik's voice holds a ten-year-old's peevishness. "I was just trying to get acquainted."

Jaye's lips turn up, slow. Her eyes stay forward, navigating tight curves on tires that bite the road's surface. "So, tell me about this adventure we're on." Deliberate, she includes herself. They are in her truck, after all. "Who is Zolo?"

Feet thud back onto soggy mail. Nik's back straightens. Words trickle out. "Law enforcement brought Zolo in to the animal shelter where Dad and I volunteer. He was chained out at an empty house the previous renters owed money on."

Jaye looks at her, but now Nik's head is turned away. Her fingernails press into the skin of her palm, leaving visible marks.

"A leopard Catahoula, scared of everything."

Jaye keeps her voice light. "So chasing mountain lions or range bulls—not his thing?"

"Not at all. Slinks back against the leash when he sees a rifle. Lies in the snow when he sees cattle. Even though that's what they're bred for."

"He ran away from you?"

Nik's scathing answer rakes Jaye's cheeks. "Woman from Parodice said she'd work with him." She rubs her hand down her arm. "The yard had a solid fence. I approved the adoption, even brought the dog to her. Her car was in the shop, she said. Said she'd get him chipped too. But he got loose first day there."

In the shadow of Nik's anger, Jaye stumbles forward. "When was that? It's a ways from Parodice to Yahanna." Thick fingers drag loose strands of hair away from her face.

"A week already. Had two calls earlier. Turns out one dog they had seen was black with white, not the other way around. The other was long-haired, not short-coated. Female and friendly. Jeez. Couldn't get any more opposite."

Jaye snorts. But her words are empathetic. "People want to help."

"Long drive for nothing. Not helpful."

Jaye hears this woman with her expensive clothes rejecting the locals. But exactly the kind of help Phelan gave her today, and Nik tried to excuse him. She pushes out a breath. "At least the latest caller thinks Zolo is still running?" Not found on the side of the road with his eyes pecked out.

"If this guy isn't wrong, Zolo's traveled almost eighty miles already." She leans her head back into the seat.

Jaye goes silent. She watches the mostly buried buck and rail fence flicking past. The snow is too deep for a mountain traverse. Traveling the canyon's highway, though more feasible, is almost certainly deadlier.

As if conjured by her thoughts, a small huddle of ravens and a single eagle ignore the truck's passage, intent on the roadkill and stench that brought them all together. She sees only a rabbit's hind leg, torn free of the carcass. Lifted wings over bright snow won't protect her hitchhiker from seeing the smattering of cinnabar blood.

Nik smears a wet trace down her cheek, though when Jaye glances her way, she fakes an itch.

Even snow covered, the pavement echoes between Jaye's ears. They finally crest out of the mountains, passing Woody's gas station at the Rim, high desert plains on the other side a whole different world. She needs a different conversational angle. "So, your brother has a son?" Could be handy. Parents can always be manipulated by—or through—their kids. Might be good to know more.

"My roommate at U-W was Finn's mom, but she . . . died."

"I'm sorry to hear that." Jaye feels her skin flush pink. "Recently?"

"No, soon after he was born. Twenty-one years ago already."

She hears fresh tension in Nik's voice. Tries to find a way to loosen her. "A good feat, raising a kid on his own."

"Phelan's always been lucky with money. He could afford help, even though he was still a student too." She swallows, and picks at a dried-on mud splash on her knee. She rubs a hand hard across her forehead. "Had nannies later." The words pulse in her tight neck.

Jaye can tell she's gone from bad topic to worse. She switches gears again now that they're past the long climb out of the valley. Recalls another name from Nik's few words in Phelan's office. "And Bart? Is he your son?"

Nik's head jerks up. "How do you know Bart?"

"He totaled your car, you said? Why you need my taxi." She waves at the Dodge's brown hood.

"My husband." Nik pauses, then a surprising grin. "Of his father's Fogarty Property Management Services, based in Teewinot. Bart and I invested in a new branch in Moon Valley. 'The Reliable People.'" A choked laugh lurches out. "He borrowed my car last night because the county Mounties already know his custom Camaro too well. And the smell of his breath."

Jeezus. Strike three. Jaye should be out of the game. But she takes a chance on that grin, keeps going. "I take it you've seen him in light the advertising team has not."

"Bart said to get Zolo adopted before I got any more attached. That sure backfired."

Jaye watches her, attention now on the endless snow, speckles of sage poking out. She feels Nik's eyes swelling with her need to see. "Any distinguishing characteristics?"

Her hand waves across the landscape. "He looks like all of that. White with grayish patches, Ice-blue eyes."

More miles, more silence. Jaye wonders if Nik's attachment is as much to being the savior as it is to the one she might save. A biologist stuck in Moon Valley, apparently in charge of eldercare, no longer part of the urgency of wildlife populations dwindling to nothing.

The Scent of Distant Family

Across the wide swells of landscape, they point out to each other the emergent shapes of mule deer, in groups from six to sixty. Antelope are even easier to spot, their shade of brown more red than the sage or the deer and closer to the colors of sunset, which spreads already, a whip at her heels. She drives faster, eyes scanning.

Muffled, a song snippet rings from Nik's pocket. She fumbles her phone out. "Finn—is everything okay with your gramps?" She presses the thin rectangle into the far side of her head. "Oh good. Thank you. I'm so glad you were home."

Jaye's eyes flick toward her, but Nik doesn't notice. She's turned toward the mountains, stretching in a long south-reaching line beyond the Rim as the truck continues away from the sun.

The graying day gnaws at Jaye's earlier excitement, adrenaline dump swallowed, chased by a bitter pill of distrust. She hears Nik's voice, but words go gray too, overwhelmed by echoes from Phelan's lame excuses. No, she doesn't beg, but if someone wants to invest? Venture capital. Shit. What does she know? Progressive thinkers could have found out about her efforts. Her hopes for the new ranch. Crazy new ways. Someone has to try something different. Something regenerative. The buzz of the day, and hopefully of the future.

"Of course I promise not to tell your dad. Crossing all my fingers. Out with the news already."

Jaye risks another quick glance. Nik's shoulder-length haircut hides her face, but then she turns, catches Jaye looking at her.

"Kiran's going to India—a tiger sanctuary? Tell her congrats for me!" An audible swallow. "Interviews for Africa *and* Australia? Yeah, I can see why you're so thrilled."

Jaye has often imagined Australia. A horse loping along under her, grassland scent rising from damp ground where water hides from the sun. Nik turns even further away from her, hunching her shoulders as if pulling a curtain.

"Sure, we can work on mock questions. Don't let it stress you out."

A few more sympathetic sounds, ritual leave-taking. Jaye's right hand scratches absent-mindedly along the knuckles of her left hand, which rests on the steering wheel. She lets silence shroud the space.

"Watch out!" Nik braces one hand against the dash and points with her other.

At a high gallop, a mouse-brown horse with thick black mane leads a small herd across the highway.

Jaye stomps the brake, and the truck fishtails into a halt, sideways across both lanes. Five horses pass in a stream of legs and tails, then swerve as one, like a flock of swallows, to leap over a low spot in the barbed wire ranch fence on the far side.

Jaye hits the gas again, spinning in the direction the horses came from, trying to distract two long-tongued coyotes. She leans on the horn. The truck reverses as the coyotes look between road and horses. A heavy black horse at the back of the herd whirls and stops, head high.

No horses being wintered near here. She's sure of it.

Nik catches her eye, then looks back at the herd. The black horse wheels and races after the rest, who have slowed up, knowing the truck turned their pursuers away.

"Lead mare looks like old Spanish lineage." Jaye muses out loud. "But wild horses are way on the other side of Parodice." Behind the grulla mare, the four others string out, in no apparent panic. They flow across the landscape, a kaleidoscope of manes lifting and falling. "That's the stallion at the back. Classic mustang herd structure."

"Mustangs?"

Jaye just keeps her eyes on them while she straightens the truck around and moves onto the highway's shoulder.

The Scent of Distant Family

"Wouldn't they have a freeze brand?"

"If they've ever been caught at a roundup, yeah. But then they wouldn't still be out here either." The horses drop to a walk, then two of them, nonchalant, dip their heads to the ground and lick at some exposed tips of grass.

"The BLM keeps everything they brand? Even if they don't get them adopted out?"

Jaye nods. "Holding facilities, usually. Land's capacity doesn't keep up with the numbers."

"I never worked anywhere with wild horses. And they aren't officially wildlife. Range managers get to sort that one out." She, too, checks for traffic as the truck eases back onto the highway. "I imagine keeping the peace with ranchers gets tricky."

Jaye comes from rancher stock, but her kind of ranching is a different beast. The idea of capacity, though, flinches the hairs on the back of her neck. Range damage comes from fast-food burgers, human insatiability. Not the horses. Not even the cows. The herd walks and eats and walks, the grace of their strides impossible to ignore, until their movement fades into distance. Jaye breaks the silence inside the cab with a rarely spoken memory. "Last day I saw my grandmother, she climbed aboard her grulla mare, Tess, like that one. Cancer got Grandma the same night. Tough cookies, both of 'em." She puts the Dodge in gear. Not far now.

Nik breathes slow as the truck picks up speed. "In memoriam, then. I'll call her Tess."

The horses dip out of view behind the land's curve. Jaye's mouth a straight line. Nik has no right to name a free horse like that. Even if Tess sounds right. She stares forward, works to keep her voice neutral. "Grandma's Tess was a wild one, for sure. But that day, she took good care of her person."

Finn

The frenzy of microwave popcorn exploding from their kernels slows down, and Finn releases Kiran from his one-armed hug. Points her at the machine's control panel. Keeps one finger crooked through a belt loop, keeps talking.

"We wanted to talk with you about these internships. But Kiran needed to give an answer today, so it's for certain. Her parents are so excited for her."

She gingerly opens the greasy bag, steam rolling across the kitchen and pooling up against the cold windows. No cold where he might be going. But no Kiran either, so no warm. No family meals with her parents teasing him, her kid sister challenging them with random trivia questions. No hot fingertips tickling his palm, tracing his lifeline, tiptoeing toward his amorphous beginning.

"I wanted your input. That's why we came all the way up here."

Charlie laughs at the small blizzard tipping into his lap, Kiran's bowl slipping from her hand. "I'm sorry, I'm sorry," her voice chokes out through Charlie's giggles, his ready joy infectious.

Finn licks his lips. Brushes a drop of popcorn steam off his forehead. He listens to Nik's voice, that songbird chatter it's taken on since she returned to Wyoming. As if her heart always beats too fast, unable to register how her expectations have unspooled. What doesn't change, though: her useless words. Prevarication, that's all he's gotten from her or his father, for years, when it comes to Australia. His mother's homeland.

Finn's eyes flicker to the door, assuring himself Phelan isn't within listening distance. "Well, don't say anything to Dad yet." Australia won't be an approved direction for his internship. Neither is wildlife conservation an approved educational, or vocational, direction. But disappointing his father is only leveling the score. While Phelan has

The Scent of Distant Family

always appreciated the world's natural wonders—frequent excursions to beachside resorts and bird-bejeweled Amazonian canopies from ziplines—doing what it takes to keep all that from disappearing isn't something he's interested in.

Nik's words sparrow away in Finn's ear. Kiran's arms circle around him now, her chin digging into the back of his ski-tired neck, her small breasts a pressure behind his shoulder blades. Poor Nik. Bart again. Basshole. A moose, for Chrissake. Leaving her without a car. Leaving a small orphan in the winter-white, winter-dark woods.

Phelan

The Rover shines chemically blue lights down the canyon as he drops toward Moon Valley with his dad. Nik is the one doctors should examine for brain function. He couldn't make a scene in the office, but what the hell? There's always more dogs. He can't understand her. But he needs to understand Jaye Hawkins, so maybe Nik's little escapade can help him out.

He tries to talk with his dad. "You watching for wily wapiti out here under the cottonwoods? I can't believe the state feeds them this close to such a busy highway. Sure blows the illusion. Everyone will know they aren't as 'wild' as they're made out to be."

Charlie stares intently into the dark. "They can be hard to see in the cottonwoods. But coddled by government handouts or not, when they step into a highway, wrecks get real. No good for anyone, not even someone pulling a semitrailer."

Phelan's foot lifts off the gas, ever so slightly. "Your whole career, you never hit one, did you?"

"Just lucky, I guess."

"You are a lucky guy, true enough. You have a good grandkid." Phelan came home to the dense smell of fake butter and a party he wasn't expected to be part of. "Finn's sweetheart makes good popcorn."

Charlie's voice turns wry. "Sorry they had to get back to school so soon. Leaves you stuck bringing me home, since you insisted on taking away my driver's license."

"Serves me right, I suppose." Phelan tries to joke, but he isn't about to take on that kind of liability. His father likes to complain, but even Finn admits Charlie's driving has gotten erratic, along with his moods.

"Helpful to have a driver *and* a spotter." Charlie is conciliatory tonight. "Still, you could drive a little slower through here."

Phelan has never understood Charlie either. He managed to have fun even when he worked long-haul driving. He insists on living slow and says that's how he makes space in his life—which seems absolutely bass-ackward to Phelan. Most of his vacations have been working vacations, taking Finn along to experience new resorts wherever they spring up. More often than not, his son makes it into the marketing photos.

Charlie spots nothing, says nothing, and they make it to the valley, slowing for what passes as downtown in the village of Dust, where his parents made their home so many years ago. "New sign?" Phelan almost laughs at the sparkling gold letters where the town fathers announce their elevation and unfortunate name.

"Still trying to pretend this is the mother lode." Charlie gives a snort. "Council oughta change the name to Nugget, if that's how they want to be."

"Flour gold, gold dust, same thing. No nuggets in this one-pony town." Phelan drives away from the brief storefront glare, into darkness. Tries to turn his dad to happy thoughts. "But there's silver in the sky. You can always wish on the stars."

The Scent of Distant Family

"I'm not sure which would've been the first out." Charlie's voice holds an unfamiliar uncertainty. "Maybe wishing on the whole skyful works better."

The changing star seasons, another disappearance from a memory no longer to be taken for granted. "What do you need them to do?" Phelan reaches to touch Charlie's hand, clenched in his lap.

Charlie twitches. "Wishing Nikki can get her dog back is all."

Phelan sighs, frustrated by this singular inexplicable obsession that seems to have the whole family under its spell. Out of all the problems in the world, this is what he'll wish for? The Rover rolls over packed snow as the roads get narrower, until they finally pull up to the front of the house. The door at the top of the stairs opens, and a face stares out at them.

"Where's Nik? My hell, it's late. What's going on? I've been trying to call her for a couple hours. I thought they must've gotten held up at the hospital."

"Hold your dump trucks, Bart. Let's get Dad inside first."

Charlie brushes past him on the stairs while the rant continues. "Good thing I ate at the staff meeting." Bart is holding a glass, sloshing tawny liquid onto his fingers.

"Nik got another call about the dog." Phelan touches Charlie on the shoulder and heads into the kitchen, where he rattles pots out of a cupboard.

Charlie stands in front of the pellet stove. "I can't see a fire. I can't hear a fire or smell a fire."

Phelan hears him from the kitchen, but Bart pretends not to. Charlie lowers himself onto the stool, one hand touching a cold cast-iron edge.

Phelan's not letting Bart off that easy. He keeps his voice pleasant. "Nik says you totaled her car. But you got out okay at least."

He opens a can of beans.

"If I totaled her car, I doubt I'd be as okay as this." Bart stretches his arms wide.

"Meaning what?"

"I'd hate to call your sister a liar, but—"

Phelan slams a pot onto the stove. "Because she isn't one."

"Well, I wasn't the one who wrecked that car."

Phelan sees at least one logical problem with this line of thinking. "Nik, too, is perfectly okay. She came by the office to borrow my car."

Charlie must've decided the kitchen would be warmer until the fire got going. He settles on a stool pulled up to the tiled island. Bart speaks in a soothing voice to him, as if Charlie had been the one to slam a pot down. "Nicole is always perfect, isn't she, old man? Her driving, her cooking, her caretaking, her choices. Perfect, perfect. Always."

Phelan ladles warm baked beans into a thick bowl and settles it in front of his father. He pours the rest of the pot into a second bowl and removes two big spoons from the drawer. With a titanic gurgle, the pot descends into the sink full of soapy water. He ignores Nik's poor choice of a husband.

Charlie blows air across the steam rising from his spoon, saying nothing.

Phelan waits. Bartlett Beecher Fogarty the Third—Charlie likes to say the whole thing—won't be able to keep his trap shut.

"I'm the one making a real income here. I need to keep my license. It would be her first wreck. And anyone can hit a moose in the dark."

"Anyone with a gut full of tequila can." Phelan hasn't heard about the moose. That's what it takes for her to finally stand up for herself.

Bart manages to not hear him either. "Nicole was more worried about a little moose than about getting a new car. Not like it has to go to college to learn how to be a moose."

Charlie interrupts. "These beans are good, nice and thick. Nikki never puts brown sugar in hers, even though Maggie's recipe calls for it."

"Do you need anything, Dad? Some milk?" Phelan is done with dinner and the conversation. He stands to pull a glass from the cabinet.

Bartlett Beecher Fogarty the Third pours another whiskey. Neat. "Anyway, there was no wreck. In fact, there is no car." He stands, too, looking out into the milky starlight across the snow.

Phelan doesn't try to make sense of Bart's ramblings. Charlie drinks his milk, and Bart goes to the bedroom, turns on a television.

Charlie points out the window at a jumble of muddy snow, heaped and well tracked. "Nikki won't get any insurance payment for the car."

"Holy shit, he wasn't joking." Phelan whistles. "Property management companies come with a choice of wreck-erasing equipment, don't they?"

2

Nikki

As the horses disappear, Nik refrains from lecturing Jaye on the difference between wild and feral. She returns to squinting at the landscape for a landscape-colored dog. They pass through a small hamlet, a church and bar and a couple blocks of ramshackle houses, with assorted vehicles parked—or stalled out or collapsed—next to each. Nothing but a lack of ambition within. Miles of sage beyond. Deer and antelope pepper the darkening space, and an occasional eagle wings by, looking for mangled carcasses left by oil field traffic.

Nik is more aware than most how unique these mule deer herds are. She remembers the surprises and marvels science can uncover; no one suspected the record-setting length of their seasonal migrations. Gas frackers and developers are required to leave migration corridors alone, even if driving a mindless water truck is the best life someone out here can imagine. But she cringes away from the much-touted marvels of modern medicine and the puzzle Charlie presents. She wishes the doctors would leave them alone.

Finally, Jaye wrestles the steering wheel up her own road, the truck's unweighted back end sliding. The wooden sign for Sage Winds Ranch still looks unweathered. The long driveway to the ranch buildings is plowed, but barely, winded drifts narrowing the two-track. Snow from the next storm will be impossible to move, and according to the Sprucedale station in the truck, more storms are moving in.

Nik sees large corrals where horses sniff through the end of the day's hay. Some have wandered out the far gates into white pastures. Braided stream channels must run through, bare shrubby willows edging irregular courses. A shaggy chunk of black-and-brown dog trots toward them from the lodge's wide front porch. Jaye spins the truck into an about-face before she stops. "Got stuff to do here, but like I said, the truck's all yours. Can you find your way back?"

Nik is surprised to realize she's not at all sure she can. She doesn't know landmarks on this side of the Deheya Range, and unmarked roads head to oil and gas wells, gravel pits, communication towers. Seldom to houses. She sits, silent. When she was a kid, Charlie always drove out here, and she kept the binoculars up to her eyes, watching for birds. If only Zolo sat beside her, she'd feel more confident. Of course, if he sat beside her, she'd have no reason to be here. Her logic is as lost as the dog.

Jaye, at the opened passenger door, tugs open the glove box and spreads a map out in the air. She points at a blue-inked circle. "You Are Here." She grins. "Should have cell service in this driveway, but elsewhere it gets spotty. You might want to call your reporting party and see if he has any road numbers or maybe what direction your dog was headed."

Nik pushes past her and circles the truck, erratic wind gusting at her, blowing hair in her mouth. She slides behind the wheel.

"You can drive a stick shift, right?"

Doubt in Jaye's voice gives Nik momentum. "Yes, thank you." Her voice cuts cold as the disappearing day, sun behind the mountains, though the air holds dispersed light. "No need to wait up. Where should I go if I get in late?"

The Scent of Distant Family

Jaye glances at the mountains and shakes her head. "Take a left at the front door, go past the room full of couches, first bedroom in the hall will work." Jaye touches the front of her hat, almost a salute. Maybe simply *Good luck*.

Nik has both her hands on the dirt-sticky steering wheel as she faces the emptiness ahead. She gives a reckless nod and clenches her teeth as she lurches off. What did she expect? A guided tour? When they met, this odd woman with her work clothes and fields full of horses was arguing with her brother. She drove a virtual stranger all the way here and is willing to loan out her truck into the trackless evening, on a goose chase after a dog she doesn't know.

When Nik reaches the ranch sign, she calms down enough to drop the truck into neutral and calls the guy with the latest Zolo sighting. He picks up, eager to describe what he saw. When she tells him, as best she can from the map, where she is, he gives her suggestions for which road numbers he thinks are being plowed. A smart dog would stay on the plowed routes, save some energy. She feels a surge of possibility and thanks him. "I wish you the best," he says. "But I'm down to Salt Lake for a few weeks. Won't be around to help watch for him."

She jiggles the stick until it finds first gear and rolls forward. Coming off the Rim, the land felt like one long descent but at closer inspection reveals itself to be comprised of endless swales and waves of hills, some mounded, some flat topped. Like the ancient sea that rocked here in the days of dinosaurs, the land carries movement in it. The truck's radio signal shatters into nonsense, and she gives up on the company of human voices. The roads lull her with straight sections, then surprise her with sharp corners and hairpin curves. After a while, she isn't sure if she might have missed a numbered junction—or two?—while she was pumping the brakes and trying to stay on her side of the narrow way. Her hopeful feeling drifts and thins like gas fumes in the air.

Watching for road quirks and road numbers is hard enough in the low clouds that flatten the gray light to an even dullness, but she is looking for a white-and-black dog too. She thinks of the companies that make camo winter wear for those guys who can't enjoy being outside without a rifle in their arms. Coyote hunters.

Loose dogs seen in the backcountry can be shot without question, just like coyotes and foxes. Dogs run wild game, stressing them ever closer to starvation. Sometimes they kill outright too, especially if they run in packs. Zolo's adopter, Tara, didn't say if his rainbow collar was still on him when he got loose. It might save him, if a hunter decides to take pity on someone's pet. Or it could catch in the brush and trap him somewhere he'll never be seen again. She reaches the top of a swale, and wind shakes the heavy truck. She kicks it out of gear and pulls the emergency brake on. Heat pours toward her from the dash. She lets it soak into her face while the wind shudders outside. A Catahoula has such short hair.

The mountain shadow and the overcast erased her ability to judge time, but now she realizes night is fully here. Only the reflective snow keeps the landscape within her range of vision. Her forehead falls to the steering wheel. She stays motionless long enough to feel its imprint on her skin. She is such a sucker for what someone else thinks she needs to do—the video of her memory shows Finn's face when he first saw Zolo online, his immediate insistence that they bring him to Dust, help him gain confidence. Finn's confidence in her disrupts her hopelessness, and she slides out of the truck. The wind slams the door behind her. Jaye must think she's stupid to imagine she'll see much in the dark.

She bends to the ground, using the headlights to examine the crust for signs of animal passage. She is in luck. The many hooves of a deer herd show up, breaking through. At 120 pounds, she weighs about the same as a doe in good fall condition. And though she only has two feet to spread the weight between, her rubber-bottomed boots are wider than a cloven hoof. She follows the tracks off the top of the swale, and in the blue light, she sees no sign of her own feet's passage.

Finn's mother was so young, had traveled so far from home. Nik was the same inexperienced age and couldn't anticipate the day when that wordless infant would find so many ways to ask about his missing mother. She tried to do the right thing. Maybe she was wrong then too.

Wildlife will travel high, where the snow is blown low. But they will bed down low, where the wind scuds away well overhead. She walks back to the truck and climbs in. She drops into low gear to ride down the swale without touching the brakes and pops into neutral, leaving the heat on while she steps outside again. The snow here is easily a foot deeper than on the ridge, and she peers through the dark, up the ephemeral drainage and down, seeking the shape of anything sleeping under the big sage or, warmer yet, beneath any willow brush supported by underground moisture. Nothing.

She turns to trudge back to the truck, and a gray flicker crosses the headlights. Tall ears shine black in the bright. Even though Zolo's black ears flop down along his white cheeks, her stomach leaps at the movement. The critter leaps too, long hind legs pushing off. Finn's phone call has conditioned her brain, making foreign animals not just possible but likely. The lights and shadows conspire to convince her she sees a wallaby. As it beelines right for her, she starts laughing. Jackrabbit. Of course.

At her human sounds, the big rabbit veers away and in two more jumps disappears entirely. She wonders at the strangeness of this world for an Australian exchange student like Finn's mother, Robyn, or for a shelter dog like Zolo. Will he eat jackrabbits ? Surely the Game & Fish people will forgive a dog for that. Ranchers used to have huge rabbit drives to corral all the jacks they could find and flog them to death—intent on saving every last sprig of grass for their cattle or sheep and frugal enough not to waste bullets. Nik wonders if that practice stopped because ranchers, like a lot of people, are more ecologically attuned these days or if the number of rabbits simply never recovered from such devastation.

Against the wind, she pushes the door open and clambers in, but instead of driving anywhere else, she rests. She turns off the headlights. She wishes for coffee, and just the thought of that fresh-ground smell brings saliva to her mouth. The coffee is an illusion, but she pulls a water bottle from her shoulder bag and twists off the lid. Methodical, she takes a sip, breathes, and repeats, thinking about Zolo. If she had as many people helping her as used to take part in rabbit drives, she could map out a grid to find the dog. Alone, what were her chances? What were his?

Vibrating with the running engine, the map slides off the bench seat onto the floor. She longs for a big blue X marking the spot where her treasure could be found. Her blue-eyed darling. Truly her foster failure, not because he stayed with her but because she let him go. After that first routine call to check on his adoption, Tara refused to return messages. Even though a lump of bile rose in her throat when she heard he was missing, Nik had been excruciatingly polite. Tara didn't echo the effort.

She wrenches the lid back on the bottle and chucks it onto the passenger side. She'd tried a few times to find Robyn's family. Those phone calls had been equally unproductive. Though she'd successfully found traces of several species almost lost to science, hunting people was clearly not her strong suit. Driving out of the snowy creek, squinting into the dark blankness, she misses a gear and grinds her way to the top, then she smashes her foot on the gas and the truck fishtails along the straightaway.

Anger and driving, not a good combination. Right. It's not even her truck. Her foot eases up, and she exhales, tears leaking down her face, her breath shaky. Not even her dog. But—her promise. Finding him the right home was her responsibility. Finding him a safe home, his forever home, as they say in the shelter business. Finn has his forever home, and yet curiosity leans him toward Australia. Nik feels her family scattering. In the starless night, Zolo is homeless, and she is adrift, with just the bulk of the mountain range to maintain her bearings. Well, partially. She considers the curves and the corners she might have lost track of, and while she knows she's not going east or west, she can't even say for certain anymore if she's going north or south.

She can't say for certain if Zolo is moving north or south either, though continuing west over the mountains seems the least likely. If he really came this far, if the report is even accurate, rather than merely hopeful. The man on the phone didn't sound loco. Her waterworks wear down. She sighs, pushes her sleeve against her nose, and drives, unable to see much beyond her headlights. She's run across less than a handful of ranches, and she's peered into every pool of light shed by every building and gas flare. The binoculars in the glove box have been handy but unproductive.

Stopping seems like a bad idea. But driving seems little better, and she sure can't drive and read the map in the dark. She finds another bare spot on the top of a ridge, though she can't tell if a plow cleared the pull-out or if the wind did. Enough—Charlie would tell her this searching is a waste. He doesn't like waste. She turns off the engine and fumbles on the floor for the fallen map. She doesn't usually need reading glasses, but maps are the worst, and in the weak cab light, she narrows her eyes, feels the skin wrinkling at their edges. Road numbers seem to have shrunk over the years. She feels herself shrinking too, down and down some more, smaller in the black night without the mountains than she was in their shadow. Her once purposeful self, pointless as her dog chase. She shivers.

The whole day collapses in on her, and weariness layers thick on her bones. She is ready to beg. She tries her phone, but Jaye was right. No service. No surprise. No help. She takes a few slow sips of water. She screws the bottle top on securely, no wasting. Leaning her back against the dashboard, she tips the bench seat toward her without getting out in the cold. Behind the seat, like any good rancher, Jaye keeps a neatly folded blanket and an extra wool hat and gloves. Nik would cheer if she had the energy. She cocoons into her new gear, bunching clean rags under her cheek where it rests against the passenger door. Grateful, her eyes close, and she tries to keep sadness on the far side of her eyelids.

Her mother's voice, singing, drifts past her. *When the dog bites, when the bee stings, when I'm feeling sad . . . .* Zolo never bit anyone, but everyone imagined he was just about to. Dogs and people both bite when scared. Nik was the only volunteer willing to take him out for walks. Finn reminded her that Zolo just needed someone to care about him. She built his trust over time, running forest trails together, trying not to tangle in the retractable leash.

She remembers her surge of joy the first time he pounced on a ball she rolled toward him in the fenced backyard. He's playing!

She wanted to shout it but didn't dare ruin the moment. She called Charlie outside. As instructed, he resumed playing the fiddle he'd been messing with inside. She wanted Zolo to know everyone was having fun. At the sound, Zolo stopped running around, ignored the ball, cocked his head. He tipped his nose high and howled along with the fiddle. She copied him, not a full-on howl but wordless sounds to match the music she knew well. He kept it up a long time, but finally Charlie quit, laughter shaking his fiddle. She fell in the old grass, and Zolo flopped beside her, not quite touching. Under the autumn calls of nutcrackers, Zolo's chin rested on the ground, his eyes closed. His breath blew warm across her ear. She let her breath sift past his nose, let him take the scent of her into his lungs.

He never cared to fetch, but he liked to grab the Nerf ball and play keep-away, tail high and wagging. Same as with people, you can see a real grin in the eyes. When she first met Robyn, the grin in her dark eyes lit her whole face. Finn has her eyes, without question. Zolo's eyes crystal blue, brown eyebrows accenting his white face. She knows her face is whiter than usual, even without looking. Cold, yes, lost—yes. In a place without any people, she locks herself in the cab. Because if a person did turn up out here, what kind of person would he be? And would she be able to tell?

She completely misjudged Tara. The day she handed Zolo off is branded on her memory. Zolo sitting bolt upright the whole way to Parodice, his eyes catching every raven winging overhead. His tail thumped against the seat when she sang, trying for upbeat tunes. The ache in her chest rose to her throat as they got close, and she dropped into silence.

The aching night surrounds Nik now but not with silence. Wind greets the sage gently, but the solid barrier of Jaye's truck creates an angry whistle. Tara had greeted them at the door of a little redbrick house. She let Zolo come to her without crowding him. She offered him a biscuit, let him chew it on the carpet, leaving slobbery crumbs behind. They stepped to the yard, tidy wooden uprights fencing a neat plot with shallow snow. Zolo checked his new boundaries with his nose. Deferring to the husband who followed her back to Dust, Nik discounted her own raw need. The only dog her father ever liked had become the companion her husband no longer was. Afraid she was being selfish to want Zolo for herself, Nik chose to trust this woman.

Zolo pays, night after night, for her mistake.

She wriggles lower in the truck but doesn't open her eyes. If the moon wasn't hiding and her eyes were open, she could see her breath right now. The blanket isn't warm enough. She layers the blanket over the hat, then pulls it back below her ears. If Zolo approaches the truck, whimpering for company, she wants to be ready. Even with Jaye's thick gloves on, she tucks her hands between her bent knees, trying to get warm.

She worked with Zolo, knowing she needed to find him a home with someone else. That was the deal. Bart insisted she was too busy taking care of Charlie to keep a dog. Bart insisted Zolo couldn't sleep in their bedroom, so he made his way from Charlie's floor up onto his bed. Zolo carries no extra weight to hold him over until he's found. She can't bear him thinking he's been abandoned. She tucks her chin and breathes warm air under the blanket. In her imagination, she spreads the wool over both of them, and they share each other's heat.

A low growl penetrates the cab's metal walls. She lets the blanket drop as she sits upright and pushes the hat away from her ears. In the dark, her eyes are uselessly wide open. Another, longer growl . . .

is followed by a flicker of orange light in the distance. The ground carries the reverberation of an approaching diesel truck.

Jaye

In front of the hay barn, she parks the tractor and rests the plow blade on packed snow. The driveway is ready for the incoming storm, and under the barn's floodlight, horses chew hay and chase each other in the pasture. "Polenta, jump." The mountain dog hops off the tractor onto a snow berm and stands on it, overlooking her spread. Jaye surveys the scene, too, her head still spinning with the possibilities an investor could bring, though wary of an unsought gift. But Wyoming banks have proven suspicious of "progressive" ideas. Ecology of leadership, high desert permaculture, horse therapy. So many ideas in the world, and she knows they can work here. Commodity prices increase inversely to their commonness, and nothing's increasing in rarity as fast as nothingness. Wyoming's open space is a good investment. But business start-ups are notoriously . . . unstable. Sage Winds fits that pattern.

She clambers down, and several cats curl around the legs of her coveralls. They know it's their turn next. Cat food emerges from a metal trash can. Jaye shakes kibble into bowls balanced in the stack of bales, scratches each of them behind their ears. Even the small weight of a cat adds to the pressure for success. Failure isn't just selling off a bunch of equipment or an empty building. She might be single, but all these critters count on her. This is their home.

She kicks snow off her boots at the side entry hall and hangs her coat from a deer antler. Polenta pushes past and heads for her bed in the living room. Jaye hasn't even got the water turned on in the kettle before her phone is ringing. Selina.

"¿Cómo estás? Chores done for the night?"

She sets the kettle on the stove, louder than she intended. "Just got in. How's the land of the friendly ghost?" She waits for the gas to light up before she turns toward the jar of tea.

"I'd rather be in Cheyenne. Ten degrees warmer than Casper right now, and the wind's slower by ten miles an hour."

"And . . . the husband's cooked dinner and done the dishes and folded the laundry."

"You sound bitter. What's up with that?"

"Hungry?" Jaye spoons tea into the steeping ball.

"Me? Oh—you. Yes, you always get cranky when your blood sugar's low. Maybe you could hire a cook."

Jaye would love to have the funds for that. "Did this call have a purpose?"

"See what I mean?"

"As usual, I have no idea why you're so mean." Jaye sees her own half-grin reflecting off the windowpane, the night outside stormy dark even without snowflakes. She'd much rather see Selina's face, even though a frown is what she hears.

"Quit. Just quit."

Selina's voice shows her thinning patience, but Jaye only pauses long enough to haul in a quick breath. "What you always wanted, isn't it? If I'd just leave the crazy ranch thing behind . . . ." Old arguments. Tired arguments, but still not put to bed.

"Jaye, dammit. You are on a roll. I assume your conversation this afternoon didn't go well."

"Wrong assumption. It didn't go at all. Delaney couldn't talk. He'd forgotten about another appointment." Boiling water sizzles over the silver tea ball, and steam curls above her mug like a beckoning finger.

"Or wouldn't talk. Maybe he's stringing you along for some reason." A silent pause. "So, are you going back?"

"Tomorrow morning at eight." Her chapped lips burn on the tea, and she grimaces.

"Convenient. So you leave at five thirty."

"Feed horses at five. Yup. And feed Delaney's sister breakfast at four thirty, I suppose. If she ever brings my truck home." Jaye feels a tiny satisfaction as she sinks into the soft rocking chair. Nik's urgent need, her own quick offer to help. Sleep would be helpful.

"His sister? How the hell did that happen? And where did she take your truck? To the bar?"

Jaye knows she only imagines jealousy. "Hah, could well be. Sure don't know how she'd be looking for a lost dog this time of day." Selina would be grateful if she found someone.

"Okay, I'm not sure how much that explains, and since you'll just say I gave up my right to know, I won't ask." A pause. "But I can tell, okay? So I'll tell ya again, good luck with tomorrow's discussion. Or negotiation. However it turns out."

Jaye knows she's being a shit, but a part of her enjoys shooting arrows at her ex. She pushes that small part into the hole it crawled out of. "Mighty kind of you. I'll bring some throat lozenges, so I'll be well lubricated." She has no idea how to talk to investors. She just knows she better not screw it up.

"Better grease than the Waterin' Hole, no doubt. I'd best go slave over my story, since that's what they pay me for. Let me know how it goes. Buenos noches, sweetie."

"Nos vemos." Jaye presses her mug hard against her upper lip. The small pain fails to cancel the skepticism she hears echoing between Selina's words. She walks in halls of power and shakes her head at Jaye's naïveté.

She sighs and flips open the file folder she pulled out of the truck before letting Nik drive off with it. What resort developer would take a chance on a place as remote as this? As purposefully remote—and likely to stay that way. Her ideas don't show any income, nothing to lure someone to approach her.

Three times she re-sketches potential layouts before she sets the cold tea on the floor. Stretching, she paces to the dark windows and wills her truck to pull into the drive. She plunks herself on the floor next to her dog, picks up the brush from its usual spot, and gets to work. Polenta's tongue hangs over her pink gums as she stares into space. The brush eases through long hair, smoothing out snow mats and removing the occasional stem of straw. Jaye tries not to wonder if Nik is lost. Tries not to wonder how she'll get to Phelan's office if Nik doesn't make it back in time.

Nikki

She shrinks lower in the truck. Maybe the smart thing to do is pretend no one is in here. She might be able to curl into a ball on the floor of the passenger side, covered with the blanket. She isn't in the roadway, after all. No one pays plow drivers to check on stranded motorists, who could be drug dealers parked in out-of-the-way locations. If she plowed roads, she sure wouldn't be stopping. She'd just get on the radio—they must be equipped with radios—and call in a deputy.

The rumble increases in volume until it's less doglike and more *Tyrannosaurus rex*. The truck shudders, and so does she, knees trembling as she folds herself over the soggy mail, hanging onto the wool blanket like Linus. She fusses in the dark, checking to be sure all of her is hidden.

Her breath is shallow. She forces herself to suck in more air, so she'll have a good supply if she does need to be still. She hopes the driver is going too fast, climbing the slick incline, to stop at the top. She thinks about that radio call for a deputy. The plow gears down for the final approach up the hill. She knows its headlights have to be picking up the Dodge's metal by now. Even squished together, her legs shiver, and her arms, wrapped around them, can't stop either. She thinks of all those stories about unsavory law enforcement officers, or even people pretending. She probably wouldn't open her door for the law either.

She hears the plow's engine ease up. This is a minor summit. The driver should change gears and let it fly on the downhill side. A good theory maybe but not happening. The plow stops. The rumbling stops, too, though the growl remains.

She gulps air. Please, just call dispatch with the plate number. Call Jaye, get her to come out with a deputy. Then she'd feel safe.

"Hallo? Anyone in there? Everything all right?" Footsteps crunch through the snow, and a man approaches.

He has a strong flashlight, and through the blanket, Nik can tell he's aiming it at the windows. Hopefully, he'll make a cursory visit—quick check, due diligence and all that.

He's at the truck now, knocking on the window. "Hallo?"

The light is more intense, and Nik fears her trembling limbs will betray her. He knocks on the passenger side. "Anyone home? Holy shit, what's that?" He jiggles the door, and she feels her backbone rocking.

The locked door gives way, opening so fast both of them are taken by surprise. Nik's legs and arms fly upward, and she grabs the stick to keep from rolling out the door. The plow driver steps back so fast he trips on his feet and lands in the windblown snow, cussing and scrambling to get upright again.

"What the—?"

Nik flings the blanket off her now, needing her eyes—if not to feel safe, at least to feel like she'll know which way to run. But half-sprawled on the ground, a large man, made larger with layers of winter gear, blocks her exit. She crabs herself farther into the truck, until her back is against the locked driver's side door. Her breath rushes in and out like she's been practicing sprints.

"Who the hell are you? Are you stoned or what?" The man stands upright now. He takes a step away from the door, cautiously, so he can keep his eyes on her as she moves to the other side.

She wants to pull the door closed and start the truck and hit the gas. No way a heavy plow would keep up with her. But she knows she won't win a wrestling match with this guy. Despite his age-weathered face, he's six feet, easy, and built like a bear. And he's mistaking her for a kid.

"I asked you a question. Or aren't you trained well enough to respond when elders speak to you?" His hand hovers by his hip.

She can't see a gun anywhere. But he looks like he'd feel more comfortable if he had one. "No." She can't spit anything else out at the moment. The refrain—*No is a complete sentence*—repeats behind her forehead.

"No, you haven't been trained? Or no you aren't stoned?" Now he's bending his knees a little to get a better look at her in the dome light.

Too many questions. "I was just tired. I've been looking for a lost dog." She tries to make her voice deeper, less girlish.

"In the dark? You better come up with a better story than that."

That pisses her off. "I haven't got a better answer because it's the truth. I'd rather limit my search to the distance covered by these headlights than not search at all." Her voice reverts to normal, and her anxiety leaks into it, building to a high, choked—angry—sob.

The big man picks the discarded blanket out of the snow and sets it on the edge of the passenger seat. "Why are you in Jaye's truck?"

"Why didn't you tell me you know Jaye?" Her body uncurls. She hardly knows Jaye herself, but relief smooths her breathing.

"Shit. You thought you were scared? I saw a body under a blanket on the floorboards of a friend's truck. How freaked out do you think I was?"

Her words tumble out through strangled laughter now. "She's working with my brother. And my husband wrecked my car."

"And I doubted you about looking for a dog? Either I'm getting old, or none of your stories makes sense." He flicks a single long braid over his shoulder and reaches a hand into the cab. He holds on to her glove for an extra couple of seconds, studying her face. "Name's Russell."

"My name's Nik."

"Tell me about this dog then." He holds the edge of the door, still open.

"Skinny hound, mostly white. Super-short coat, bright-blue eyes. I had a call he'd been spotted." Her voice settles again, less girl and more mature woman at least, as she makes her business clear. Nonchalant, she reaches for the water bottle. It is a better weapon than nothing.

"Where was he lost from? I haven't seen anything. But not many animals who don't hole up and cover their ears when this thing comes their way." He points a thumb at the plow.

She is grateful he doesn't mention her own behavior. "Parodice. Six days ago."

He whistles. "Pretty steady traveling, if true. I imagine you're done being tired now. I can let you get back at it. You people from Parodice." His head shakes as he turns away. "Scared the bejeezus outta me."

She calls out before the door slams closed. "I'm not from Parodice." Like it matters.

He faces her again. Then he walks around to her side and motions for her to roll down the window. "You as lost as your dog?"

"How'd you know?" She presses her back into the seat, hoping this door doesn't have a weak latch. She takes a sip from her water bottle.

He points at the wrinkled map sticking out under her legs. "I can drive ahead and lead you to civilization if you want. Was just cutting back drifts anyway."

Another pulse of relief washes through her arms. She extracts the map and folds it down in her lap. "It was too hard to keep track of all the road numbers and watch for the dog too." Another sip. "At least for me." She sticks her arm out the window and gestures into the darkness. "Can you get me to Sage Winds?"

"The roads shop is past Yahanna, so you're in luck."

She gives him a thumbs-up. He lumbers aboard his plow. In her headlights, his braid sparks with gray streaks.

The adrenaline rush woke her up, for sure, but now she's drained, and even without the effort of trying to track where she is, by the time he pulls up Jaye's ranch road, her arms are limp and her head thick. Too bad Jaye spent the night bucketing the driveway wider— Russell could have used the plow rig on it. He has no trouble getting through and turned around. When Nik slides out, though, he turns the plow off.

She stands below his open door. "Don't you have to get back to the shop?"

"I do but not this very second." He swings out and down to the ground, agile for someone as big as he is. "I radioed Jaye while we were driving. Figured she'd be up worrying about you. She invited me in for a snack. If you'd care to join us." He waves toward the door, where Jaye stands dark against the house light.

Her voice streams across the cold air. "Well, c'mon in. You must need sustenance by now."

Nik looks back and forth between the two of them. Jaye has a two-way radio? Her legs remember how to work.

Russell kicks back in an easy chair, Jaye's dog already stretched out on the fire-colored circle of rug where his big boots settle.

Jaye delivers soup to two small end tables. "Squash and red pepper, if not too spicy for you. Figured the heat might be welcome."

Corn nuts rustle in Nik's coat pocket. She sinks into a rocking chair next to the second bowl. "Kind of you," she murmurs, rising steam washing her face but doing nothing to erase her over-tired confusion. The first spoonful releases a sharp burst of eager saliva.

Russell savors each sip and pauses in between to stroke the sleeping dog. "Good stuff. Glad you were still up."

Nik watches him, letting the puree slide down her throat, hoping it can burn off the residual humiliation, curious about their relationship.

Russell smiles, spoon in the air. "No one else likes my nocturnal schedule much." He points with the spoon. "A fellow insomniac."

Jaye sits down with her mug of tea. "When I was looking for someone to talk with guests about local wildlife, a friend mentioned Russell. He brought a little saw-whet owl along, and they became instant celebrities."

He nods at an antlered rabbit mount on Jaye's bookshelf. "Teach people about jackalopes too."

Straight-faced, Nik answers. "It's almost breeding season, isn't it? Good time to see 'em strutting on stolen sage grouse leks, showing off." She doesn't know where the energy for a joke comes from, but Russell's burst of laughter rewards her effort.

"Yeah, I keep telling Jaye that February's a great time to bring tourists to Yahanna."

Nails click against wooden floor, pulling Nik's attention to the dog, still flat and sideways, dreaming of a day's labor chasing magpies. "How'd you come by a saw-whet?"

Russell puts a hand on Polenta's long-haired back, without waking her. "Came to me as a nestling, after a windstorm knocked over the home cottonwood. My wife and grandkids kept her supplied with grasshoppers. Didn't seem she'd be fit for the wild, after being with us, so Game & Fish gave me an education permit."

Nik watches the dog dreaming. An owl must be good company for a plow driver. "Do you ever come over to Moon Valley? My father would love to meet her. And you, of course. He'd want to thank you for rescuing me, I imagine."

"You'd have made it here fine come daylight. Or found your way to Fossil or Sprucedale and a toasty motel."

Jaye speaks up. "Oh, but I have an early-morning appointment."

"Right." Nik's face heats. She looks around and finds the clock, worked into an old draft horse collar hung on the barnwood wall. "Not long 'til we need to be leaving, is it?" The futility of her night's quest crashes against her ribcage. With Charlie at home, she can't stay away longer.

"No rush. Relax and eat. Nothing like a good ole all-nighter to sharpen the brain." Jaye leans back. She's on her home turf.

"My brain's soft as the soup." Nik's head feels frayed. She listens, distracted, to a blurred litany of names—people, animals?—they both know and whatever each of them are up to. No one requires her to pay attention. When they're done eating, Jaye rises to clear the bowls. Nik stays in her chair, feeling out of sorts.

Jaye comes back with a ledger, neatly sketched drawings in several colors of pencil. "What do you think? If this investor really has capital to sink into the place, I figured I better have some options to present." Before the ledger is placed in Russell's lap, Nik sees a north arrow pointing to the top right corner.

He hunches over the pages, studying layouts, comparing what he sees with the legend to sort out what she has in mind. "Ah, greenhouse. Good location. Near the compost, not far from winter's manure pile. Mm-hmm."

"Can I get you two some tea?" Jaye spins toward the kitchen before either of them answers.

Nik feels the despair of her day dragging her deeper into the rocking chair. While Russell is focused on the careful pages, Polenta slides her belly along the floor, moving closer.

"Here you go." Jaye sets the tea down but doesn't sit down herself. Russell looks up, ready to offer another comment, but again Jaye disappears, leaving only a small swirl of cool air and dog hair behind.

Polenta wriggles a little closer. Now the dog is within reaching distance, and she puts both paws on one of Nik's feet.

Russell starts to share an observation but pauses. "This is interesting." His finger sits on a green circle on the page she can't really see. "Humph. So is that." Tilting his head at Polenta, he turns back to the drawings without explaining either of his thoughts.

Jaye enters the room, carrying an armful of clothes on their hangers. "I suppose showing up smelling like horses doesn't look so professional either. Nik, any advice?"

Nik tries to focus her attention on the collection of western shirts and their pearl snaps. Through her own thick socks, she feels Polenta's slight pressure. "Bright and bold maybe. Purple and russet together? Looks confident, don't you think?" What she thinks is Jaye looks nervous. Despite her earlier posturing.

Jaye won't settle for one expert opinion. "Russell?" She hefts the plaid that Nik suggested and waves it through the flickering light from the woodstove.

"These drawings show him what he needs to see." He lifts the ledger, still open, with both hands. "I like the smell of horses." Then he closes the ledger, carefully, looking from Nik back to Jaye. "What do you two think about a card game?"

"Are you kidding?" Nik looks at his wide smile and knows he isn't.

"Heck, yeah. Why not? It's already after two." Jaye drapes the shirts over an unused chair and strides to the bookshelf to choose a deck.

Nik can see they've done this before.

Russell swings the end table around by Nik so she doesn't have to move. "Wouldn't want to disturb the dog. We can join the two of you here."

But the dog is disturbed. Polenta sits up, and now she rests her chin on Nik's thigh, eyes examining her face.

The dog's voiceless question rustles like ripples on a reedy shoreline as Jaye shuffles slick red cards. Wolves know when an elk or a caribou in a herd is unwell. Dogs, too, can sense something wrong. Nik flips through the possibilities. Her father, brain waves scrambled. His need for her. That could be it. Her marriage, fast losing traction on black ice. Or Zolo, poor southern-bred hound.

"Your turn, sleepy."

"Sorry." She pretends to study her hand. Soft fur and a solid jawbone settle on her forearm. She reaches for another card. She feels Russell's eyes on her but doesn't look up. Jaye draws next.

The game flows around her, cards laying down and drawing up. This motion, too, feels wavelike, small sounds of gathering and receding. The dog doesn't return to her rug, even as Nik leans forward or settles back to wait for the next move. A wet nose continues to push at her. To nudge toward something she's not seeing.

"You're not bad at this, for someone who's half-asleep." Russell shuffles this time, after a Nik win.

"We played a lot when we were kids." Cards slap on the table's smooth surface.

"I only learned to play after I moved here." Jaye sips at her tea and leaves her cards until they've all been dealt.

"These younger generations." Russell gives Nik a conspiratorial wink, shaking his head with mock disappointment.

Nik pictures her brother when they were young, green eyes dancing as he bluffed his way through game after game. Polenta sighs. Nik lays down cards and picks them up, unseeing. Time condenses, and three generations of Delaney menfolk play cards at her mother's kitchen table, her mother's humming nowhere to be heard.

Polenta sits up, lifts her head. Nik feels, instead, the weight of a secret she and Phelan share. One they haven't discussed since Robyn's baby, smelling of mashed bananas and talc, was left motherless. Forever after, Phelan acting as if a stork delivered his son to him.

"Beginner's luck, then. My game." Jaye rises, stretching, as she gathers their cards together.

Nik rubs her eyes, then adjusts her focal length to check the time. "Almost made it through the night. You going to be okay to drive?"

"No problem. Let me get a pot of coffee going, though, because Russell's going to need it. Here, shuffle up one more game."

Russell spreads his wide hand on the table, then pops a knuckle. "I'm going to need it? Shit, I get to go home and sleep."

But she's already off to the kitchen, already jittery without a drop of caffeine in her.

Russell gets up and stretches, too, pulling one arm with the other to loosen his shoulders. "Don't see her like this very often."

Nik assumes he's talking about Jaye, but when she looks up to respond, his eyes are on Polenta. The dog leans against her hip, eyes half-closed. Nik pushes her memories away, pushes the dog to her feet. Even invisible, some burdens are too heavy. "Maybe another game is more than enough." She steps toward the dark windows, wanting the feel of cold glass on her forehead.

He yells toward the kitchen. "Got a travel mug I can borrow?" Then he faces Nik. "I'll keep my eyes out for your dog. How do I get hold of you if I hear anything?"

Nik stands, too, and extracts her wallet from the same pocket where the corn nuts are stashed. She extends the bright-yellow package first. "A token of my gratitude?"

"Don't mind if I do. Nothing like a good crunch to set off a creamy soup. And to keep a driver awake."

She flips out a green-and-white business card and hands that to him as well.

"Webmaster, eh? For the Forest Circus. Who woulda thought?"

"I know. No logging boots, no fire line boots, no cowboy boots. Just the computer screen and me. But I work from home, so I can help my dad." She doesn't mention her previous life—traipsing through spruce-fir forests or buttery grasslands, collecting data to design protections for vulnerable animals. Now she can't protect a single hound.

"Good for you, then. I'll find an excuse to bring a little owl over to your side o' the mountains and meet him. He raised a daughter of persistence." Russell turns to accept the mug from Jaye. "Keep your truck between the snowbanks and outta the rivers, okay?"

"That's the plan. And thank you."

Nik notes Jaye's head tilt in her direction. Her face flushes like fireweed leaves. She knows Jaye's more grateful for the return of her truck than for its temporary driver.

Russell swings off into the night. The diesel fires up, and the big yellow equipment rolls back to the road, blue and amber lights flashing, Nik's pulse following their rhythm. The satisfaction, the usefulness, the solitude. It is possible to envy a plow driver.

Jaye shows her to the kitchen, oversized for feeding summer guests and updated with stainless steel shining crisp on all the counters. They fix their own mugs of coffee. Jaye drinks hers straight black. Nik adds real cream, a needed comfort. Like ocean salt brings small wounds sharply to a person's attention, the night has opened the scab over her self-doubts. The possibility that good intentions aren't enough.

They stand sipping in the kitchen while Nik tells a shortened version of her attempt to rest on the side of the road. "Did you get any sleep before Russell called?"

"I had lots to do, like I said. So no, hadn't gotten that far." Jaye points down the hallway. "You could shower if you want before it's time to leave."

Hot water has energy to share. Nik's legs are heavy. "What about you?"

"I'll run out and get the nags fed." She smiles, but her topaz eyes don't brighten. Nik watches the surface of her coffee shiver, as if blown by an anxious inner wind.

Jaye

Dawn is still far east across the high desert when they slide into the truck. Today Polenta perches between them, dodging the stick as Jaye shifts into reverse to pull around and face the road. "Got everything?"

"I didn't bring anything." Nik swishes coffee around her mouth. "My teeth feel shaggy." She hugs Polenta's hairiness close. "I can't stop thinking how Catahoula coats are so short."

"I'm sorry." Jaye keeps her eyes on the snowy road. "I wish you could have found him and brought him home." It's the time of day when wildlife move between the hills and the water, and they're almost impossible to see until too late. She keeps spare toothbrushes for guests but never thought to offer Nik one.

"Maybe I'll get more calls. My number's on all the shelter's posters anyway, since Tara doesn't have a functional vehicle."

Jaye doesn't mention that Nik doesn't have one either, but her passenger seems too tired at the moment to catch this problem. Since Nik's phone is also out of juice, she wouldn't be getting any calls today that she can't, in fact, drive somewhere to check out.

A fuzzy mitten covers an involuntary yawn. "Or maybe someone will say something to Russell."

Russell seldom bumps into people. Jaye checks the gas gauge. She needs to stop anyway. They can get the word out at Woody's.

Nik pushes herself more upright in the seat, leans away from the untrustworthy door, toward the dog. "Help me look, okay?" She leans her head on Polenta's head.

"Can do. Go ahead and sleep." Jaye doesn't know if the request is to her or to her oddly mesmerized dog.

"No way." Nik's mouth stretches open. "But who knew how exhausting it is not seeing what you hope to see?"

Agreeable, Polenta keeps her eyes open, sitting upright to support Nik's sagging. When Jaye approaches the plowed lot at Rim Rendezvous, she slacks off the accelerator. She turns in with a gentle swerve. "I always fill up here. Hate to see this guy have to close down."

Nik slides to the ground. Jaye runs the nozzle and watches Nik scan the gentle curves of hills, the edge of mountains dark with trees. Lean and lithe, this strange woman arches her spine backward, then bends forward to spread her palms onto the tip of her boots. Jaye takes a deep, cold breath.

Wind careens over her cheeks, traveling from far across the high sage—nothing between here and the state's invisible southern border to slow it down. Nothing but Phelan's poor scheduling to keep her from an investor's charmed touch on her dreams. Someone else believes in what she's trying to do, in this place considered a cultural backwater. The wind is as frigid as one would expect at seven thousand feet in February. Like always, she taps the nozzle twice on the top of her gas tank before replacing it.

They head inside, and the bell on the door jangles. "Hello?" Woody's voice. But no Woody.

"Hey yourself. Where are you?" Her head swivels.

"Hawkins, that you? Behind the counter. Can you come back here a minute?"

He is sprawled upside down through a trap door into the crawl space. Since he has no hips to hang a belt on, his worn jeans are pulling away from zebra-striped boxers.

"Nik, meet Woody." She grins.

Nik remains speechless, lips tight.

His voice is muffled, and he's too distracted to ask who Nik is. "Would you, uh, have a minute to help me with something?"

Both women try to get clarification at the same time. "With what?" and "Just one minute?"

"I've got to get something out of here. But I can't quite reach it. Would you just sit on my ankles so I don't fall in? No ladder down here."

"Something?" Jaye feels the small air flow now, surprisingly warm. But the hairs on the back of her neck are lifting.

"I know it's a weird request." Even muffled, his words exude guilt.

Jaye feels Nik's eyes on her, but her own gaze is locked onto the little black square of hole.

"What are you trying to get out?" Nik has to ask.

Grabbing at the sides of the hole with knobby fingers, Woody folds himself partway up, his face smudged. "Rubber boa."

Jaye stares at him. "Great." It could have been a jar of spaghetti sauce, but no, her baseless suspicions were exactly on target.

"I don't want the little guy slipping into the store when people are around."

"We're people." Jaye mutters it, but his ears are still good and he drops his eyes.

"I'd sure appreciate it." Then he notices Nik. "Oh. Hi."

Nothing else makes it out of his mouth, though he usually struggles to keep from talking too much. Jaye recognizes his reaction. They are both like rural high schoolers—a new person in Nowhereville almost always seems more attractive than they might elsewhere. He folds back into the hole, and fighting off her involuntary shudder, she leans on his left leg. Nik has her hands around his other ankle. They watch the reflected shine of his headlamp swing.

"Woody, can you even see him?" Jaye hopes the snake has found some tunnel to prairie freedom.

"Could be a her, you know." Nik's tone leans toward condescending.

Jaye wonders if her phobia smells like fresh sweat and if somehow a female snake is supposed to be more comforting.

"May be the world's first transgender snake." Woody's disembodied voice rises from the hole. "How would a guy know?"

He's babbling. Jaye needs him to quit already and close the damn crawl space. Her skin shivers.

"Males have internal hemipenes on either side of the cloacal opening, which gives them a thicker tail, a more abrupt taper at the end."

Jaye stares at Nik, who gives her a shrug.

Her tone hits petulant. "It bugs me when the default for all animal genders is male."

To go along with her unreasonable fear, Jaye now feels fully chastised. Woody can have this newcomer.

A heavy sigh rises through the floor. "Nothing. But she's in there, tucked into a dark corner somewhere." So he had heard their discussion.

He attempts to back out of the hole. He rolls sideways and scrabbles upward, wriggling, protecting the large tongs he grips in one hand. His face emerges red, with worried hangdog eyes.

Jaye rises and scrambles backward, knocking Nik's bag of corn nuts off the counter. Like an embarrassed cat, she pretends she was just getting out of Woody's way. She grabs the coffee cup and takes a swig, eyes still not moving from the floor's hole, gaping open now as Woody stands. Her hand trembles.

Woody sets his flashlight on the counter, his breathing short and fast. "Can I ring these up for ya, then?" He doesn't meet Nik's eyes.

Nik tugs her coffee loose from Jaye's fingers. "Sure, but make it two coffees."

Woody hands over the change and inclines his head toward the back of the deli.

Jaye takes the hint and the escape route he offers. Watching from the coffee urn, she sees him set a commercial-sized cast-iron fry pan on the floor, covering the hole. "Nonvenomous snakes like Guthrie are on the people team. Nothing to be worried about." His words, obviously, aren't meant for Nik.

Jaye pictures a thick, gray-brown snake, goatlike eyes unblinking in a goat-sized head. "Guthrie for a girl?"

From the door, Nik adds to her snake lecture. "Wyoming has lots of nonpoisonous options, like boas or wandering garters. They're good at garden pest control."

Woody pulls his hair out of a green rubber band that looks like it came off a bunch of broccoli stems. "She decided to hibernate in the crawl space. Her dreams have been keeping me company most of the winter. But she woke up early."

Nik's disdain isn't well hidden. "And crawled through the wall to see what you have in the deli?"

He gives Jaye a hurt look, and she defends herself. "I had no idea I was driving around with a snake expert."

"All I meant was," Nik looks around the closest aisles, "Guthrie's not likely to come up here during the day, anyway. Maybe she'll go back into hibernation."

Jaye strides toward the door. "We better get going." Until that happens, the cast-iron pan is round, and the hole is square.

The Scent of Distant Family

THE TRUCK'S ENGINE PLAYS ITS LULLABY. JAYE GLANCES over to see Nik's eyes closed and her head fallen sideways against Polenta's shoulder. The dog is smitten with this stranger. Maybe she senses Nik's commitment to animals or just that she seriously needs help. But even after her restless night, the woman's untidy haircut still looks expensive. The tires slip as the truck swings through a shaded curve, and Jaye's heart lurches.

When she's finally through the narrow canyon and the road straightens out in the wider valley, she checks on Nik again. Still sleeping, her lips damp. The missing dog is unlikely to fight all this snow. With jackrabbits on the desert, it makes sense he'll wait there. Spring will come eventually. She wonders if his westward movement from Parodice is an effort to return to this woman who is so intent on finding him.

Steam lifts off open water in the middle of the icy river, and in the low spots, fog collects into hoarfrost on every twig of cottonwood tree and chokecherry bush. The crystals hang huge, like miniature forests growing on the branches and lifting up from the drifts. Here in the bottoms, no wind disturbs their overnight growth. Little sunlight threatens to melt any of this cold beauty either. She rubs a hand over Polenta's head, slides fingers into the soft hair of her neck. Her hand falls close to Nik's cheek, and she jerks it back.

Nik, asleep, is an undeniably attractive woman. Like Selina. Jaye's record of attraction is not good. City girl looks are a poor match for risky ranch life. City girls need their cities, with all those people who can keep them looking sharp and even more to admire the effort. She rubs her eyes and wishes Woody good luck.

A magpie floats over the windshield, and a raven flies above the river, paddling through the silver sparkles of cold air. Polenta turns her head to watch. Her motion disturbs Nik, who pushes upright. She looks out both sides of the truck. "Not past the junction?" She fluffs the flattened side of her hair. "No. Duh. How are you on time?"

"If nothing's avalanched, we should be right on the mark." Jaye won't give Phelan any excuse to avoid her today.

"I have to tell you again how much I appreciate this. Not exactly how you expected these two days to go, I imagine."

"I don't mind surprises. They keep life interesting." Jaye gives her a dry smile. The main surprise—that anyone wants to invest in Sage Winds, in Yahanna. Her stomach twists. To be expected, unfortunately—not finding a missing dog in Wyoming's open expanses. She doesn't share those expectations with Nik, who sags again into the bench seat.

The familiar miles roll by with their white uniformity, and Jaye counts herself fortunate to be keyed up enough to stay awake. The flow of traffic increases. Jaye arrives in town just before her appointment, and as the truck backs into its parking spot, Nik wakes up. Groggy, she pushes against her door in a groaning stretch.

"Careful."

She springs to center again. Pulls slender fingers through her hair. Nods toward the office and gives her a thumbs-up.

A half-smile opens on Jaye's face. She can't interpret what her own smile is saying. She brushes seat belt wrinkles out of her bold plaid shirt and grabs her ledger of drawings and options for the future.

The Scent of Distant Family

3

Zolo

Under his belly, earth rings with quickening heartbeat, and morning sun freshens through holes in old log building's cracked chinking. Little light inside, but sun soaks narrow logs outside, and heat wafts from wood. Zolo's bones loosen. He shakes his head, and flapping ears sound like summer, like leaves clapping. Earth's pounding heart draws him to his feet, and he stretches, nose pointing to sky, breast-bone low. The ground shivers. Zolo lifts each back leg into air and shakes it. Good to be loose when earth sings. Out empty doorframe pokes his nose.

Even in cold, they smell lightly of sweat but also green breaths in silver shines of steam. Earth's drummers pound along ridgeline, glorious movement, manes and tails touched by their own wind and by sun's melting honey. Drummers melt Zolo's loneliness into a scent of belonging, breaths mingling. Earth's dried grass gives legs their drumbeat. Life circles, puppies curled nose to tail. Air carries mustangs: like breath, they rise, touching sky, and like ravens, descend, ringing earth. Wild horses, belonging to each other. Belonging, here. They run close together, jostle of shoulders, nose nipping at hindquarter. Zolo motionless but for his nose. Air moves into him thick with horses and crushed sage and hot breath of summer in bent blades of snow-cured grass.

Horses disappear down long swale, source of swirling water, alive with mountain's slanted energy. Zolo leaves cabin behind, trots again toward mountains. Sun warms his back and blinds his eyes against brilliant slopes ahead. But thin heat lifts world's stories from sagebrush as he passes through, and his nose reads. Hole of warm vole. Plunge. A nest of twined stems is half-stuck to his muzzle, and its contents, whole, plummet to his gut. Grateful, his sharp nod sends neatly woven grasses tumbling over snow. Other voles deeper, drifted over, not yet in his circle.

Zolo trots and, downhill in taller snow, lunges into rocking lope, trots some more. In woody branches of bitterbrush, his own doggish scent, the only one of its kind. Cold-blue shadows cast by low sun pull him forward.

His nose twitches. Primal recognition surges through his feet. He stops. Sniffs. The scent is, by a minuscule amount, stronger. Warmer. Approaching. Still as a snowdrift, he stands and knows. Earth accepts him. He tips his head toward warmth and hears soft breaths of wide feet schussing over snow. He hears sharp teeth tearing leaf. Smells his life coming closer. His tongue trembles behind his lips.

Tall ears flick, as if they hear muscles tensing. Zolo doesn't wait. He springs into air, owl silent. Jackrabbit can't hear him there.

But bulging eyes are set wide on hare's narrow head. Unidentified movement begins the chase. Zig and zag, over and under, sprinting, bare hints of rabbit ghosting over sage. Zolo doesn't need scent now, eyes locked on runner, his supple body twisting and doubling back, launching forward.

The jack spins quick maneuver left, and Zolo, bending around boulder, lands suddenly on top of him. Teeth on neck. One shake and another, harder. Long legs slacken, go still. Zolo's tongue slides in and out between wet teeth. He pants. A raven's call, water drum, burbles through sparkling air as day's wind begins to lift. As Zolo's life begins, with breakfast.

Charlie

The last, brightest stars linger while he drinks orange juice and swallows his pills. He watches the world surface from the morning dark. A pale halo traces the top of the first ridge of mountains. He isn't hungry yet, but he knows who always is.

Bundled up in layers of long johns and sweatshirts and a poorly knit blue-and-gold scarf, he follows the yard fence out to the barn. What is now the cat room comes complete with a couch and a dorm-sized refrigerator and an old radio with a long silver antenna. They hear him coming, of course, crunching over the snow, so he has to slide in, moving his feet carefully.

Cats twine around his ankles, tails crooking over his knees. To get bowls and food lined up on the table, he shuffles across the floor to the cabinet so he doesn't step on anyone. The sound of kibble dropping into bowls revs the excitement up a notch, and cat voices fill all the choir roles: the black longhair is bass, the brown tabby covers tenor, and two orange tabbies hit the baritone. He holds a bowl in each hand and waves them around, orchestrating. The Siamese, of course, sings high soprano, a torti performs mezzo, and the lady in blue provides the contralto. Charlie teases, not releasing the bowls. The tenor, not amused, plants his claws in Charlie's fortunately well-covered thigh.

He places seven bowls in a wide semicircle, then stands back, arms folded over his gentle paunch. Satisfaction. He looks out the window, where the sky is a handful of freshwater pearls, touched with dusty rose. Maggie loves her roses, the pinker the better. He steps out the side door to admire the sky show and almost trips over the snowblower. He doesn't remember leaving it there. He remembers

Nikki with her new dog out here in the yard. When she brings him home, the cats will adopt him too.

Charlie decides to clear the dog a path around the yard. This one's not fuzzy like Maggie's ranch dogs. He studies the blower. He can't find the starter cord. He pats around the machine, then remembers the electric ignition. He can't remember if he checked the oil when he parked it. He unscrews the dipstick. Fine. Tries to remember where the choke is—going to need it to get this baby running in the cold. Finally, the sweet purr of the engine, and he leans on it to walk into the yard. His breath is huffing, but he is happy. He has so much fun watching Nikki and the dog. If only both his kids could be so happy.

"Dad, what the heck are you doing out here?"

Phelan is angry, again. He wears a brown satiny robe and thin black socks. Neither look warm. He's hopping over the snow in his socks.

"Dad, that thing's too heavy for you. You could fall. Why are you up so early?"

"Cats were hungry. Where are your boots?"

Phelan turns the engine off, and the yard goes still. "The driveway is plowed. And Nik must've cleared the path to the barn yesterday."

"Where's Nikki? She lets me use the snowblower."

Phelan grabs his elbow. "I'm freezing my buns off out here. Come back inside."

"Nikki lets me."

Phelan drags him through the snow. "She does no such thing. Come on, I've got to get to work."

From the pocket of his robe, a phone rings. The man can't be bothered to put on boots, but his phone's in his pocket.

He checks the number. "It's Home Health." He tries to scrape snow off one sock with his other sock. "Hello? No one's available? I know, yes, I heard. We should have had an appointment, yes, but

The Scent of Distant Family

something came up." Phelan gives Charlie a nervous look. "I understand, yes. No, I think for today we'll have to figure something else out."

Charlie pushes through the back door, and Phelan is behind him, hopping on one foot while he strips the wet sock off the other.

Charlie bangs around the cupboards pulling out the coffee grinder and fresh beans. He plugs it in and watches his son's mouth move behind the noise.

Someone's bed head appears in the kitchen doorway. "Too loud, too loud. Get the instant coffee."

Charlie grins. "We don't use instant."

Phelan slaps a small glass jar on the counter. "Here it is." Under his breath, to Charlie, "Play nice. Please."

Charlie tips the fresh beans into a filter and fills the coffee maker with water. He was done grinding anyway.

"Bart, I've got a huge favor to ask. I've got to meet a client at eight o'clock. Can you hang out here until Nik gets home?"

"Since I had no idea she wasn't coming home last night, I have no idea when she might be home today. So, no. And I'm the boss. I have to line the crew out for the day."

"She's supposed to be at my office by eight." Phelan pours nuked hot water into a cup and stirs coffee crystals into it before sliding it over to Bartlett Beecher "the Bed Head" Fogarty. The Third.

Charlie knows it must be killing him to play nice.

A confused look crosses under the messed-up hair. "Is there no cream?" He eyes the driveway. "I thought you said she borrowed your car."

Phelan motions for Charlie to check the fridge. Charlie turns in the opposite direction, pushes mugs around in the cupboard, searching for the one he wants. Phelan gets the cream. "You can wait for her, right?"

Bart stirs it in and sips. "Who did she go chasing dogs with?"

"A ranch gal from Yahanna had a truck she could use. And you're the boss, right, so delegate whatever you had for the morning." He's ironing a rose-pink shirt. But the laundry soap makes it smell like lilacs.

Bart frowns. "Fine. You want to take off, me and Charlie got things covered here."

"Seriously?" Phelan's hand pauses.

"Not such a good idea," Charlie says, pointing at the iron.

Phelan pulls his hand up, examines the shirt for damage. "Nik should have a car reserved so you won't have long to wait." He pulls the shirt on without another thought.

Fogarty starts a shower. Charlie has another thought. While Phelan gets ready to go, he fills his travel mug and pulls his boots on. He doesn't have to be stuck here. He better make a pit stop first, though, since, knowing his son, they won't be stopping anywhere. He gets out of the bathroom just in time to see Phelan's Rover disappear beyond the snowbanks.

Tess

Emerging from the creek's rising milky breath, her clear eyes take in the jumble of splashing hooves and long-boned legs defining her herd. The Sentinel, her stallion, on the opposite flank, flared nose also on alert. But winter is a season safe from the bear who ate last year's foal. And though they've traveled along the lower edges of forest, where the smell of predator might surface from old piles of bones, no other horse herds wander this far from the clay hills. No younger stallions will challenge him here.

She shivers the last drops of star-silvered creek from her whiskers and a breeze-tossed forelock plays between her eyes. She watches the big-boned mare pin her ears at her almost-grown daughter, whose thick coat is powdered in creek frost. The oldest mare taught Tess this business of making decisions. It isn't for everyone. Choosing wrong has consequences.

But the right choice can land her herd in magic like this. The mountains with all their water, sharing in runnels, in spreading marshes and in lively channels defying the cold. Grasses and sedges thrive in broad pathways where water seeps from underground. Wide space where people seldom appear, where horse legs can stretch. Sharp sun balances the cold, especially as the days lengthen, tilting between darkest winter and wet spring. The mares paw and nibble and move. Sentinel, without putting his head down, scratches cotton-wood bark loose with long teeth, and Tess listens to his crunching, content.

She walks. Snow, hiding her dark forelegs, cascades away from her with a small sigh of crystal music. On the creek bank, leafless trees clack bare twigs together in gentle percussion overhead as she rubs the back of her ears against a white trunk. She smells sun streaming into the bark of these trees, green just below vision. She hears these trees in the bright morning churn cold air to sweetness, a promise from folded golden buds at patient branch tips. Her nostrils quiver. Her herd begins climbing out of the bottomland, flowing upward as they eat and walk and walk and eat, sampling old leaves that skid across the top of snow.

Her tail blows past her hocks, even though she is stopped, on alert again. She feels the give-and-take of the ground as her herd steps and nibbles and moves upward. Through her legs, she feels the roots of their prehistory in this place, and she feels ghost toes clustered above the solid hoof that remains a part of their movement across continents and back. She tosses her head at time and bares her teeth in a wide yawn before joining the current of horses moving toward wind and grass.

At the top, an old boulder balances, partly over the steep edge but leaning toward the broad shrub steppe. Beneath its lee-side curve, the filly finds a spot of green, warmed from the rock's reflective shield. Tess catches the scent of bunchgrass released as blades are torn. She moves close, happy to absorb the smell and leave the taste for the three-year-old. They pause together, Tess looking over soft snowy plains and her younger charge turned in the opposite direction, still chewing. Tess angles her head to scratch a small clump of matted dirt from the filly's withers and is repaid in kind. Their heads nod in unison as their teeth scrape, pushing away tangled manes to reach higher along each other's necks. Yes yes and yes. Forever is as present as the rabbit on the face of the moon.

Nikki

Phelan's secretary, Becky, tells them Phelan couldn't get anyone from Home Health. Nik imagines the foul mood he must be in. Becky drives her to the airport for a rental, leaving Jaye to wait on her brother again. Hopefully, she finds breakfast somewhere.

The Jetta's front-wheel drive handles well on the snowy road back to the house. Nik is confused to see Bart's Camaro still in the driveway but not Phelan's rig. Did Bart convince Phelan to trade now?

She walks inside, kicking her boots off in the tray by the entry. She peeks at the kitchen, then steps to the living room. No one. She checks Charlie's room and the guest room, most recently used by Phelan, its original occupant. Bed left unmade, like their house was a hotel and she was going to wash his sheets after just one use.

"Hello, anybody? Dad, where are you?" She glances at the open door of the bathroom. The house still has a just-showered smell of shampoo and a soft humidity.

"Oh, hi, honey. You didn't take long." Bart emerges from their room wearing his terry robe and fleece-lined leather slippers. He gives her a peck on the cheek. "How was your sleepover?"

She traces her finger down the imprint of a wrinkled sheet on his forehead. His hair is still damp on one side. "Where's Dad? Becky said I needed to get here fast so Phelan could leave."

"I couldn't figure out why Phelan was so worried about you getting home. Logical for Charlie to drive to Teewinot with him and, whenever you were ready, come back with you."

"But . . ."

"That was the plan." He strokes her arm. "You didn't answer me about your night." He settles his other hand on her hip.

"Phelan took Dad up to Teewinot, but I left before they got there?" She is going to dissolve into a muddy puddle on the floor. "Now I'll have to go back again and bring him home." So much consecutive time behind the wheel has got to be illegal.

"You look beat, honey. I'm sure your dad's fine up there."

"Buttering popcorn." What might look like a smile twitches across her lips, but she knows it's mere exhaustion.

"You should go to bed." He adds pressure to the hand on her hip. "I took the morning off. If you need a sleeping aid—"

"Let me call Phelan first and figure out when he needs me to pick Dad up."

Bart follows her into the kitchen. She plugs in her phone and calls while it's attached to the wall. "Just like when we were kids, right?" He twists loose her first button, but she bats him away when Becky picks up.

"Hey Becky, Nik. Just wanted to make sure Dad's not being a bother up there. I must not have noticed Phelan driving north when I came home. I could really use a nap before I head back for him."

"He's not here, Nik. I thought your husband was watching out for him."

Her vision goes blue, like a computer screen or the ocean. Her stomach swallows itself. She remembers to touch the phone's red button.

"Why did you say he was with Phelan?"

"He isn't?" Bart pulls away. "But Phelan left, and then Charlie wasn't here, so I thought, I thought they'd come up with the obvious plan."

"Get dressed. And get looking."

She stuffs her feet back in her boots. She almost falls running out the front steps. She is yelling. Charlie's hearing isn't what it used to be. "Dad? Are you out here?" She checks the driveway for footprints telling her he's left the property. But she might have driven over the evidence. "Dad?"

She heads for the garage, then hears Bart coming out the door. She points. "Garage, then check the road. Look for footprints." She turns for the barn. "Dad? Where are you?"

Someone fed the cats at least. She can't tell if it was her father or her brother, but she follows tracks along the fence. She sees the snowblower parked in the backyard, halfway through a circuit of the fence line. Nothing makes any sense. Why would someone call her when they found a long-haired, black, female dog? Why did a locked truck door fall open? Why does her husband make everything harder?

She opens the cat room door. Cats look up, wondering too—why she's so upset. Nik counts five cats on the couch, with Charlie, who remains completely asleep. His quiet snoring has never sounded so beautiful. Her legs give out, and she slides down the side of the couch, her head finding a resting spot against the covered arm. A blue cat sidles up and climbs into her lap. She opens one eye, her breaths coming short and fast. "Agnes, darling, you've all been taking care of him, haven't you?"

Agnes rolls over, curving into a ball, rubbing her back on Nik's belly. No need to panic. All is well. Nothing like cats to keep everyone calm. A whole room of professional nappers at work. Nik listens to her father breathing, the cats purring, her own heart settling into their serenity. Her lungs billow in gratitude. Her body relaxes, though she won't be able to sleep for a while.

She breathes. She doesn't count the minutes but feels their fullness, their lack of concern with any of her concerns. Her bones remember sitting like this on the floor of their college apartment, baby Finn swaddled asleep on her lap, oblivious that his mother is gone. Whenever Nik needed someone to hold her, her mother wasn't afraid to sit on the floor. They sat on the floor together when her old brown dog died, her best friend through the tough years of junior high.

Charlie stirs. "Hi honey." He reaches over and settles a sleepy hand on her shoulder. "I always wonder when we'll get to meet Finn's other grandparents. It doesn't seem fair that we've kept him all to ourselves."

Her heart clenches. Finn could have told Charlie about going to Australia. Taking a chance, then, that Phelan will find out. Maybe the changes she sees in Charlie aren't obvious to everyone. Like right now, she's pretty sure he's not talking to her. She picks his hand up and holds it against her cheek, saying nothing. His breathing deepens, Agnes matching his rhythm.

Finn's other grandparents don't know he exists. Their daughter so full of promise when she came here. Before she left, demanding Nik's promises. Her eyes close.

The door, however, cracks open. Her dry eyelids drag upward, and she sees Bart, face pale, suddenly realizing Charlie is safe. He sucks in a breath, but she cuts him off, both hands waving at him as if he's a charging bull.

Instead of yelling, then, he hisses at her. "Why didn't you come tell me you found him?"

"I was just so relieved. I needed to sit a second."

"Because it's always about your needs." The volume of his hiss would wake a hibernating bat.

"Bart, please. I had a long night."

"Oh?"

"Don't you have to get to work?" She is so tired.

"I can't have this conversation in a whisper. Get out here where we can talk."

Nik wishes he would just come in and settle down beside her. He could really use a cat in his lap. She pats the floor.

"You'd like that, wouldn't you? Me going into anaphylaxis?"

Nik's body is a thousand-pound hay bale, unwilling to move. "Can we talk tonight?"

"I don't even know if you'll be here tonight, do I?"

She sighs, gives Agnes a kiss, and lifts her to the back of the couch. She touches the top of her father's head, about the only place without a cat sprawled over it. Then she turns, follows Bart to the house. The snowblower, stranded behind the fence, still stymies her.

She sits on a kitchen stool, both so she can keep watch out the window toward the barn door and so she'll have to stay awake or fall off. Bart strips from his clothes, snowy and sweaty both, strewing them behind him as he stomps into their bedroom for drier options.

"Feel better now?" Nik has poured him a cup of reheated coffee, pale with cream. She gestures toward where she left it on the gray countertop. "Tell me again how this mix-up happened."

"Looking for a way to blame someone? I told you, I was in the shower, and when I came out, Phelan and Charlie were both gone. Seemed pretty obvious."

"It wouldn't have occurred to you to call Phelan and check on the change of plans?"

"Phones don't work in the canyon."

Nik sighs. Her stomach is too cramped to try coffee, so she sips from a glass of tepid water. She wants to say more but sips more instead, pushing words down with the water. The pause just isn't long enough. "Why didn't you bother to check around for Dad if you, in fact, weren't able to reach Phelan before he got to the canyon?"

Bart busies himself pulling his leather belt through the loops on his office pants. Then he steps behind her, places his hands on her shoulders. He squeezes. "This was a scare for you, Nicole, I know. But it's over now. You going to be all right if I go to work?"

Damn, he was good. At discounting her emotions. She counts the seconds, as if she were back in the field, observing the social behavior of vultures. She knows she's hard on him. "It was kind of you to offer to watch him. You didn't have anything important at work this morning?"

"Nothing Ben can't handle. Or if he messes up, nothing I can't fix again later. So tell me about your sleepover." Hands strong from working out at the gym, he presses on her tight muscles.

She laughs. "Not much of a sleepover, since there wasn't much sleep involved."

His hands go still. "Really?"

He is such a teenager. Always trying to cover up poor decisions with his stupid suspicions. "Jaye had to do chores, so she stayed home, and I took her truck to look for Zolo. All those oil field roads—absolutely crazy making. I got lost. Go figure. Not lost, really, I mean, it's obvious where the mountains are, but I couldn't figure out how to get back to her ranch."

"Her ranch? Is she not married?"

"I didn't see any evidence of a husband, but I didn't think to ask." Her focus had been Zolo. Frustration fills her. "The question didn't seem as relevant as, say, you asking Phelan where Dad was."

He pushes away from her and slams his half-finished coffee in the sink. "Can't let go of that, can you?"

Brown coffee droplets dirty the kitchen window. "Sometimes I think you would be happiest if Dad wandered into a snowbank and never came out." There. She's said it now. Her ribs press on her lungs. Her watchful gaze falls to the floor.

His voice is casual, though, his anger already released. "You have to admit, Nik, this parental caretaking gig puts a cramp in our style."

Her phone rings, and she leaps at the sound. She checks the caller. "Phelan?"

"What the hell's going on now? Becky says Dad isn't there?"

"He's here. Bart just didn't know exactly where." Her voice changes from accusative to soothing, as she tries to ease any judgment Phelan might make against her husband, even in the middle of her own argument.

"One hour of his time. That's all we asked of him."

Phelan was on duty, but because her husband botched things up, she was to blame. Silenced by cultural standards she never lives up to anyway, she keeps that observation to herself. "You know how

Dad gets. He hates being watched like a baby."

"Nik, Bart's a wreck. You need to get him straightened out. And I have to get to my next meeting. So we'll talk again soon."

She sets the phone down and turns back to Bart, his last words still ringing in her mind. "My style," she meets his eyes this time, "is about taking care of family."

"If that's so true, I wonder if you actually put me in the same category."

"Oh? I let you take my car when you asked."

"And it's only fair Phelan pays for a rental until we can buy a new one. Since he's fine letting you sacrifice your income. The car rent covers your eldercare wages." He slips into his driving boots.

"Because you can't tell the insurance company you wrecked the car?"

"You know they'll jack up the rates. And your part-time income is paltry. We both need me to be able to drive for work." He paces back and forth in front of the door.

Her income is meager and a sore spot, though not the biggest loss when she gave up her career. And her working from home saves them from paying someone else to stay with Charlie, who really doesn't need much care. This is hardly a financial argument, but if that's what he wants—"Until you figure out how to manage your financial outflow to something resembling your inflow, you can't really complain about my contributions. Especially since you're living in Dad's place for free."

"Not by choice. By choice, I'd quit this whole popcorn stand of a state and do property management in a beach town somewhere. We never even ski anymore, so what's the point?"

Exhaustion makes her malicious. He only ever skied enough to get to the lodge for a drink. "The point is, my family's all here."

"Your point, then, makes my point for me. After four years of marriage, you still can't consider me family." He slides on a pair of thin black leather gloves. "You talk with Phelan's son more than you talk with me. I hardly know you. I certainly didn't know you had a friend in Yahanna you might spend a night with after some random call about a missing dog."

He needs to leave. Nik could just say so, and he would go. But if more communication is the key to a stronger relationship—"Finn is twenty-one years old. He grew up without a mother, and Black in a Wyoming ski town. You don't think he's still trying to work through that kind of challenge? He's your family, too, if you'd claim him."

"I'd rather have a chance to claim my own kids."

The same old argument. She would only adopt. He would only procreate. But with Phelan's son, there is more to it. "Finn's just not white enough for you."

Bart is already halfway out the door. "And after your 'long night' in Yahanna, I have to wonder if I'm just not woman enough for you?" He gets his parting shot. He almost runs over Charlie, halfway up the front stairs.

Nik is at the door behind him, but when she sees Charlie, she freezes. She is grateful Bart doesn't take his anger out on her father. He stomps to his Camaro in a rigid silence, waiting until he can rev the engine and spin his tires to add emphasis to his argument. By then, she is at her dad's elbow. "Did you have a good nap with your harem out there?" She forces her breaths to slow down, her voice to sound cheerful.

"You weren't home to clean their boxes. They hate dirty litter."

"I know. I'm so glad you could take care of them. Want me to take your coat?"

He shakes his head. "I just need some hot chocolate. Then I

have to finish the dog run. And you have to do the cat meds. I can't remember them all."

"Dog run?" She looks over the fence at the snowblower.

"So you can play with your dog out there. Getting pretty deep." He is at the sink, filling a kettle.

One mystery solved, sort of. "Dad, that's why I spent the night at Jaye's. The dog is missing over there somewhere. I was looking for him, but he didn't turn up."

"I know." His voice is testy. "Place needs to be welcoming, whenever he does come home." He warms his hands beside the kettle as the water starts to make small jumping sounds. "Next time, I should go with. I can help you look."

"I sure could've used you last night. I got kinda lost. But you could drive those roads all day and always know where you are." She would cry, but she's too exhausted even for tears to fall.

He spoons cocoa mix into his mug. "Don't know why you left me with Phelan then."

Nik can't rightly say why anymore either. "You were in with the doc. Someone called who thought they saw him, and I wanted to get there right away. But there's just no getting to Yahanna fast."

"Next time, we'll find him. And he'll have a trail here he can run on." He lifts his mug as if making a toast to his prediction.

"If we get a next time, Dad. It's already been a while." She looks out the window at the white, white world, the drifts bending fruit bushes in the yard. If they get a next time, she won't defer to Bart— Zolo will have a home. A raven, twisting over the fields, is a mere speck against the impenetrable wall between here and the desert.

His mug clanks on the counter. A creamy brown line sits on his upper lip. "Okay, I'm ready. You coming?"

"Where are we going?"

"Finish up the dog run. Can't you remember anything?"

"I'm sorry, you're right. A little distracted. But I hate the racket that machine makes. I could really use some physical activity." She points out the window. "How about I shovel a path and you fiddle on the porch like you did when Zolo was here?"

"Help you keep your rhythm going?"

She needs a hug as much as she needs the workout. So she gives him one. "Dad, you know I love ya, right?"

He strokes her hair for a minute before he goes to the living room for his old case. She hopes the wind will blow the tunes all the way to Zolo's ears.

The Scent of Distant Family

Jaye

Exasperated—closer to incensed—by waiting on Phelan again, Jaye sets off with Polenta, seeking fresh air and a fresh attitude. She was smart to bring the dog this time, to hell with random hairs on her clean brown pants. Selina's doubts fester, and Jaye's feet land hard on salted boardwalks fronting endless restaurants and art galleries. She walks past high-end clothing stores and high-end toy stores and shining wide windows showing off brilliant colors in backcountry ski gear or avalanche beacons. Finally, on the voices of ravens eating well in the alleyways, her natural optimism floats—slowly—back to her. She and her dog walk until Selina's words shrink to minor punctuation in the story of how Sage Winds finds its way in the changing West.

She stomps her way in the front door, pretending to kick snow off her feet. She doesn't pause at Becky's desk, but she does rap once on Phelan's open door before showing herself in.

He is up and at her side, sweeping her in and closing the door behind her in one smooth motion. "I am so, so sorry about this. As you must have gathered yesterday, our father needs supervision, and rural areas have a hard time with support services. It took a while to turn up anyone else on short notice this morning."

Jaye drops backward into a soft green chair. It matches the sponge-painted green walls, giving the impression of somewhere mossy and tropical. Does moss grow in the tropics? Maybe mossy *or* tropical. Maybe this is going to go fine. She places the folder with her drawings at the side of the chair. "Glad it worked out in the end. You still have some time?"

"I hoped you would understand. So few of our clients are home-grown Wyoming folks, and outsiders expect us to ignore family emergencies. They like to know we'll drop everything to prioritize their needs."

"Because people always do."

"Oh yes, count on it." He gives her a conspiratorial nod. "We have pie. Did you build up an appetite while you waited on me?"

She considers the offer. "I did, actually." She rises to pour herself a coffee from the carafe on his sideboard while he brings the pie over and sets it on a tray. She has the first bite on her fork when he begins.

"Since we're behind schedule, I'll dive right in. Our researchers have noticed your ranch's limited liability company has been delinquent in paying some of its government obligations, for a couple years already."

She chews and chews, and the small bite of pie keeps growing between her teeth.

"Of course, it's easy to understand the difficulty of attracting visitors to such an isolated location as yours. People right now are dedicated to *Destination Locations.*"

She hears the buzzwords curving into italics. "They want to be where everyone else is, you're saying."

"Yes, where they have lots of opportunity to spread their money around, different activities, a variety of shopping choices. I see you understand what our researchers are just figuring out." He motions her toward the pie again. "We've been in this business awhile, though, and one certainty is that people are fickle. The tide will change, and Hidden Gems will suddenly be in high demand."

The Scent of Distant Family

"That's what I plan to be ready for." She ignores the rest of the pie. Her eye stays on him now. "And mine is a fresh take on the tired old dude ranch model."

Phelan brushes off her claim. "Of course, today's geotourism is far more diverse than simply letting people chase steers up and down the mountain, pretending to be cowboys. Though cowboying, as an iconic personal desire, is more enduring than you might imagine."

She wills him to get to his point. But despite him putting her off for a day and a half, she is not going to look eager. His company approached her, not the other way around. Though it sounds like his company knows her finances as well as she does.

"What science shows to work best, in an uncertain economic environment—and believe me, there is no such thing as a certain economic environment anymore—is being well capitalized. Allows a business to ride out the troughs in public demand, knowing the crest of the wave will return." He sits on the front edge of his desk, leaning toward her.

Jaye looks away, turning to the tall window framing the town's ski hill and all the development at its base. This is only the small local mountain and no longer locally owned. The real game is on the far side of the river, at a village that grew up specifically to serve the international skier world.

"Joining a franchise of some kind," Phelan's voice is geared to reassure, "changes the risk calculation. Big players, secure in their array of holdings, can recognize the value of each during different moments in a business cycle."

Jaye hears the voice of the schoolteacher from the old Peanuts cartoon strip, one of her grandmother's favorites. The sponge-painted walls seem jungle humid now, vines growing over trees and a canopy of leaves so dense no light reaches the ground. She's afraid if she sits still, the vines will wrap around her neck like a boa constrictor and strangle her. She stands, almost knocking over the tray holding her unfinished pie.

"I called you in here"—Phelan stands, too, making her action seem more normal, herding her toward the window—"to let you know I have an investor ready to provide the capital your ranch needs."

"Any deal has to include a contract clause where I stay on as primary decision-maker."

"Most people feel the same. My investor suspected you would be no different." He leans forward, his hands on the wide windowsill, and his gaze follows the ski lift as it rises toward the summit. "Understandably, of course, your role would need to change somewhat."

Jaye hears the muffled trumpet sound that always sent Peppermint Patty directly to dreamland. *Whahwhah, whahwhahwah, whah.* She watches skiers streaming downhill in surfer sprays of white fluff. Surely no one can be so carefree. Dissembling—the word surfaces like a massive trout out of the depths of her school days. Phelan is a master. But the role this investor seems to envision for her sounds a lot like cook–and–chief bottle washer.

"Given your age, unfortunately, and lack of experience or notable business success—"

She turns to him so fast he steps behind his desk. "And gender, perhaps? Here's the answer. No."

Sitting once more, elbows on his desk, he props his chin in both palms, studying her. "Again, Jaye, I can completely understand your sentiment. And my investor is also prepared," he leans back and opens his palms, "to make a total purchase offer. So you would be out from under the whole proposition and could start somewhere else with less complications."

The Scent of Distant Family

The room sits with its breath held in. Jaye feels the ski hill at her back, but her eyes are captured by the green wall behind Phelan, sinking into that mysterious dark. Tropical or mossy?

"From what our researchers are presuming about the amount of red currently on your books, the offer is unlikely to be high." He holds a hand up, as if stopping her from interrupting. "More than fair, though, more than fair."

"No."

Phelan gets up again and walks to the far side of the room, admiring photographs of well-designed resorts in other parts of the world that were cash-strapped until his investors stepped in. He turns to face her, smiling. "You are, of course, just acting stubborn, as a multigenerational Wyoming rancher can be expected to act. An admirable trait, helping people survive physical hardship doled out by Mother Nature. Father Economics, though, is a different task-master." Now he's walking back, brisk, even perky, in his smooth pink shirt. "Economics favors movers and shakers, far-reaching risk-takers, not those who simply hunker down and hang on." He motions her back into her chair, and he sits opposite, his hands on his knees, leaning forward. "Look around. Wyoming is a different place now. Ready for a different kind of businessman."

She sits across from him but leans away, the back of the chair solid. "Good, then an old-fashioned business*woman* might still pull this off."

"Don't think so." He, too, leans back. The fingers of his right hand tap on the green arm of the chair. "You don't quite understand the full precariousness of the situation."

She studies him. Despite the showmanship, something about him smells nervous. A dark spot expanding under the visible arm of his pink shirt. "I don't." Not a question.

"This investor—well, buyer really, as we've already determined—is convinced his next development will be at Sage Winds. Why would you wait until you've failed so far that the IRS seizes your assets? Would you want to watch your horses loaded up on their way to the killers—because it's quick and easy to sell whole herds there? You know the government won't have the patience to sell one good horse at a time."

She isn't going to sit and listen to this. Who cares what his client's fantasies are? She stands and walks back to the window, the low sky beyond the ski area a necessary sanity. Apparently, money is a small issue, so why not move on to a more agreeable rancher? "The answer is no." She spins toward the door.

He's quick on his feet and blocks her way. "Our researchers are extremely thorough, Jaye. Outfitters in this state are all male, you certainly know, with your singular exception. Clients are mostly male, though sometimes with their families, and entirely conservative."

"Your point?"

"Scandals are the simplest way for many of our buyers to incentivize a chosen seller. With no client base, your books become a bloody mess."

"Well, that will be a tough go for them. My life is about as unremarkable as they come."

Phelan gets up and joins her at the window again, his shoulders aligned with hers. His voice is low and his eyes stay forward, beyond the pane. "I hate to say this, but we both know—given your chosen business, of course—your life, or lifestyle, is more salacious than you're admitting."

Marriages and divorces are matters of public record. And nothing's more apple pie than marriage. Jaye swallows.

The Scent of Distant Family

"If you chose to work somewhere more urban, or on either coast, it would hurt your business not a bit. But Selina Hawkins, née Cortázar, now cherished wife of Thomas Jenkins and mother of his sons in Cheyenne, is accustomed to writing the news, not being newsworthy."

Jaye hears her ex-wife's cheery "Que pasa?" in the quick honk of a delivery truck on the far side of the wall. Selina doesn't deserve to get dragged through his throwback muck. She doesn't hide her previous marriage from anyone, but Phelan would turn it into front-page malarkey. Where Selina's whole family would have to deal with it. Where it stands a good chance of destroying anyone else's interest in potential business partnerships.

"And you also spent an entire night with a married woman, just last night, I believe."

This time she beats him to the door.

Nikki

Nik still doesn't feel recovered the next morning, computer pages swimming in front of her eyes, aimless as fish in a tank. She wanders into the living room, where Charlie runs through songs he hasn't played in a while. Plaintive, the fiddle mourns something wordless. Something cellular, flitting through her bloodstream. Something tapping on the curves of her ears, tenacious. In her half-dreams, Zolo huddles, his nose on cold dirt. Alone. Cold suffuses her arms, her chest.

She surfaces to see Charlie watching her, his fiddle in its case across his knees. Her conscience lurches. "You ready for brunch?" They both prefer a lighter, two-meals-per-day schedule. But everything about her day feels heavy—the regretted words with Bart, a cold night on the couch, and muscles she abused while shoveling a path in the yard for a dog who may not even be alive. Her teeth clench.

"Tomato soup and grilled cheese?" Charlie pulls a can out of the cupboard.

She pushes air out her lips. "Sunflower seeds on your sandwich?" Her mother always added sunflower seeds. She grabs the griddle and a small soup pot.

"Of course. And pickles on the side."

Her mother pickled every vegetable she could find. Cauliflower, carrots, beets, zucchini, and of course, cucumbers, even though they had to be grown in a greenhouse. Nik thought about making her own pickles, but she had always seemed too busy, too far away, to learn how. It isn't a skill a person should have to learn from a cookbook. She carves thick slices of Monterey Jack, Finn's favorite.

Finn shouldn't have to learn about the wildlife of his mother's homeland from a book either. Of course she should encourage him to take the Australian internship. She and her father prepare their meal together without much conversation, easy in their teamwork. Something Finn never got to build with his mother. Of course, if he goes to Australia, he will look for his mother's family. A shiver travels across her shoulders even while her ears heat up.

Charlie pulls out plates and mugs and cloth napkins while she flips their sandwiches. He holds his plate out, and a crisped brown sandwich dripping with moon-colored cheese slides off her spatula. They sit knee to knee at the little round table and look out the kitchen window at chickadees and siskins, naked aspens and, beyond them, mountains. Nik blows on her soup, then scoops a spoonful off the top. "With yesterday gone, I better get more work done this afternoon, if I can. How about you? Any plans?"

"I have toys ready to get painted. If I can. Stay awake, that is."

Nik smiles. "They'll have time to dry before the craft fair?"

"It's only Wednesday. Even if it's cold, gives 'em three days before we need to set up."

Nik couldn't have guessed what day it is. She rubs her eyes. "Let's do it then. We can leave the dishes until after dinner."

They split up, and she settles in front of her computer, moving updates people have sent her through the appropriate templates and pushing them to public view. Charlie hasn't complained about not going in to volunteer at the shelter. Plenty of cats to keep him occupied here. She usually finds something of interest as she works, but today even the new bighorn sheep avoidance maps for backcountry skiers can't catch her attention. Not like she'll have a chance to get out into the peaks. Bart prefers the ski area and chairlifts, rather than having to put on climbing skins to reach the top under his own power. She presses keys and clicks on arrows and saves and reviews without reading anything.

She touches the phone number for the shelter director but hangs up before it makes the connection. She is no defeatist, and Zolo gives her a place to focus. Those soft ears between her fingertips. Those blue eyes, beginning to soften toward trust. She will not abandon him.

She hears a car in the driveway, though she isn't expecting any deliveries. And it isn't like any of them have friends around here. Even Charlie's old buddies avoid the place, afraid to upset him if they share old stories he can't remember.

She gets to the front door just as it's opening. "Phelan?"

"I'm sorry I missed you at the office yesterday. Even though you said everything was cool with Dad, I thought I should come down and check in." He pulls off his gloves, slips his coat onto a peg. "How did your trip with Jaye Hawkins go? Any luck with the dog?"

She freezes in front of his questions. They seem so innocuous. "No. No luck." He could've asked Jaye that much himself if he was really concerned. Why did he think he needed to check in? As if she'd really lost Charlie and didn't dare tell him.

"Well, have you heard anything more from her today? Maybe she saw something on her trip home?" His eyes are wide, caring.

"You thought you should check in on my search for Zolo? Or on Dad? He's in the basement if you want to visit with him."

"We can visit first, can't we? I sent you off to Timbuktu with someone neither of us knew and wanted to make sure nothing went awry."

"Nope." She pauses, unsure what to think about this unwelcome surprise. "Tough to look for a dog in the dark, is all."

"But you tried."

"All damn night. It's because of me that dog is out there in the middle of winter without a single friend." Her anger at herself snarls out in her response to him.

And anger calls anger. "It's because of you apparently that Finn and Kiran came all the way to Teewinot. But this dog was more important than dinner with them?" Phelan often issues questions as challenges.

"Finn and I can talk on the phone. We can email. Not an option for Zolo."

"Then why did they have to come up in person?"

"Kiran was offered the internship of her dreams, and they came up to celebrate with a ski trip. I would have liked to celebrate with them, but of course, they understand." She doesn't know that for a fact, because she hasn't called them today. "Finn was the one who decided we needed to foster the dog."

"Oh? What internship was that?"

They must not have invited Phelan to replace her at their dinner reservation. Or maybe they canceled it because they had to wait for him to collect Charlie from the townhouse. She sighs. "A tiger sanctuary in India. She'll be able to visit relatives; they'll be able to come to the sanctuary to meet her, see what kind of work she does. No one has much of a picture about wildlife biology."

"Finn's not going, is he?"

"You just saw him, why grill me?"

"He barely speaks to me these days. Besides, I had to drive Charlie home and stay here, since Bart's so unhelpful."

Nik snorts and mumbles. "You have no idea how unhelpful."

Phelan hears her perfectly. "You married him."

"You have no experience regarding the compromises a marriage entails."

"You have no experience with the compromises raising Finn has entailed."

She hears Phelan's jealousy. Finn wants to talk with her. "Oh, really? You mean all those times I arranged to take him on wildlife projects, while you had your mental health vacations?" She sees his mouth open but beats him to the next line. "Tough compromise, vacation without your son, instead of vacation with him?"

The pause in conversation is short. The next sentence tumbles out of him, despite an audible catch in his throat. "Have you got the slimmest clue how lonely single parenting can be?"

She glares at him, chin high. "About on par with how lonely eldercare can get?" She thinks of the awkward silences in the first few phone calls she had with her work friends after she no longer had her work. And how few second calls ever arrived. There's an extinction crisis happening—biologists are busy.

Phelan glances toward the creaking cellar door. "Good thing you always have me here to help." His capability is returned, voice steady, sardonic.

She can't bear his self-satisfaction. As Charlie's head pokes into view, she hisses her reply. "You stay here then. I have a dog to find." The freshly printed stack of flyers is easy to grab as she pulls her coat over her shoulder, and slip-on boots are made for quick getaways.

She kisses Charlie's cheek in passing, and whether he can hear her or not, she whispers in his ear. "It isn't you, it's *him*."

Without a recent sighting, her hopes of actually spotting Zolo are snowed under like last year's grass. There but invisible. The flyers might help, though, since she isn't getting any responses from Tara. And given the few businesses where she can post something in the even fewer towns around Yahanna, the chances she might learn something are fair to high. The people may be scattered about the wide country, but what one of them knows, all of them will know. Growing up in these parts, that was less reassuring. Now it might be helpful.

The rental car purrs along under her. Charlie is going to be ticked off. Or with luck, he'll have forgotten that she promised to bring him along this time. He hasn't forgotten that old story he used to tell everyone about finding her with her grandparents' half-feral cattle dog, a Corgi cross that scared not just the biggest of their Angus bulls but also the toughest of the cowboys. *I thought that crazy dog had eaten her head—she was tucked up under the dog's jaw so close I couldn't see the top of her. Yep, she's always had this way with animals.*

She cranks the car's radio volume, tapping the steering wheel and throwing her voice at the windshield. Her childhood magic no longer holds its power. Miles roll by with the music, rivers roll by with songs about rivers, and tall trees clutter mountain slopes as she climbs toward Rim Rendezvous. Guilt climbs up her chest as if connected to the road's elevation. Phelan has never talked to her about loneliness. Certainly not his. How could he be lonely with Finn there? But then, he figures she's got no reason to miss this dog like she does. She has Charlie and Bart, both. Other people's lives, never what they look like.

The snow outside sparkles like the diamond ring Bart fit over her finger. Her mother's diamond, a rainbow of grief on a sharp clarity of golden desire. Without her mother, Nik suddenly wanted what her parents always had. Bart was there, where a river's sparkle lifted onto tall buildings and shining windows. Bart toasting their Portland home for bringing together two successful people from humble Wyoming beginnings. Their cut crystal wine glasses posed for a picture framed by the Cosmopolitan on the Park. The Willamette rippling in her memory captures her gaze, and she is swept into its current, into a panic not her own. A cold she drowns in, heart pounding in her skull, casting echoes in a cliff-walled canyon. Her fingers tighten on the wheel, and the Jetta carries her, away or forward, she can't say.

She can't bear to admit her misjudgment. She needs to make this right—before it's too late. She needs to find a three-square-foot dog in a five thousand–square–mile landscape. Her fingers rake back her hair, rub her eyes. No more hopeless than helping her husband feel less trapped in Moon Valley's slim fifty miles, strung between mountain ranges. Or helping her father hang onto his memory. Or deciding what to tell Finn. She pushes the image of his mother out of her mind, an image two decades out of date.

She'd gone along with it, Phelan's insistence that Finn was just "in a phase" about Australia. She distracted, diverted, discounted, shook off. She's out of cell service now, another nonanswer. Her long-lived lies rise like fog from a fast stretch of river to haunt her. No matter where Finn goes, Australia or Africa, when she's lost his trust is when she'll have lost him.

Finn

Kiran's fingers trickle up the back of Finn's neck, spiderlike. Even though he likes spiders, he shakes her off and twists around to wrap his hand around her small wrist. "Quit it." The futon hard under his hip.

"Ouch. Jeez. Just teasing, you old crank."

He loosens his grip and, openhanded, lifts her wrist to his lips. Brushes her skin. Closes his eyes and inhales her patchouli. Phelan calls her Finn's hippie. Correction number one: not *his*. Number two: patchouli belonged to her long before California ever birthed a hippie. His eyes open to the dull gray walls of the dorm room, brightened with a cacophony of calendar photos, wildlife in every verdant shade of macaw and sea turtle and hummingbird.

"I'm sorry. Just wallowing over here." He rubs his cheek up her forearm, his head turned to look away from her. She's going away. "Indecision is a stark country."

"I'm just thinking about myself too. I can't quash my excitement. It feels good—so I want to share it." Her other hand reaches up, running the curve of his jaw between her thumb and fingers.

He wishes he could stay in the campfire glow of her enthusiasm, but always, always, his own uncertainties well up, a cold geyser. Unstoppable. "A person just has to wonder." He's never dared to wonder out loud. But Kiran's already—gone. Not like he'll scare her away.

"About?" She drapes a knee over his leg.

The small weight of her holds him to his topic. "What if my

mother didn't die? I mean, why are they so damn evasive?"

"I can't imagine that. A mother could never leave a baby as fabulous as you." She spreads her palm under his long-sleeve T-shirt, over his ribcage, riding the expansion and contraction of his breaths.

"What if I wasn't fabulous until I met you?" He flips and hovers above her, osprey like, a daily regimen of push-ups bringing him up high enough to see her from a distance. As if she were obscured behind riverine glare, a sleek trout whose sinuous silver curves come suddenly into view.

"Always you were fabulous. In thousands of lifetimes before this one, my friend." She tips her head back, exposing the pulse in her willow-brown neck. "Maybe Phelan stole you somehow. Pretended to buy a piece of red stone art from your street vendor mother, and while she went to get change, he disappeared into a Sydney crowd with you under his jacket."

Finn collapses onto his back beside her. "No doubt he's a thief, but I can't imagine he'd need to steal a Black baby. Your sister says the U.S. childcare system is chock full of kids waiting for families."

"Not as unusual as it sounds. At least back in the day. Kids had their uses. Domestics or farm labor." She pushes up from the floor, fluid, and slips toward the refrigerator. "Juice?"

He ignores the offer, flipping again onto his stomach, cradling his head in his elbow. Why won't Nik call him back? He needs to choose soon, or he'll lose both options and be stuck waiting tables in Teewinot, making ungodly amounts of money pretending to be friendly to strangers.

Kiran snuggles again alongside him, raising up on an elbow like a cobra to sip from her mango spritzer. Smelling her is always a feast for his senses.

She pokes a finger at the back of his head. "So what do you think the great mystery might be?"

He crosses both arms in front of him, his chin bouncing on the back of his hand while he talks. "I think about all kinds of unsavory things that could run in my veins, right? Maybe she was addicted to something and couldn't take care of a baby. Maybe she mastermined some elaborate swindle and sits in prison as we speak."

"Phelan and Nik would choose not to share that, I suppose. They wouldn't want to taint your potential. But still, unlikely." She pulls her shirt off and rolls onto her back in one graceful move. Then the spritzer is pouring slowly onto her belly, a thin serpentine trail that Finn must follow. He tastes the ripe fruit, and carbonated bubbles burst against his eyes.

Phelan

"Hi Dad—how's painting?" Phelan forces his voice to sound normal. He's had lots of practice over the years. People like normal.

"What're you doing here?" Charlie watches the Jetta's taillights disappear out the driveway.

Phelan forces a smile. People like smiles. "I needed to talk with Nik." He tries to settle, like normal, on a stool. "Nik doesn't care, of course, what I need." Damn how being around a parent can turn a person into a child. He picks up a random pen and taps it on the counter, searching for a rhythm. Some song he can fit himself into.

"Where'd she go?" Charlie leans at the sink, washing primary colors off his hands.

Phelan stands up again, pacing. He looks at the driveway, too, as if his eyes can pull her back, a cartoon character superpower. "Chasing after that stupid dog again." Damn how being around Nik seems to sap all the power he's earned in a twenty-year career.

"Her dog is smart. He's just scared, so he doesn't do what people try to tell him." Charlie pulls out the recently vacated stool and perches on it, his feet still on the floor.

Phelan never did reach his father's height. He carries Maggie's genes for smaller people, though her family made up for it with political stature. Ranchers ruled the range. "Dad, the dog was never hers."

"Apparently, he wants to be." Wiping his hands on the towel hung over the oven handle, Charlie leaves pale streaks of watered-down crimson.

"He's a dog. What he wants doesn't count much. Even if—and this is a huge if, not a bet I would lay on the table—she finds him, she'll still have to find him another home." Phelan strides to the back window, where he can see the barn through the fenced yard.

"It's my house. That's my barn. If I say he can stay, he can stay." Belligerence rises in Charlie's straight back and in the strength still obvious in the arm pointing across the property.

Phelan pours a glass of water, takes a sip. Finn told him how Bart feels about the dog. Not his battle. "Want some?" He tilts the glass at his father. Distraction is the devil's main delight. Nik has distracted him from the goal his boss gave him. Fine. He needs a day off anyway.

Charlie has his hands on a tall metal bottle. "Water for a road trip?"

"Nik's already gone, without you." Phelan winces at his easy cruelty.

"We can go too. The other direction. Long time since I've driven around the valley. Don't you want to see your old stomping grounds?" Busy at the sink, he doesn't meet Phelan's eyes. "Since you're the one who took my license away. It'll be fun."

The last few days have been no fun at all. Finn's surprise arrival and speedy disappearance, a night with Bart. And yesterday, starting off with Jaye's refusal, even when he threatened her ex. The woman who now has a husband and sons whose classmates would come up with a long list of creative names for their new mother. Phelan turns to Charlie. "Grab some coffee mugs too. It's cold out there."

Despite constant population overflow from increasingly expensive Teewinot, Dust still has no elementary school. In the next town south, they pass the renovated long brick building where Phelan first discovered his love of numbers. He rose all the way from those primary-colored wooden blocks to Algebra I in this building, one of the elite students who were so lucky to have Mr. Walsh in their still-tender years. "I got pretty fast at ducking thrown erasers in sixth grade."

"Your teacher played baseball when we were kids." Charlie's attention roams over the ball fields, now snow-covered and empty.

But the valley's old pastures and hayfields are not. They drive higher, this river flowing backward, south to north, and Phelan sees ranches now mostly turned to ranchettes. Old barbed wire cattle fencing replaced by fancy buck and rail paddocks for all the fancier horses that seem to be part of the required yard decor. One thing he didn't inherit from Maggie's family, that whole horsemanship thing. Manure was manure, and he didn't care to get involved with it.

A completely new elementary school was built in the center of the valley, pulling kids from the hamlets east and west of the river, all the way to the Idaho border. Charlie directs him to turn off the main highway, toward the lowlands along the water. "Look at the size of those houses. Let's drive out there." An ice fog erases whatever cattle must still be wintering in the bottoms. He watches a tractor mechanically spin off a long line of hay from a one-ton round bale. The valley's famous wrestling teams used to get strong from winter work on the ranch. Nowadays, not so much.

Phelan drives out of the fog on the far side of the river and pulls up next to a huge wrought iron gate—locked. He admires the graceful art in its sign. TRUMPETER SWAN ESTATES.

"Even geese don't have families big enough to fill all those bedrooms." Charlie grew up in this valley full of families with six, eight, sometimes thirteen kids, and he's still impressed with the size, as much as the stonework. Kids used to share bedrooms.

"An entertainment center for each member of the family, perhaps?" Phelan is only half-joking. The clients he works with definitely need their entertainment. He pushes away the disconcerting thought that sometimes, unwittingly, he might be it.

Charlie laughs. "One way to avoid fights over the remote." He points up a different route, toward the Idaho mountains, less imposing than the steep, bald-headed beasts on the Wyoming side. "What's up that?"

The locked gate here bears another intricate iron design. "Timber Horse Trails. A resort? Looks like this place plans to stick around awhile. None of those rotting wooden arches for them." The sign features a solo logger working with a draft horse to twitch a huge dead tree out of the forest. Time-shares maybe? The houses up here, no smaller than the ones near the river, are built with horizontal stacks of those huge former trees. A consistent aesthetic, like the all-brick college campus Finn visited in Minnesota a few years back, when Phelan still hoped his fascination with wildlife would pass. He never suspected that a devotion to wild places would lead his son to such negative judgment of the career that makes their lives possible. A hole opens in the overcast, blue emerging, brightening the world, if briefly. The central lodge is an architectural reflection of the mountains, with steep roof pitches at varied angles to each other. Must employ an army of local kids to shovel the shingled valleys clear after a storm. People like resorts, visiting them or earning money at them. Phelan's career serves many. It is honorable work.

Charlie remains silent, but the frown on his face deepens. He points again. "Go that way, then."

"What're we looking for?" Phelan doesn't have any particular memories of this rounded hill. A bonfire party or two. Parties he's probably worked hard to forget. They find another side road and swing onto it through high snow berms.

"Your great-grandparents' house was here. One of your mother's cousins got it. They wouldn't have sold out."

Phelan considers that. His mother was one of the youngest ones in the crowd of cousins, so maybe her cousin's kids sold out. "That old house was probably thick with mold." Hanging on was not healthy.

"Her cousin had lots of kids. Hard to keep up with the housework."

Phelan remembers suddenly. Some of those kids were downright nasty. "The kids must've sold. Too many of them to all make a living growing hay."

"I only have one grandkid. No one can blame me for all this development. This is crazy."

If Nik had kids, Finn would have cousins. But yeah, no kids is lucky, since she married Bart. "You get grand-cats. All appropriately spayed and neutered." Nik is crazy but maybe not as crazy as Moon Valley.

Charlie settles back against the padded headrest. "And maybe I'll have a grand-dog soon too. That will make Nikki happy."

Phelan presses the gas hard enough to spin the Rover around in the snow. Time to keep driving. He wasn't here to make Nik happy, and he doubted the dog could do it either. Finn sure isn't making him happy these days. He misses his son already, that sweet one from just a few years ago. He's glad to imagine the current one out on his own. To imagine what, or who, might fit into the empty nest.

They make it to the valley's main town, Callisto, and the only non–gas station option for coffee. Phelan hopes it doesn't live up to its Cowboy Coffee name. The first time his grandparents' branding crew offered him a mug, he practically choked on the unfiltered grounds. "Coming in?"

"Don't we need gas? Me and Finn get coffee there." He points down the block.

Phelan pulls his door closed again, refastens his seat belt. Finn must have made more than one trip back from school that he didn't know about. He pulls into the road, grateful for the lack of traffic, his eyes not quite focused. He turns in, easing up next to a pump. Charlie's large hands curve around their mugs, and Phelan hands him a pair of fives. "Get whatever you want for snacks."

Two fresh-baked molasses cookies, soft and cakey, rest on the console, two mugs in their holders. Charlie probably doesn't remember that Phelan only likes crisp cookies. Or maybe he does. "Where to next?" This trip down memory lane isn't turning up the memories Charlie is after. But at least he's not just sitting in the house.

"Still south. Out to the Pinnacles. That's where Nikki says her friend used to live. But I don't remember Hawkins. Seeing the ranch will jog the memories."

Phelan's face goes cold, despite the gulp of rank coffee that burns his throat. "She told you about her trip?"

"She found a guy with an owl but couldn't find her dog."

"*The* dog." Phelan tries to be funny. "Guys with owls have to be a lot more rare than dogs.", He senses his failure.

"*Her* dog is pretty rare. Those eyes, especially."

Phelan feels the old familiar sense of his father's disappointment, disapproval. Charlie's never-spoken "you'll never get it—you don't fit in here." Silence fills the miles until they ease into a plowed pull-out by some mailboxes. "The Pinnacles." He waves his hand at the jagged cliffs that bring the ranchland below them to an abrupt edge. Lining that edge is a double string of tall condos, their backs to a private airstrip and a series of hangars. Their blank, many-windowed eyes reflect dark trees rising steeply behind white fields. Charlie whistles, eyes almost as blank. Phelan's shoulders lift and drop again. "People have to live somewhere." They usually have to work, too, and now telecommuting makes it possible.

"No cattle?" Charlie looks around the fields. "Elk used to steal hay here, since the ranch stole their bottomlands. Did you know Hawkins?"

Phelan's people had done the research. "One in my class but not friendly enough that I ever came out here for anything." The research wasn't so honorable. He wouldn't remember a Hawkins in his class without someone telling him. "You weren't in the valley that much when you were trucking. No reason you should remember."

"I grew up here too." Peevish, Charlie takes a super-sized bite of the second cookie. "I want to remember."

Phelan prefers to forget. He put his staff's research to dubious uses. He still hasn't gotten the results he is paid to achieve. Like his own son, he doesn't much like the man who plays that kind of game trying to get those results.

Charlie points with the remainder of his cookie. "I remember that peak over there. Me and my brother saw a wolverine up there one summer. Yeah, summer, but on a snowfield that lasted into July. No wolverine would live there now. Couldn't bear to see the valley like this, even from four miles away."

Phelan doesn't ask how he could know. And doesn't doubt him either.

"Just imagine all the snowmobiling." He waves his cookie at an open-sided, covered barn where long trailers—toy haulers—were parked.

"You and Mom loved snowmobiling. I could never keep up." He never saw a wolverine either. He wonders if Finn ever has.

Slumped back against the seat, Charlie looks older than he should. "You're an important guy. How're you going to fix this?"

His father's not only losing his memory. He's delusional.

Nikki

After she crests out across from Woody's gas station, only willows along buried waterways relieve a ubiquitous sage and snow–scape. She'll need to switch to a country station to match this view. Good music for self-castigation.

She can't help but look for Jaye's group of unusual mustangs. What she sees, though, are the usual—antelope herds whose tawny sides splotched with white so perfectly match the sunstruck land, they become visible only when they move. Then Nik's gaze follows them, trying to see whether, just maybe, a dog who also wears snow-season camo might be following them. Not to eat but to learn from. They would know how to take advantage of landform microclimates. But they would have little reason to share their knowledge with a predator-shaped student. She chews on her lower lip. Her reasons for marrying Bart seem spurious now. Emotionally driven, people can be so unreasonable. Maybe wild animals, too, act in ways not always susceptible to reason.

The antelope disappear as she follows a road sign north toward the Neaippeh mountains and a well-advertised restaurant and convenience store. A place she remembers being popular with snow-mobilers, who might take note of a dog running far from any ranch. Snow berms edging the roadway are higher here, closing her in, the radio stuck on songs of loss and loneliness. The simple act of giving voice sometimes can be enough to dispel whatever pain the lyrics relate. But she doesn't know these songs and can't sing along, so that option isn't available to her. Like her friends aren't available to her. Busy. And far away.

She knows one person who isn't so far away. And whose new dude ranch doesn't yet include winter visitors. She should call Jaye and see how yesterday's session with Phelan went. Maybe new invest-ment will allow her to be more of a four-seasons operation. A wide spot opens ahead where the plows push the berm over the edge, toward the river. Why not reach out, make a new friend. Jaye hired Russell to talk with guests about wildlife, after all. They must have something in common.

She feels guilty for idling, spewing unnecessary greenhouse gases, but being lonely is bad enough without being cold, too. The little car vibrates under her as she listens to the dial tone, radio off. The sky's clouds begin to coalesce, white all around softening to ivory. Clouds lower into mountains, road blends into meadow. Finally, a voice breaks through.

"Sage Winds Ranch." A pause, with some heavy breaths as if Jaye is outside, doing heavy work.

Nik waits for more words, but none surface. She needs to make a move, but friendship feels like an unfamiliar art. "Hi, Jaye? This is Nik. Of the lost dog? I wanted to, uh, thank you again for your help. And um, see how things went for you after I left for Moon Valley. Any luck with the potential investor?"

The heavy breathing stops, but it isn't interrupted by words. A silence that somehow sounds sharp escapes from Nik's phone.

"Are you still there? I'm out by Dora, close to the Stage Stop. Maybe the connection is no good?" Nik wants to ask her for more ideas on places to hang signs.

"I'm still here." Jaye's voice, wry, dry. Like snow when the temperatures drop and pull all the moisture out.

"Oh, good. Did Phelan like your drawings? See some possibilities he thought his client would want to be part of?" Nik is out of her league, dealing with businesses. Wildlife work is rarely about dreaming up new things, more about trying to protect vestiges of the world's former richness.

"No."

The sentence is so short, Nik almost doesn't register it. She's still trying to think of the next thing to say to keep a conversation alive. The silence that follows Jaye's sentence is what she hears. "Oh." Not enough to inspire a response. "I'm so sorry. It seemed promising there for a bit. The ranch will be fine though, right? Not like you were counting on outside money?"

In the wordless gap, Nik hears what Jaye would never open up to say, especially not to a stranger. "Jaye, I really am sorry. I know what it's like to get your hopes up." She wants to say something about Zolo. She hopes Jaye will say something about Zolo. Or something about how close Dora is to Yahanna, after all, and coffee is on if Nik wants to drop by. But she says nothing. The connection drops, even though she hasn't moved a muscle. Only the car shivers under her. She puts it back in gear, foot still on the brake, and stares through the endless gray. She could call back, at least say a proper goodbye.

A small motion catches her eye. Distance unreadable, her heart startles toward Zolo. But the motion isn't a houndish lope. A hop, but not large enough for a hunting coyote. Slowly, her mind sorts out that the movement is nearby and belongs to a small creature. She turns the car off and steps out. Long flopping ears. A domestic rabbit, rather than a wild snowshoe hare. A Lop. A mini.

"Hello out there. Are you looking for someone?" She squats on her heels, the shearling lining of her boots cushioning her, arms stretched forward. "Can I give you a ride?"

The little rabbit eyes her for a moment, then decides. The answer is yes—and small hops turn to energetic bounds, hind legs stretching longer than Nik would have imagined. She prepares herself for impact, but the bunny stops on a dime and begins nuzzling the pockets of her jacket.

"Oh, sorry." She's apologizing again. Must be her theme song for the day. "Just dog biscuits, I'm afraid. But we can find something for you at the restaurant, I'm sure. Will you come?" She fits her arm under the soft cinnamon haunches and lifts the almost weightless rabbit to her chest. The bunny snuggles against her quilted down jacket, so she settles her new companion inside its folds. She leaves the radio off and hums old lullabies instead.

At the Stage Stop, she holds one arm under the rabbit against her stomach and gathers a few flyers in her other hand. Miniature or not, the extra being adds courage and purpose to her stride.

She pushes the door with her shoulder and, in the sudden cessation of wind, realizes she can stand upright. She shakes her hair back around her shoulders, and the shopkeeper calls out a cheery greeting. She waves, the flyers fluttering in her hand.

"What you got there?"

She leans her hip on the counter and irons the papers with the edge of her hand, awkward with the Lop still hidden against her belly.

"Another lost dog? I'm sorry to hear that, but sure, you can post one there on the corkboard." He points toward the restrooms, where a large bulletin board covers the wall between the two doors. He opens his mouth to say more, but a crowd pushes through the door, thick in their snowmobile gear and raucous in their lingering two-cycle deafness. She escapes toward the board and uses available pushpins to post Zolo's photo on both ends of it, hard to miss no matter which restroom a person uses. The rabbit never frets, despite her clumsiness. They seem to be in agreement about the need for secrecy, with loud voices debating deli sandwiches versus a sit-down lunch. Nik sees two other lost dog notices. A Labrador and a border collie—both much better suited to winter. On her flyer, the Cata-houla's anxious expression turns her stomach.

She pushes into the restroom, freeing the bunny onto the counter. She'd heard no women's voices in the lunch discussion. "Stay right there for a minute, all right?" As she reemerges from the stall, however, her luck runs out. The restroom door opens, and a young girl enters the space. Their eyes meet, and then the rabbit sits up, drawing all four eyes at once. The girl squeals, and in the same moment, the rabbit leaps at her. Nik is too slow to step between them. The girl crumples to the floor, gasping, but the rabbit clings to her chest.

"Cygnus. You're back, you're back." Between gulping sobs, words jumble out.

Nik pauses. Not an attack. A reunion. She waits, gives them time. The bunny rubs soft ears along the girl's damp cheeks. She finally speaks up. "Cygnus?"

"Where did you find him?" The girl's voice suddenly clear and strong.

"About three miles south. At least he's small enough to stay on top of the snow." Nik thinks about Zolo's thin legs, thinly haired. He's light but not featherweight.

"Snowmobilers go way too fast to see him though. Especially at night." The girl sits on the floor now, legs in a wide *V* with the rabbit in the middle, searching pockets.

"Has he been gone long?" A cinnamon bunny stands out in the snow but she's right, not so much in the snowy dark.

"Two nights. I couldn't do any schoolwork. But Dad wouldn't let me look very far. Three miles. That's a long ways for such a little guy."

Ah, yes. Nik realizes the girl isn't wearing snowmobile gear, just jeans and tennis shoes. Dad must be the man at the counter. "How'd he get loose?"

"He didn't. Dad's got a supercool latch on the bunny run. Even Cygnus can't get it open."

Nik hears her pride, but she's missing the logic here. "He was three miles away."

The girl pushes upright, scooping Cygnus in one arm. Like a miniature adult, she straightens her back and holds her hand out for a shake. "Emory Whalen." Her head cocks slightly, waiting.

"Nik Delaney. From over to Dust. At least, that's where my dad lives, and I'm living with him."

"Dad and I live here, right now, with Cyggie."

Nik waits this time. Emory has more to say. She opens the door, and Nik follows her into the store's aisles of colorful packaging, holding back the day's hovering gloom. Returning to childhood, Emory skips ahead to the counter, holding Cygnus high in both hands.

"Whoa! Where's he been hiding?"

"He was three whole miles away. Not hiding." She sets him on the counter, where her father runs his hands through dark fur. Then she

The Scent of Distant Family

turns to Nik with a flourish. "Mrs. Delaney says he was just out there on the snow for anyone to see. But she was the only one who did."

Emory's dad turns his eyes to her. She hadn't noticed before how blue his eyes were. Darker than Zolo's but every bit as striking, especially with his deep-brown hair. She's almost embarrassed by the gratitude she sees in them. "Nik is fine, really."

"Miller. Miller Whalen, and we can't thank you enough." He steps around the counter to grasp her hand. "Here you are missing your own best friend, but you stop to pick up ours and bring him right to us."

"That last part was pure luck. I didn't know who was looking for him." She wonders why she didn't see a poster on the corkboard.

Emory solves that mystery, waving a flyer at her. "I was just adding a reward. Mrs. Connelly let me shovel for her yesterday so I'd have money to offer." In her other hand, she holds out a small wad of dollars.

"Oh, no, not needed. Seeing you two together is reward enough." From the counter, Cygnus stands up, leaning on Emory's back with one tiny paw. He sniffs her ear, and she giggles, pulls him over her shoulder into another whole-body hug.

"You better get him to the kitchen and see what Gretchen has for carrot tops." Miller has one hand on the top of her head and turns it slightly toward the staff door. She needs no further instruction.

So much for commercial kitchen standards, but unlikely to see a health inspector out here. Nik's wholesome sense of satisfaction is tempered by a selfish tug of emptiness. She hopes the tears in her eyes appear as happiness. They are hot enough to hurt, after the cold outside.

"How long has your dog been missing?" Miller respects her privacy by stepping back behind his wooden countertop and shuffling a stack of receipts on a small stainless spike.

"Going into a second week." The words aren't as clear as they could be, but the pain is.

"Ouch. We've seen a lot of notices going up lately." He picks up a stained coffee cup. Sets it back down without drinking.

Nik's antennae go up. "Emory seems to think the bunny didn't just escape?"

"Strange time of year for dogs to run off too. Was yours in a fenced yard?"

A fenced yard was a requirement for placing Zolo at an adopter's. She nods, cautious.

Miller's cobalt eyes look into hers. "That's a pattern with the others too."

"Meaning?"

"Nimble fingers can reach over the top and open the gates." His broken fingernails drum on the counter, a quick riff.

She stares at their motion. Who would do that?

"A gal named Tara got released from jail a few weeks ago. Apparently, she doesn't like to see anything penned up." Miller's voice sounds empathetic.

The rock that had lodged in Nik's throat drops hard to the bottom of her gut. "Tara in Parodice? Do you know her?"

"My wife knows her. They were cellmates. Alex is still there."

Zolo

Music to his ears, music rings in multiple tongues and different pitches, all happy, all eager. Zolo is on his feet in one breath. He exhales without joining his voice to the others. Behind the baying joy is another sound. He doesn't know that sound, but despite the high whining, he knows it is not dog. He cocks his head and listens. It is a long way behind.

He can no longer resist. He tips his nose up, and song pours out, creek leaving mountains, gravity pulled. Creek song leaps and with it Zolo, over rocks, through sun and snow. Hounds are giving chase, and he chases them. He has been so lonely.

Nose in air releases voice; air releases their scent. Hounds, hounds, and ahead of them, a long cat, bounding. Zolo stretches stride, tail flat out, and he breathes wide, lungs filling, buoyant with dogs and songs. Heart pushes and pulls and throbs with dogs and ecstasy of chase. Snow splashes from spread toes, snow sheds from slick sides as he swims through windward side of sweet-smelling trees.

With running and baying and excitement, he forgets. Whine creeps closer, and yes, fear, but dogs are ahead. Dogs slowing down and song speeding up, pitch climbs with mountain, and with mountain's lion, now spitting as they stretch, front paws on cliff face. Frustration barks, interrupts baying song. Zolo stops in lee-side tree hole, watches, listens. They jump and bark and ignore whining getting closer, passing him. Whining loud until suddenly silent, and men's voices surface in space still ringing with dogs.

"Did you get a picture at least?"

"Shot a few, but I'll have to see how they turn out."

"Because there's no following him up that."

A crisp whistle smells like metal, cuts hound song. Zolo can see hounds but not men, hidden behind trees. He trembles. Indecision.

"Let's go. That's all we'll do here." Another whistle blast turns the dogs.

Toward Zolo, they turn. And one nose lifts. Four noses lift. Zolo's tail begins to wag, high and happy.

Until they run.

First one is on him, knocking into his shoulder. Another right behind, teeth slashing at his hindquarters. Two others run so fast they leap pack mates over his sprawled form in snow. Zolo hears men's voices, and he hears teeth and growling and under it all a whimpering. He twists and panics and somersaults, and pain whistles sharp, toothy, through his leg and his lungs, and men's voices yell, and his pain echoes confusion, and he rolls away from heaviest dog, slides past another, looking over shoulder at advancing men. Zolo gathers his legs and pain and confusion, and mountain pitches him downhill, stumbling over drifts, limping under loud squirrels. He breathes hard, without music, without hounds, into cold desert draw. Only sadness, deeper than mountain, bigger than mountain lion, follows him.

Nikki

The Jetta squirms around in crystal snow churned up by snowmobiles traveling on the roadway. Nik follows a business sign pointing toward the local feedstore. Only a couple trailer houses in the vicinity, but surely the gray distances include more scattered ranches. A person would have to be a true fanatic to even find animals to set free. Of course, getting them from animal shelters can add to the volume. She wonders how many other shelters have fallen prey to Tara's sincerity. She wants to bang her head on the steering wheel. Stupid, stupid, stupid. She wants to rub her red eyes in the soft cinnamon fur of Emory's rabbit. The spot where Cygnus snuggled against her belly stays unbearably cold, despite waves of heat from the dash.

She manages to find a post office, alone in its narrow valley but for a weathered cabin with quilts hanging in the front windows, then a pottery shop, which likely does all its winter business online, but a lady with gray hair piled loose as a cow patty on her head accepts a flyer anyway. Nik backs away from conversation, "more flyers to get up," and crawls into the little car. The main highway is ahead. She drives, open vistas stretching across endless space before sagebrush meets the mountains, but she feels trapped by her own wishful thinking. She imagined Zolo home where it wasn't going to exist. She missed any signs that Tara might be this person Miller described, the kind of person who throws family pets at the mercy of the world's endless hazards. The car's tires chant at her: STU-pid, STU-pid, STU-pid. Her chest aches. A wind blows a red box along the edge of the highway, and she pictures Zolo, the once scaredy-dog, coming out of his hermit crab shell to jump on it, to bite at it and growl with his own playful imagination. Behind the box rolls a glistening black semi with matching trailer, its grille painted, white teeth dripping with vermillion blood.

She turns her head away.

She's almost to the Rim Rendezvous, and she doesn't want to talk to anyone—Tara's deceit souring what she feels about all people. She was right about local gossip, but it wasn't helpful. Maybe Woody has heard something more useful. Besides, she needs gas.

When she goes through the door, its loud clang of dangling bells tap-dances on her strained nerves. He has another customer in the store. Without even pretending to look around, she stands and watches while he dishes up a meal from under the heat lamps. He nods at her but then does a double take.

"Oh, hey, Jaye's friend. I'll be right with you." His face, striped with loose strands of hair escaped from the rubber band, pinkens.

Nik wonders if his snake ever surfaced.

While his customer steps through the door, he brushes his hands off on faded jeans. "What can I get for you today? Nik, right?"

She hands him a Zolo flyer. "I didn't have any of these with me before." STU-pid STU-pid. "But I'm hoping you can keep your ears to the ground and let me know if anyone happens to mention seeing him. He's really distinctive."

Woody studies the photo. "So he is. Even without the blue eyes—if you just saw him from a distance." He picks up a tape dispenser and walks to the front windows to give it prime display space. "I can put 'em in a couple places if you want to leave me a few others. He's shy, it says?"

"Yeah, he probably won't let anyone else catch him. That's why I keep coming over here looking."

"Where do you live, then?"

"Down in Moon Valley, near Dust."

He whistles. "Putting in some miles for your dog. But I'd do the same."

She better ask. Being polite won't hurt her. "You have your boa somewhere safe yet?"

His face brightens. "Wanna meet her?" His eager wave invites her to his living quarters at the back of the store. "Forgive the mess. Bachelor pad, you know."

He's Jaye's friend, after all. And shit, she's exhausted. She wonders if Guthrie really is a girl.

She steps through the door, and he moves to a corner cordoned off as snake zone. It smells . . . like something that eats rodents. She breathes through her mouth. "So Guthrie's going to live inside for the rest of the winter?" The boa's tail tapers evenly toward the tip.

"Can I get you a drink? Have you been out putting up flyers all day?"

She turns to where Woody indicates a rocking chair and imagines the view without the cloud cover. She sinks onto the pillow tied on

The Scent of Distant Family

the chair's seat. "Hot tea a possibility?"

"Piece o' cake. Do you want milk? Cream—or soy even?"

He's overly keen. But she's surprised he thinks of a nondairy option that doesn't come in a paper packet of suspicious powder. He ducks back into the store, and she lets her eyes unfocus under the distant and hidden mountains. Her body feels bruised. She is torn knowing Zolo is lost on the desert and knowing she can't— like Woody probably would—just camp out until she finds him.

"Here. Hope that's a good amount for you." He hands her a thick mug, the Marine Corps Amphibious Attack Unit label over a lime-green muscular beast she'd have to guess was a salamander. Maybe that's where his interest in herps comes from. The black tea is colored chocolate as a spring river.

She half-closes her eyes in the steam. "Thank you." A blurred murmur.

He eases into another chair nearby and begins patting tobacco into the bowl of a carved pipe. "D'you mind?"

"Your house, no, of course not." The tobacco's warm cherry scent comes as a pleasant surprise.

"Guthrie doesn't seem interested in returning to hibernation. Maybe she isn't able to. I've ordered frozen mice from Rock Springs."

She leans her head against the chair and listens to the sounds of a second match scratching, Woody puffing the flame into life. She tugs her wallet from her back pocket. She hands him a small stack of her business cards people can take, even though her number's on the poster.

"Make sure people have it when they see him." He nods. "Good idea."

He said when, not if. An optimist. She knows she should be on the road. Phelan will be livid. Charlie has a right to be. Not much incentive to return and face the music. She rocks the chair back and forth, her feet rolling from heel to toe. She thinks about Tara.

Woody takes a few more pulls that sound strangely like surfacing fish and inhales deeply. "Anybody seen him anywhere?"

The rocking soaks into her muscles. His gray eyes wait, patient. She tells him what she learned from Miller, and though he related the story without any judgment, she hears contempt slide into her own version. When she stops, he puffs a few times more in silence.

"Miller's good people. He'll ask around for you. And Emory, too, with all her school friends."

Of course, Woody knows them. What's fifty miles out here? She holds a sip of tea in her mouth, warming her teeth. Poor Emory, without her mother. Miller single parenting, like Phelan. She wonders why his wife is in prison.

Pipe in hand, Woody rests his elbow on a bent knee, smoke curling toward the windows. "So Zolo was a shelter dog? How'd you get him to trust you?"

The flyer has the shelter's logo on it, their number as well as hers. They weren't likely to trust her judgment anymore, not after she mistakenly trusted a former inmate. She has no business to judge Miller's wife. She doesn't like to think about Emory, though, having to visit her mother in handcuffs, watched over by people wearing guns. In a place that clearly wouldn't welcome rabbits. "Time, I suppose. I fostered him almost four months." She wonders how long Miller's wife is in for.

He puffs again. "More than enough time to make things worse, so if he trusts you, you did something right." Watches a pair of smoke rings not quite fit inside each other. "How long did you say he's been missing?"

The Scent of Distant Family

Finn's trust feels more fragile every day. "Almost two weeks." Her empty mug has lost its heat. Finn's mother gone two decades. She rubs her hands against her kneecaps. Presses her thumbs hard into tense tendons.

"I wonder," he says around the stem of the pipe, "if this Tara didn't break parole or somethin'." He puffs twice. "Could explain why she isn't answering your calls or posting anything."

Nik's back straightens. "She's springing animals from homes she perceives as prisons. I think she's just ignoring me. She's probably done the same with who knows how many shelter groups."

"Could be." He puffs, and his eyes focus out the windows. "I think she only recently got out." He inhales deeply. Takes the pipe out of his mouth but then settles it between his teeth again and doesn't say anything more.

Nik feels the snake behind them, unblinking. Her lungs constrict. She wants to blame Tara. Or her parole officer, who could have put her back behind bars and turned her dog loose to save himself any effort. Nik wants Woody to take her side, but she's just making up stories. She doesn't know Tara. She doesn't even know any parole officers. Damn. "Or shit, who knows?"

He turns to her now. "Doesn't get you any closer to finding him. I'm sorry."

Her lips tremble.

He stands up to take her mug. "Refill?"

She needs to say no, but her head nods. So many kinds of trapped, like inside someone else's image of who you are. Inside a feared image of who you might be, some inherited tendency. Inside the intense emotions of an unforgettable ordeal. Or even in a long-ago promise, one that maybe no longer serves its intended purpose.

Finn would have to wonder about his mother. Of course he would make up stories.

Woody hands her mug back, steam soothing her dry skin. "If Zolo's moving, he's visible. And unusual enough for people to take note."

She can tell he's trying to bolster her hopes. She wonders how many people he has done that for. "How long have you lived out here?"

"Since I got out of the military, a good long time ago." He leans on the wall where he can look down at the dull-colored snake or out at the invisible mountains, either way. "Always something new to learn about the place, or people."

Woody's words, unselfconscious, sound like contentment. Nik stares at Guthrie, who wouldn't survive an hour if she left her little space of pretend summer. The boa seems unconcerned about danger outside her cardboard. "Jaye sure freaks out around her."

Again, he passes no judgment. "We all have something, don't we?"

Winter leans against his windows, and her lips tighten. She can't be his kind of mellow. Her *something* is Zolo, and getting him to safety. Bringing him home, as Charlie would say. A hiking companion, someone to sit by her side while she works in her solitary space. At least flyers are now posted across the countryside, and people want to be helpful. Even Phelan is being helpful, if under duress. Bart has decent employment. Charlie is still painting toys. Finn still wants to talk with her about his future. When the time comes, she'll know what to say.

5

Jaye

Even two days later, the same disbelief that gripped her in Phelan's office hovers over every breath, and because her limbs still throb with the same anger, she chooses to snowshoe across the wide pasture, dragging hay in a heavy plastic sled. She has to push her muscles hard to keep them from shaking. She has to push her energy to exhaustion to make possible the slightest amount of sleep. And she has to save every last cent—not one bleeding penny is going to run a tractor when her own human power can feed this whole herd. Sage Winds Ranch does not need outside investment.

She and the ranch have everything required for success. Open space to experiment in and strong legs to pull dreams forward. If it takes all day to scatter feed over the snow, great; the night will be shorter. She won't let this place fail. If it takes a lifetime for income to cover expenses, she'll have had a life full of watching wild ideas bloom, as different as Indian paintbrush and sunny balsamroot. If wind drives snow pellets hard into her eyes, her tears will be that much easier to explain.

One leg sinks into a soft spot, and the sled loses all its momentum as it runs into her, the rim of its leading edge a painful prod. Polenta circles back, tail wagging. Cautious, Jaye switches her weight onto the other leg. She extracts her foot, but the tall boot stays in the snow. She drags the sled alongside and sits on the hay while she pulls the boot up and stuffs her leg back into it. Pulling a glove off with her teeth, she tightens the drawstring cord at the top. Polenta pushes her nose against Jaye's fingers and gets a distracted scratch under her jaw. Cold air sears her chest, and she drags it in deeper. Horses swirl around her now, Polenta dancing between their flashing legs. Jaye flings two handfuls of snow, too cold to pack into balls. It scatters into powder in the air. Rainbows of sun sparks spook the hungry horde, and horses wheel away, heels close to the sled.

Jaye shakes the first thick hay flakes into clean snow but doesn't pause to watch anyone eat. She'll need to make four trips to spread out enough feed for these hayburners. The biggest and bossiest turn their ears back and claim the early run without challenge from the others, who run back to the barn with her while she loads and returns.

The donkeys bray when they first see her and every time she goes back for more. "That's what you always say," she says, swatting the taller jenny on her shoulder. The two donkeys are the last to eat, but the three ponies, who are even smaller, bluff the more laid-back horses, who share piles near the end of the line.

"Step back, this load's for you." She digs her feet into the snow and gets the refilled sled moving fast enough for a bit of a jog. A donkey leans onto skinny haunches and bursts forward in a short, rocking gallop. Polenta, with her wide paws, runs ahead, egging them on with quick barks. A pony bucks past, a paint in soft tan with white on his side in the shape of China. Jaye flings the hay, and one hefty chunk bounces off his neck. He stops and grabs a quick mouthful, shaking his head at a shy brown gelding, still waiting. Finally, everyone eats, and Jaye stands still, breathing hard, enjoying the satisfaction of a well-fed herd.

No one is going to steal this from her. Phelan has never seen a hunkering down like she can hunker down. She can save the cost of having a crew come in to shoe this bunch, even if it takes her three weeks each time to get 'em all done herself.

Things were different in Moon Valley. The debate about selling out caused her parents' divorce, even though they were united in disgust at all the chopping up of old farms and ranches. But if a person gives up on a place like this while it still has a chance to hang onto what makes it desirable . . . she wouldn't forgive herself. The other side of the Deheya range sinks under its growing population, but on this side, people don't suck up all the air. In this part of the country, people might be out here for work, running drill rigs or driving log trucks or what-have-you, but they don't generally live here, and endless yard lights don't erase the stars.

Polenta hops into the empty sled and stretches down on her front legs. Jaye waves a hand at her. "Not a chance. You have four legs, and I have two. You should be pulling this thing and letting me ride." The dog hops back out, unfazed. Jaye starts trudging. "You're as entitled as *Mister* Delaney." Her breath sizzles out between grinding teeth.

Not even to her dog can she put into words the entirety of Phelan's chicanery. Ha. School vocabulary returns. Must be because his ploy feels so unbelievably adolescent. The trudging, the crunch of snow under boots, the smell of horses and alfalfa, these bring back the reliable feeling of school days, when she didn't know how fast everything can change. When she had no clue how disingenuous people can be. Before the cultural habit of deference to those with money had taken hold. Barely remembered words just keep coming. The stability promised in high school lied. The world is so much more complicated.

Polenta barks, and looking up, Jaye sees her dog poised at attention ahead of her. They both look beyond the pasture fence toward an odd rumble. Way too cold for rain and definitely not thunderstorm season. Polenta whines but doesn't move. Jaye can't see anything yet, but the sound grows. And then out of the gray horizon, she does see—a rolling motion across the sage and snow clouding like summer dust. As they approach, individual horses appear out of the cloud. Leading the way is Tess, the wild grulla mare.

Like her dog, Jaye stands frozen. Their freedom fills her. She notices her whole herd is staring as well, but remarkably, none of them have left their hay to chase along. The snow is deep enough, and they are domestic enough, and the alfalfa is sweet enough. The grulla doesn't seem to notice them, doesn't swerve her herd toward their fence to consider getting hay for themselves. She leads beyond the horses and past the fences, her head high and her dark tail streaming behind. She seems to know what she wants, and it isn't here. Behind her, a bay and a strawberry roan follow in the snowy pathway she carves. The thunder rises through the ground into Jaye's legs, and she feels it in her backbone.

A smaller horse plunges off to the side, throwing snow with her nose and heels, toying with winter. Jaye laughs, watching her. The heavy stallion is, apparently, used to her antics, and he pushes her along from behind. She spins, but he's fast enough to cut her off and drive her forward again. She rears. A beam of sunlight bursts through the overcast and touches her sorrel coat with flame, and Jaye wishes she had a camera. Any visitor, or prospective visitor, would be enamored. As simply as Nik named the grulla mare, the name Razzle tumbles out like ripe berries over ice cream. It was her grandmother's nickname for her.

Then the horses are gone. In the charged air behind them, snow swirls, and Jaye sees a flash of her grandmother's long hair, gone silver in a matter of weeks when her cancer settled in. She sees her grandmother, on that last morning in her brave body, climbing on through her body's torment for a final mountain ride with her mare. By midnight, the family was gathered around her bed, and she was telling them all to keep courage. A scared kid, Jaye closed the memory away. Seeing her grandmother's face again, she finds a curiosity there she hadn't noticed.

Whatever her words might have meant back then, she knows exactly what they mean now.

"C'mon, 'Lenta, if you want a ride." She gives her dog a whistle and claps her hands, waving her toward the sled. The dog jumps in, then, catching the excitement, jumps out. "What, are you chicken?" Polenta leaps back in and braces her legs and barks. Jaye hears it—*about time you figured this out*. She laughs. "Hell, girl, sometimes my brain's slow as water flowing uphill." Another bark. "Right. In winter."

She stashes the sled in the hay barn and follows the packed trail to the house. She slaps her hand on her hip, calling the dog. She doesn't want her to consider following those mustangs. She does, however, want to tell someone about the bold little herd, expanding their allocated range farther north. Of course it's Selina she wants to tell.

"Jaye, I've been meaning to call you."

"You, my friend, will not believe who just came to visit."

"Why won't I believe? No, just tell me who."

"Because they haven't been here in fifty years or so." Jaye uses both hands to pull her wet socks off. Her phone is tucked between her shoulder and her cold chin.

"No, no, that was the why. I said just tell me who."

"Well, now you have the why. Give me a few guesses."

"Um, your brothers? Your parents? No, right, they hate winters. And they only *act* like they're that old."

"Unfair. Your family hates winters too."

"And they'll all soon have their wish—the season will fall into the rising ocean, never to be seen again. But I digress."

"Remember the picture of my grandmother you always liked?"

"Of course—sitting on that gorgeous horse. You aren't going to tell me her ghost stopped by?"

"Okay, I won't tell you. Though it could be true. The mare, though, Selina, the mare. She's reincarnated as a BLM horse, and she's leading a little herd. Here, in Yahanna."

"Must have bailed out to get away from the new drilling down on the Red Desert."

"Plenty of old drilling going on around here. Who knows why she came. But she's every bit as gorgeous as my grandmother's."

"Going to try catching her?"

Jaye stops talking. She eases down on the hard floor, knees bent and backbone supported by the wall. "Ahh. Sorry, I needed to rest my back. Been hauling hay by hand with the old sled. Great exercise. And no, I'd never think about trying to catch her."

From Selina's end of the phone, the sound of wine being sipped. "She'd never be as beautiful if she was caught, would she?"

A heart thuds in a weary chest. "How come you're the only one who ever understands me?"

"Seven years is not nada, right? Someone else will come." Selina breathes, then sips again. "Why, pray tell, are you not using the tractor?"

Jaye knows where her power sits now. "You wouldn't believe how pitiful the Delaney guy is. He completely lied about having an

The Scent of Distant Family

investor to work with me. Just some big-money dealer who wants to buy me out for whatever reason. And when it doesn't work, he decides to threaten me."

"Take away your firstborn son?"

"Something about as ludicrous." Jaye takes a deep breath and a gamble. "He's going to expose me, and you, as lesbians."

Selina gasps, then hiccups, then bursts into laughter. "That's all he's got? Oh, Lordy, isn't he precious?"

Jaye rests one bare ankle on a bent knee and breathes out. She should have known she could count on this woman. "But what about your boys? You know how high school can get."

"They think you're more cool by far than I am. They've totally got the chutzpah to call out any idjits. Does Delaney think this news is going to send your clients running away to more traditional outfitters in Cody?"

"Sounds like you know his type?"

"Cheyenne's loaded with 'em, sure. They don't have a clue what fossils they are. Worse than you hauling hay by hand. You'd think at least one of your horses could pull a sled and get the feeding done in one run. Aren't you worried the herd bosses will eat faster than you can haul? Poor burros will starve."

Polenta heaves a sigh as she loses her human pillow, Jaye standing up again to watch her herd eat. She hadn't considered using the horses. Selina has a point.

"Well, darling, the boys need me to run them to practice. I suppose whatever doesn't kill you makes you stronger, but I think your horses are lazy prima donnas, making you do all the work. Next time, get a picture of the ghost mustang for me."

"Give my best to Thomas and the guys. And, Lina—thanks for being you."

Charlie

The community center is jam-packed. His table is somewhere in the middle of the room, in the middle of several lines formed by back-to-back vendors, separated from the purchasing crowds by ten-foot folding tables, covered in throwaway plastic spreads, uniformly red. Craft items include greeting cards with hearts on the front, bedspreads with embroidered hearts, or fat pillows stuffed into fabric hearts. Too many crafters try to capitalize on the holiday. Metal melted into heart shapes. Wood carved into hearts and painted in art deco boldness. Heart candles, heart cookies, heart-heavy and artery-busting chocolate fudge oozing with strawberry syrup. Just because the show lands in February.

Charlie stands behind his wooden rocking horse chairs, his kid-sized wood boot pulls painted to look like angry bulls. The bulls, at least, have blood-red eyes. The twisted-metal guy next to him is doing a brisk business. He tries to make Charlie feel better.

"Maybe parents haven't fallen into the trap of buying things for their kids to celebrate Valentine's Day. Just sugar. Because we all know kids need more sugar."

Nik laughs. "Barbed-wire heart wreaths for the front door, though? These ladies at your table aren't worried about their kids."

"Nope. Making a clear statement for their hubbies."

In some circles, Charlie was known as "Maggie's husband." His wife's personality always the powerhouse. He put in a lot of hours in the basement. He is more tired than he thought he would be. "Can't people buy now and wrap things up for whenever someone has a birthday? Or buy early for next Christmas? Does no one do that anymore?"

"Of course they can," Nik says. She wraps an arm around his back and hugs him against her hip. "Though foresight seems to be a lost quality in our species."

"Instant gratification. That's our world. People prefer the adrenaline kick of a good Black Friday brawl." The wire twister guy leans forward to show a customer the price tag on a heart-shaped ball of fencing wire.

Nik's phone breaks into song. *Frankie Sinatra*. Charlie detests rap, but this ringtone means his only grandson. He perks up.

"Heya Finn." Nik presses her free hand against her free ear. She listens for a minute, her forehead scrunched in concentration. She squeezes Charlie's shoulder, points outside, and returns her hand to her ear again as she slides past him into the crowd. "Hang on, sweetie. Let me get out of this noise."

Charlie watches her go. The guy next to him is still talking to a customer. A teenager stops in front of a small wooden train engine and rolls it back and forth. "That's awesome. You built that?"

His mother chucks him on the shoulder. "C'mon. We need to pick up your sister." The kid slinks away slowly, doesn't meet Charlie's eyes.

"Delaney—is that you? Good to see you, man, it's been too long. The highway's not the same, knowing you aren't on it anymore. So this is what you've been up to in retirement?"

A hand claps him too hard on the back. A face swims at him. A no-name face. A Volvo trucks ball cap with grease stains on it.

The metal building buzzes. Charlie freezes. He longs for the smooth cacophony of cats in his barn. "Yeah. This is me." His arm stretches across the table, his kingdom of wooden creations. His almost-a-smile wooden.

"Well, great work, man. Everyone's gotta have some kind of gig, right?"

He nods and looks across the crowded space, the sugared kids. He wants his couch. He's been here long enough. He can try again at the fall craft fair. When he's rested. He heads out to tell Nikki.

"Grampa will love having you here. We'll see you tomorrow, then." She turns when she sees him. "What's up, Dad?"

"Finny's coming?"

"He's going to stay for a few days." She tucks her phone back in a pocket. "School's out for Presidents' Day, so he'll make it a long weekend at home."

"In Teewinot?" Charlie doesn't want to drive anywhere. Just home.

She shakes her head. "He'd rather stay down here with us. If that's okay." She starts for the metal building.

"Of course it is." Charlie turns toward the car.

"You need more inventory?"

"I need a nap. Let's go home." He has to raise his voice because he's halfway across the parking lot.

Nik looks at the door, then looks toward the car. "I'll be right behind you." She pulls out the keys and springs the locks for him, then heads back in to the crowds.

From behind the little car's framed window glass, he sits in the passenger seat and watches people flow in and stroll out, rose-colored plastic bags hanging from clenched hands.

Tess

She celebrates this place, its long golden mornings. By starlight and in sunshine, they graze and move, move and graze. In the blind spot at the end of their muzzles, tongues find what eyes can't see, bits of grass hiding at the base of sage or between twisting bitterbrush and hawthorn. Strong legs get them from brush to brush, ridge to windy ridge. In darkness, they pass thumping drill rigs, cement choking the soft earth at drill pad after drill pad. They remain invisible to trucks speeding alone on drifted two-tracks. They see every horizon and under the shaded eaves of every deserted cabin, and with senses beyond their eyes, they peer into dark spaces where a collapsed roof might shelter danger. They begin to know this place.

The Sentinel seems thin, but he is alert to every nuance of sound. She trots around the other mares, and he watches her come. She reaches over to sniff at him. Her thick mane blows past his eyes.

They rest together, facing the sun, knees locking them upright. The Sentinel touches her nose, and she tosses her head. She's got it covered—a soft whuffing from her nostrils assures him. He lets himself onto the ground, legs bent under him. His head rests on his heavy chin, leaving his ears high enough to sort through the sounds around them. She blows into his ears, but he won't relent. Even at rest, he will help.

In a sunbeam, she closes her eyes but only to focus on the sounds of winter desert. This particular voice of west wind sighing over snow. Snow across snow, a swishing slide. The mares' teeth grind, and their delicate lips murmur, sorting good feed from bits of pebble or shredded sage bark. Snorts blow snow away from a sweet patch of blond grass blades. A bit of young water flowing in the creek's narrow trench chatters with exposed old roots that hang, heavy with spray-ice, from short banks. She hears, beyond the hilltop, bounce of bark-gray deer, split toes thrumming through the ground. Silent beat of suspension as much a part of the music as the reconnecting thump. Presence as much a part of life as action. They glory in simply being. Here.

Her eyes open again, her head up. She lets wind into her body, its many messages registering along her nose and on the bellows of her lungs. The world sings to her in iron smell of sun-warmed snow and in hallowed heat of lively horses in front of her. She steps away from the Sentinel to lower her muzzle into shallow water. A gift, this place.

Something in the creek tumbles at her, and like a cat, she leaps. From the air, she recognizes gnarled sagebrush, come loose from its mooring. Like a cat, she pounces and grabs it in her teeth, shaking her head. She lunges up from the creek and sees the youngest, wide-eyed, ready to flee. Snorting, Tess chases the filly, brandishing her toy.

To her credit, Razzle senses the lack of real danger and whirls at her. She rears back, reaching her own head toward Tess's strange treasure. They wrestle, the ball of pungent twigs between them, then Tess opens her mouth.

Legs scrambling, the filly fails to find purchase in the snow and falls back on her hindquarters. Surprised, she sits like a dog, forelegs splayed in front of her, holding her prize. In this moment of stillness, a magpie swoops down and perches on Razzle's sloped back. Her mother, the big bay, uninterested in games, chews and searches for more grass. Tess charges, head low on snaking neck, to steal the brush back.

The filly's legs gather under her, and she springs up, turns aside, in one motion. Tess overshoots, stops and rears and squeals. The Sentinel wakes, lunges upright. He shakes his head and stretches his nose low along his forelegs, hindquarters high. Razzle prances—sagebrush to sky. Tess ignores her now. The herd is ready to move.

Phelan

He hasn't been so uncertain in a long time. The carry-on not big enough for options, but he isn't about to waste any time at the

The Scent of Distant Family

airport waiting for a suitcase. Colorless weather here as oppressive and unchanging as legally sanctioned corporate theft, but he doesn't need to let this winter trap him in Teewinot. He knows he's crazy to fly to the other side of the world for such a short visit, but for once, this isn't a business trip, with pleasure on the side. Focus on pleasure, and maybe let business slip in during the long flight to the South Pacific. February is the best month to visit Melbourne, by all accounts. At least, by Oliver's accounts.

The communally run vineyard Oliver codirects is green and leafy, right now, and downtown boasts a hopping nightlife. Phelan's company donates to the organic vineyard for green points with their clients, but he's paying for this trip himself. Winery tours by helicopter sound wonderful, but it is downtown he's really looking forward to. He holds a trio of favorite shirts, each of them a statement, a mood. Each with its own potential. Especially this deepest blue, the shimmer of green flash like a dragonfly. A power shirt that he doesn't wear to power lunches.

Finn, with his steadfast insistence on secondhand jeans, wants to be just another guy. He doesn't want his father hovering or his father's money protecting him. Phelan checks the time, but that taxi out the window isn't his. His son is set on separation, as a twenty-one-year-old should be. Bully for him. Two decades is a lot of time. No matter how fast it goes.

Phelan skimps on pants, since black is black and functional in every possibility. A pair of swim shorts, however, takes up little space. Out the window, the taxi pulls away into the gray dribble of falling flakes that fail to freshen exhausted snowbanks. Everybody loves a change this time of year. This time of life. Not a crisis to contemplate the blessings of one's hard work beside emerald waters, under a citrusy sun. Give him an umbrella in his drink, but don't steal the sunshine off his starved skin. If he decides to make a real change, it will be after this necessary splurge.

Green points are one of Phelan's specialties, a marketing angle he has a particular talent for finding. After all, he lives with a son who's always embracing the latest progressive craze. Phelan's never been tempted across that line. But he's never before felt that his own efforts needed disguising. Maybe he needs a green scrubbing, like a well-used pan that grease won't slide off any more. Gunk stuck on his old shine.

If Finn doesn't like his dad's money anymore, maybe he'd like Phelan better without it. Sure that sounds like crazy talk—and isn't that what midlife is for?

Nikki

Nik had located some older kids to pack up the market display and paid them from the box with Charlie's change to deliver everything out to the house. Charlie, angry or confused or both or neither, she couldn't tell, was distracted and cheered by news of Finn's visit. Now he snoozes with the cats in the barn. Bart dips chips in front of the game in the living room, so the kitchen is all hers. She chops and sautés and stirs, assembles and bakes and listens to her music. She plops prep dishes in the sink, wishing she could set them on the back porch for a dog to clean off. The phone startles her.

"Woody?" Her glance flickers out to the living room, where Bart meets her eyes. A cheer rises from the television, and he looks away.

"I thought you'd want to know, even though the report isn't super fresh. But some mountain lion hunters ran across your dog the other day, so he's still in the neighborhood. Seems to be following the edge of the mountains north."

The Scent of Distant Family

"Did they say anything else? Does he look healthy?" She steps around the corner, where the sounds of the game grow distant.

"Nothing else really." His report stumbles to a halt.

She suspects he might be withholding something less positive but hangs on to the phone anyway. "I'm so glad you called." The steam off the stove heats the whole room, and her face warms with it.

"You doing all right?"

"I feel so guilty." It's easy to be stoic until someone sounds like they care. Her throat tightens.

"You aren't guilty. You are amazing, all the effort you're putting in for him. He's a lucky dog."

A choked half-laugh makes it past her lips. "He probably doesn't feel that way. Damn, it's cold these days."

"Guthrie doesn't think so. She's not hibernating anyway. And maybe your dog feels that extra warmth from someone giving a shit. I bet he can. Animals sense so many more things than we do."

She leans on the wall, silent, unable to cut off the connection. She can feel the days stretching toward more daylight, even though the temperatures won't start playing springlike for another month. "Let's hope so, then."

"Well, I'm sorry to call at dinnertime, but the hunters were just here and saw your poster. You probably have a meal to serve."

If he's fishing, she might as well let him know he's right. "I do, in fact. Better get out to the barn and collect my dad. He'll sleep through to morning otherwise."

"Ah, okay then. Here's to your hound—Semper Fi!"

Always faithful. Zolo, *her* hound. "Thank you. Thanks a ton. Call anytime. I appreciate it."

Good old Agnes snuggles in the crook of Charlie's knees. Nik slips into the cat room and sits on the carpet in a half-lotus. Her left leg doesn't make it to full lotus anymore, but her back still feels good when she sits like this. She's a lousy meditator, but anyone can practice breathing, so she does, watching the cats clean their whiskers, toss fake mice between their paws. The house needs vacuuming, but she knows better than to do that during the game. She counts cat breaths; she counts her dad's breaths. Maybe he's dreaming of her mother. Their marriage meant everything to him. And to Maggie, whose wide-ranging recipes still hold the family together. But Nik longs for her mother's advice. Her own marriage smells like it's burning.

"Dinner—" she calls softly. The two cats who had balanced themselves on each of her thighs look up in unison. "Sorry, not yours." She untangles her legs and stands up, shaking out her knees. She touches her dad's shoulder. "You getting hungry?"

In the kitchen, they are greeted by an aroma of onion and mushrooms in garam masala spices. Charlie, restored, helps set the table. Nik calls into the living room as she passes the door. "Dinner's on. Joining us?"

She doesn't have to break the news about Finn's visit to Bart because Charlie can talk of little else. He has plans for his grandson.

Bart breaks in. "Why isn't he staying at Phelan's?"

"You know, kids that age need to make space between themselves and their parents." She spoons up another chickpea to nibble on.

"That's why he's at school, isn't it?"

She wishes her mouth was too full to respond. Instead, she has to rely on willpower to keep her lips pressed together.

Charlie, still chewing, answers. "Phelan will come down here to visit."

"Not exactly better, in my book." Bart lifts his rum and Coke, jingles ice cubes against the glass.

Bart and Finn could bond over their common distaste for her brother, but she withholds the suggestion.

Charlie pays no attention to them. "The moose calf has been hanging around the crabapples. Me and Finn'll trim the trees and take branches up in the woods for her. She'll just get hit by a truck if she stays around here."

Nik can't sit still, and she goes to the counter for a glass of wine. She stares out the window, looking for the calf, but what she sees is her reflected self. She imagines Bart, staring at her, and in her head, his voice. *You always assume the worst about me.*

"I have an idea, honey." Bart leans back in his chair. "This is perfect. Since Finn will be here with Charlie, how about I take you somewhere for a romantic Valentine's getaway? Our private sweethearts' holiday."

She assumes this gives him a perfect excuse not to deal with either Finn or Phelan. She takes another sip, large enough to qualify as a gulp. She returns to the table and lowers herself into her chair. She counts her breaths. One, two. She needs to work on their relationship. Three. They need time together. Four. She hates to admit it, but she isn't ready to face Finn or Phelan either. "We haven't done anything fun in a while." Five. Finn is still undecided about which internship to choose. Let him ask Phelan for advice. Let Phelan face those consequences. And six. "Can I pick where we go?"

6

Finn

Finn stomps through the front yard on Charlie's old snowshoes, carrying the pruners. He came to Dust with his list of plusses and minuses, ready to sit Nik down for a real discussion. Which internship makes the most sense for his future or regarding his past. And she was out the door with Bart as soon as he arrived. He fills a huge black plastic bag with cuttings and drags it behind him from shrub to tree. Charlie leans against the side of the house in the sun, his heavy coat over his new university sweatshirt, bundled under wool hat and scarf. He likes supervising.

"How about this one?" Finn points with the pruners, his voice raised.

"You betcha. Might even use the bow saw on the big branch to your left. See the crack?"

"I can cut it off, but it won't go in the bag." As he switches tools, Finn puts the pruners on top of the sack so they don't go missing in the snow.

"We can stash it by the garage. Nikki'll drag it out later. She's a sucker for a motherless calf."

Finn nods and gets to work, the sound of the saw clear in the thin air, uneven, catching in the dense grain. He loves the smell of fresh cut wood, especially with the spinachy scent from the evergreen trees beyond them. He looks forward to scattering branches under the firs. They can watch from the living room to see if the calf comes down to sample their treats. Something useful about this trip anyway.

"Old canes from the raspberries need to go. Supposed to get cut out in the fall, but Nikki always waits until spring. And she's let the crabapples and chokecherries grow wild. Her mother will not be pleased."

Finn pauses, but just for a second. No sense correcting him. Two bags bulge with their awkward loads, and he drags them down to the driveway. Charlie joins him. "I can pull one." He bends down to grab the flared top where Finn has it twisted and tied.

A gloved hand beats him there. "I'll be more balanced if I haul them both. Where's the best spot?"

"Over this way." Charlie stalks down the driveway, his displeasure obvious.

He is not useless, and loss of physical strength is not his problem. But Finn knows Nik protects him from strenuous labor. In his annoyance, Charlie moves too fast, and the ice hiding under a skiff of snow surprises him, landing him on the ground.

Finn squats beside him in the driveway, hand on his elbow. "You okay? I can't believe how quick you went down."

Charlie shakes his head, gingerly. "I can be speedy when the urge strikes me." He tries to rub the back of his neck, but the scarf is in the way. He swats Finn's hands away and plants his mittens on the ground to push himself forward. He is on his hands and knees and looks around, then laughs. He moos like a cow. "It's the best moose call I can come up with."

Finn laughs now, too, relieved, and extends his arm to pull him to his feet. "Let's go try it out on your mooseling then." Then he sees the line of blood on Charlie's forehead. Fat drops land in the snow—bright as rosehips. "You're cut."

The Scent of Distant Family

Charlie brushes his mittens thru the snow, looking for something sharp. "On what?"

"Doesn't matter, does it? Your tetanus shot up-to-date? Let's get you in the house and take a look." He pulls the black bags up on the berm, out of the way, but turns toward the house.

"We have some butterfly bandages somewhere." Charlie's earlier levity turns sullen. Blood seeps into his mitten where he holds it against the cut. "Never used to worry about walking on ice."

"Times change, Gramps. Winters are icier than they used to be. I'm going to buy you a set of crampons for your boots." Finn sees more red than he likes and keeps a steadying arm on Charlie as they walk up the steps together.

In the bright bathroom light, he pulls off the soggy mitten and dumps it in the tub while positioning Charlie over the sink. They both grimace at the same time, seeing the size of the cut. Charlie washes it with warm water; Finn searches the cabinet for gauze and tape. "Hold some pressure on this, okay?" He pushes Charlie's fingers harder against the absorbent cloth, then extracts his phone from his pocket to call the emergency room in Teewinot. Good thing Phelan made sure he had the number in his contacts because his own fingers aren't all that steady.

"Who're you calling?"

Finn mimes increased pressure, shakes his head at Charlie with a frown, and steps out in the hall. When someone answers, he describes the fall and the cut. "Yeah, probably more than butterfly bandages will hold. A couple inches long." He feels Charlie standing behind him, turns and points back at the bathroom. Charlie doesn't move. "I'm not exactly sure. How old are you?" Since he's right there.

"Seventy-three. Young enough to heal a little cut like this just fine. Let me find the butterflies." Now he heads back to the bathroom.

"Are you sure? He seems fine. We walked to the house no problem, even up the stairs." Of course. Every hospital wants to make what money it can, since Charlie has insurance. A CT scan, for shit's sakes. That'll be fun talking him into. "I'll bring him in. It'll be an hour anyway." Don't want to hit ice on the road, too, and end up in the river. Shit. Not what he had planned for his long weekend break. Maybe he can get Phelan to meet them once they're in town.

Eight stitches and a clean CT reading later, and still no response from the messages he's left on any of his father's phones. "Let me just check and see if he's around." He leaves the car running to keep Charlie warm and takes the townhouse stairs three at a time. Damn, he doesn't want any more of this. He has studying to do. He has decisions to make. He has Kiran back at school and not for much longer. His adrenaline builds as he climbs. He just wants to crawl under the covers with her and not be responsible for someone else's safety.

But the apartment holds no answers either. Phelan's suitcase stands in the corner of the big closet but not his carry-on. A short trip, then. Maybe he's still in the air. But the responsibility for Charlie is not. It sits, heavy, on Finn.

He left the car running. What if Charlie decides to go for a drive? Finn feels a quick tick of guilty relief. But Charlie's disappearance is not going to improve his situation. The last few stairs disappear in one large jump, and he's in the parking lot, where Charlie's head is tipped back against the headrest and his mouth is open, breathing loud enough to drown Finn's pounding heart.

He slips in to the driver's seat and straps on the seatbelt before the reminder bells sound, but Charlie rouses anyway.

"Just us, then, I take it?"

Finn turns the heat down a notch. "Not a disappointment, is it?"

The Scent of Distant Family

His emotions as jumbled as an empty-the-fridge kind of casserole. He eases the car out on the road, pointed south.

"Not in my lifetime. You've never been a disappointment." Charlie sags into his seat. Painkillers slide his voice toward dreaminess. "You've been a surprise, for sure, but always better than an unexpected birthday party." He reaches a hand over and pats Finn's thigh. "This scar will just be one more notch on our memory stick of adventures, right?"

Finn gives him a sideways smile. "Right-o. A man with a scar has a mysterious allure, I've been told." When he was little, Charlie taught him the Irish Ogham alphabet. The ancient writing is preserved on stones, though, not sticks. So much for memory.

"Your favorite letter was gooseberry. Too complicated for me, but you were always a sharp kid."

Charlie's memory pokes him between the ribs. Ogham letters are named after trees, or woody plants anyway. Sticks. Yes, gooseberry was his favorite. Not because it was complicated but because Maggie's gooseberry jam was his favorite. Two pairs of angled lines crossing each other and one flat line topping them off. Like a cap on a jam jar. "Your favorite was willow, wasn't it? Do you remember why?"

Charlie frowns, his eyes closed.

Now Finn recalls the bunch of sticks that Charlie notched into their practice alphabet. "Four horizontal strokes. Did that mean something special?"

"Ash. It was ash." Charlie's eyes fly open. "Bright-orange berry clusters, at least on our mountain ash. I never made it to Ireland. Are ash trees different there?"

A fall hike, auburn leaves of mountain ash dark behind their small, pumpkin-shiny fruits. Charlie with his pocketknife, notching, helping him learn. "Five horizontal lines, right? Are you sure?"

Charlie's smile stretches wide, and his eyes twinkle under the cross-hatched black stitches. "Five was for our family, with you in it. That's still my favorite."

Maggie's fall decorations always included a vase with mountain ash and a porch full of carved pumpkins. "Dang, I loved carving pumpkins." His grandma favored the scary ones. "It's been a long time."

"Even longer since we learned the Ogham together. If you ever get to Ireland, you gotta go see the stones for me." He closes his eyes again. "But maybe we can get some pumpkin seeds at the gas station on the way home?"

Finn laughs, the sound floating over a soft sadness. "Your wish is my command, good sir." He can't imagine visiting the Irish stones without Charlie at his side.

HE PULLS ONE END OF THE COUCH AROUND ON THE carpet, angling it for a better view of their feeding station. "It'll be better if your little girl isn't down here munching on people's landscaping." He pats the cushions. "Your throne."

Charlie pushes the footstool around with his shin, then relaxes onto the new furniture arrangement. "How about some hot chocolate after our busy day?"

While waiting for the water to boil, Finn feeds the pellet stove. Charlie drags the quilt off the back of the couch and tosses it over his stretched legs.

Finn leaves a mug on the longhorn coaster on the side table. "Anything else you need?" He knows Charlie's readied the quilt for the cat or three who should join him soon. But with Bart in the house, no cats. Not a bad thing to forget.

"S'perfect." Charlie draws a repeating circle with the spoon.

Finn sits cross-legged in the wide seat of the easy chair. "Do you know what time the calf usually comes around?"

"Haven't worn a watch since I retired. Comes out at dusk, whenever that is these days." Charlie takes a slow swig from his mug. A package of roasted pumpkin seeds spills onto the side table, and he gathers one, chasing his sweet drink with a touch of salt.

Finn rustles and chops in the kitchen, and then returns, carrying a plate loaded with dip and baby cut carrots, small trees of broccoli and thin strips of cheddar. "When do you think Aunt Nik will come home?" He flips a stub of carrot into the air and maneuvers to catch it in his mouth.

Charlie pairs a broccoli chunk with a bit of cheese. "Sometime tomorrow. Two days is a long time."

Finn peers over the rim of his own mug. Another broccoli flower, sans cheese, feeds his nerves. Charlie's memory changes, but favorite stories seldom do.

"Tell me the story about when you first met me. When I was little like your mooseling." This was a constant of Finn's younger visits at his grandparents'.

"Oh, no, you were much younger than she is."

"But both our mothers just died." His prompt angles the conversation, like slanted Ogham letters.

"True enough. Sad, too, but sad coupled with a happy. Like us cutting branches. Happy to help someone in need."

"Shouldn't we have gone to my mother's funeral?"

"No. It would've been in Australia. Long ways."

Charlie doesn't seem to have the energy for the old story. Finn pushes a little harder. "That would've been a chance to meet my other family."

"You wouldn't remember anyone. You were just tiny."

"I meant for you and Dad to meet them. He can't even tell me if I have cousins."

"Your dad never even mentioned a girlfriend, and then he showed up with a baby." Charlie seems to suddenly remember this. "Maybe he was afraid we'd be mad that they weren't married first."

"He couldn't go to Australia for a funeral—he had a new son to raise." Finn knows this part of the storyline.

Charlie leans back against the couch cushions, hot chocolate finished. He is quiet, but his frown deepens with the prominent stitches. "No, no, that wasn't it." One hand lifts to his forehead.

"No scratching." Finn's voice is gentle.

"Poor girl. Her boyfriend ditched her when he learned she was pregnant." Charlie's hand stills on the pillow beside his nose. A finger twitches, and his breaths deepen.

Finn's breaths stick in his tight throat. A common story but brand-new to him. He gulps for air. He stands up at the window, and his heart races the dark. But dusk rises slowly. His lungs soften and slow the blood in his veins. The unknown blood in his veins. Phelan chose a responsibility not his own. At the same age he is now? Charlie happy to help. Finn's young mother died so soon after bringing him into the world. Taxi wreck—that was the story. After hearing it, Finn always anxious in a taxi. Phelan's name was on the birth certificate. Nik shared an apartment with Robyn and Phelan. Or Phelan shared the apartment with them?

He sits again, knees unsteady. He watches Charlie's chest rise and fall. He watches for a baby who can eat chokecherry branches.

When he touches Charlie's shoulder, the forest out their window has gone almost dark. One finger is on his lips, while his other hand points outside. "Your moose, Grampa. She's saying thanks. Look."

The calf has one leg stretched in front of her, and she tips her

The Scent of Distant Family

nose toward an awkward-looking knee. She looks straight through the glass in their direction.

"Hey buddy, happy to help." Finn claps Charlie's shoulder. The little moose wags a branch from shadowed lips.

Charlie doesn't seem to doubt that they are doing the right thing. His eyes shine.

Nikki

Sprucedale lies east of Yahanna, northwest of Parodice. When they pass Woody's place, she entertains Bart with the off-schedule rubber boa story. She plays up the way Jaye skittered out the door when she heard Guthrie was loose, giving him a chance to scoff at her friend.

"Doesn't she carry a sidearm?"—one of the guys who runs a backhoe for Bart's company guides for an outfitter every fall—"and you won't catch him without his six-shooter."

Nik watches the wide, rolling vistas opening to the south, scanning. Her parents always had a grandparent watch them for Valentine's Day, and Maggie often chose the Cattle Baron in Sprucedale for their destination. The place is an institution, after all. Rooms upstairs, and by request, they have scored one looking north to the Neaippeh mountains. A place of endangered glaciers, though of course, no one is marketing it that way. Yet. It could add a useful sense of urgency for people deciding between vacation options.

Bart turns to look at her. "Don't you think so, honey?"

She meets his eyes, then turns quickly back to the highway. "Careful," she says, pointing at the borrow pit on their right.

He takes his foot off the gas. "I don't see anything." He looks at her again.

She doesn't turn this time, though she knows his eyes are on her. "Antelope. Always want to be on the other side." She's botching this already. She has no idea what he was talking about. She counts her breaths. One, two. She can't help that her eyes are drawn out across the sage. Zolo colored like mule deer, half-snow and half–brushy brindle. Then she tunes her ears, at least, to focus on her husband.

They check in to their room, the king-size bed facing tall windows where a north wind bends the row of pines intended to break it. Bart is fine with her idea of eating early. "Beat the crowd, get better service." He hangs his coat in the closet with a proprietary confidence. "Besides, we'll have a longer night together after dinner." He strokes her arm.

He really is trying. Nik shivers a little and bends to turn the heat up a couple degrees. "Those windows aren't designed for winter in Wyoming, are they?"

Bart dutifully pulls the heavy curtains. "Who needs the view anyway? I have all the beauty right here a guy can ask for." He touches her lips with his forefinger, then pulls her close for a kiss.

Not like she's dressed for romance—any winter trip can go awry, so every winter trip is equipped with appropriate clothes. Silk thermals under jeans and a thick Irish wool sweater. She keeps her down overcoat on a while longer and only loosens the soft scarf, still protecting the back of her neck. Her only fashion concession is the mulberry-colored ChapStick he's rubbing off. She breaks away, laughing uneasily. "I bet we get the view along with better heat if we're in the restaurant."

"Lead the way then, m'lady." He holds the door open for her and waves her through.

When they are shown to their table, she sees he's called ahead and had four red roses delivered. He slides her coat off her arms while she bends forward to pull the aroma into her nose. She remembers the night they met at Portland's wild salmon benefit, how he nuzzled

The Scent of Distant Family

up her rose cologne. A dusky contrast with the lemon drop breath he noticed at the first kiss. They had a few decent years. He pushes the chair in behind her, and she wriggles it to a better spot, her coat protecting her lower back from the breeze that comes in when the door opens. Another early dinner table. She brushes a finger along a soft rose petal. "We'll have to wrap these up to bring them all the way home."

"They'll do fine. The staff here know how to take care of things."

"They're lovely, Bart. Such a treat."

"To go along with the meal coming our way." Their waiter arrives, in a black dress shirt with bright lavender piping over the western yoke and black jeans. They order drinks and fall silent to review their food options.

Nik's choice of location has nothing to do with the menu. She is unsurprised by the lack of vegetarian options. When the waiter brings their drinks, however, the bottle of champagne startles her. She tries to keep her smile in place as he twists the keeper loose and pops the cork. Still, the carbonated blast shoots a cringe through her shoulders.

A voice stretches in their direction from two tables over. The other early diner is a lone gentleman, even less dressed up for the steak house than she is. "Looks like congratulations are in order." He lifts his glass and waits for them to join him.

"Four roses for four years," Bart says with his prideful public voice.

"Here's to the tricky task of staying together." He takes a sip in their honor.

"Not hard when the love of your life is this wonderful woman of mine." Bart almost picks up his rum and Coke, then switches to the champagne glass.

Nik lifts her glass and touches the rim of his. She lowers her lips just until the bubbles are popping against their surface. Then she sets it back on the table. "Thank you so much," she says to the stranger, noting the Peterbilt logo on his ball cap. Charlie's old truck brand. "You taking a load somewhere?"

"Trying to. The post and pole place didn't have the order of bucks ready like they said. But the boss can't bear a deadhead run, so I'll wait." He holds his glass up and shrugs. "His dime."

"What'd you bring in today?" Bart swallowed half of his champagne in the first toast and switches now to his cocktail.

The trucker pulls off his hat to rub the thin hair under it, then drops it back in place. "New bathroom fixtures, all upscale. The fracking boom here's a real step forward for folks. All the homes are getting upgrades."

Nik worries that bathroom fixtures will be the next thing they have to update at Charlie's house. She picks up her champagne glass, lifts it toward the trucker in a clear goodbye, and angles her chair slightly toward Bart. The view from here is even more expansive than from their room, without the pines to deflect the air currents and hide the foothills. This range is so picturesque, it could be the poster child for the lament of "loving our wilderness to death." Parking here at summer trailheads is, by all accounts, next to impossible. And still, the once-eliminated grizzly bear is making its way home. In a dry state like Wyoming, a mountain range pocked with high-elevation lakes and stocked with sport fish lures grizzlies like Odysseus's sirens. Black bears no longer have the place to themselves. She fidgets, waiting for the waiter. Focus on husband. Lighten the mood. "How can you tell black bear scat from grizzly scat?"

"Is this some infomercial you had to put on a Forest Service website?"

"Grizzly scat has bear bells in it."

Bart snorts, choking a little on his drink. "Okay, probably not something you put up online. At least not on the agency page."

It's an old joke. Hikers haven't worn bear bells since deterrent sprays proved so effective. But whenever she shucks off her seriousness, Bart is a guy who can appreciate her humor. She can't imagine having the kind of husband who would complain about her telling scat jokes at dinner. She appreciates this about Bartlett Beecher Fogarty the Third, just not often enough. She's not sure, either, if it is enough to appreciate.

The champagne sits in front of her, bubbles still popping quietly into the lack of conversation. Unlike her, Bart did dress for dinner, and he polishes up well. His gray gabardine slacks are set off with the turquoise belt buckle she bought him for their second anniversary. The wool sport coat is accented with a classic bolo, silver-plated copper on dark, braided leather. His tapered haircut is shaved short on the sides but leaves the top long and loose enough for fingers to play in. Her fingers haven't done that often enough either.

Finally, their orders are taken. She nibbles on soft, warm bread, sips her wine, and smiles as Bart turns on the charm. She isn't as good an actor as he is. Fortunately, a person is expected to gaze at the mountains here. Unfortunately, the light is beginning to fade. She hopes Finn is having a good time with his grandfather and not simply feeling burdened and avoided. She hopes her dad is having a great time with Finn and not confusing him for Phelan in his youthful years. Despite the obvious differences, they share certain verbal quirks, a nervous energy, the ways they use their hands in conversation. Their names start with the same sound.

"Do you think it could work, this summer, say?"

She starts, guilty. "I'm sorry honey. I was watching an eagle.

What're you asking?"

Bart eases his tight lips with another sip and a sigh. "This overnight could be a practice run for Finn, I think. Maybe he could stay with Charlie for a week at a time now and then. Give us a chance to get away. Take a trip to Seattle or something, go see my sister."

"I don't know if that's a good idea." She pulls the crust off another piece of bread.

"Phelan would just be up the road. Or he could even be at the house at night, if you were worried."

"I imagine Finn'll be working somewhere."

"Why not in Moon Valley? Make it easy for him to spell us." Bart takes off his jacket and hangs it over the back of his chair.

She must be making him sweat, putting up an argument. "Because he'll want to find a job to help him grow his skills. Not just earn dollars."

"His skills, is it? So 'just' earning money is insufficient for a college student?" He pushes aside the empty tumbler and reaches for the champagne bottle.

"I'm not putting you down, Bart. Property management is a skill set too. Finn has other interests though, none of which he'll likely match at home." She drags her fingernails through her hair, then lets it fall in her face again. She could have at least painted her nails. She thinks she still has a mulberry polish somewhere.

"I could get him work with the company. Then I know he would have the time off when we need him."

She remembers to breathe. "How about you just go ahead and plan to visit your sister? I don't mind at all staying with Dad while you take a break."

He tries to reach across the table and grab her hands but almost knocks the roses over. She jumps to save the vase, and he pulls his hands back in his lap, where he stares at them for a second. "Nicole, you're missing the point."

She has a finger sideways in her mouth, stopping the thorn's thin bleed. She wonders if champagne counts as antiseptic. She doesn't trust the pesticide sprays that commercial growers ply the poor roses with these days. She looks up as the waiter looms, his large round tray settling on a folding stand. She shakes out her napkin over her thighs, holding the finger against it to dry. "Doesn't it all look delicious?" Her voice is a register high, girly.

Bart, his eyes less confident now, tries for hearty, talking to the waiter. "She doesn't like to fix me steaks at home. Says eating out's more special this way." He winks. "This smell is turning me into a hound dog." His napkin flutters open, and he swipes at his mouth before dropping it in his lap. He reaches for the steak knife with one hand and the sauce with his other.

Nik has no energy to chat with the waiter. No energy to continue the discussion with Bart. No appetite for the overly thick alfredo, its obvious lack of vegetable accompaniment disheartening. A colorful splash of carrot isn't too much to ask, is it, or thick rounds of steamed, out-of-season zucchini? The steak is layered with onions and mushrooms, but no, the pasta is just pure gluten and rich dairy.

A few bites in, and her stomach cramps. Eyes hard, she rises and excuses herself. As she passes the trucker, she sees the name Darnell embroidered in primary blue on the pocket. She gives him a wan nod and keeps moving. In the restroom, she paces. She knows Bart will be ticked off if she can't eat and more pissed if she's actually sick after dinner, though there's a huge flat-screen TV in the room. She is fine; she just needs to calm down. Finn expects her to counsel him between his overseas internship options, not to offer him work with Bart, along with eldercare duties as assigned. She splashes cold water on her face and looks up, dripping, into the painfully bright mirror. Even without liner, her eyes are accented by a charcoal smudge. Thank Wayne for the hairstyle that's intended to look casually disarrayed. She shakes her head back and blots her lips. Like desert arroyos growing deeper with time, these lines around her mouth. Not the feature she should be highlighting with extra color. Her cheeks could use some, but she isn't the purse-carrying type and doesn't like to clutter her pockets with makeup. Like Bart won't clutter his pockets with the car keys he always has her stick in her coat pocket. Wouldn't want to mess with the elegant style of his pants. She pinches her cheeks, then steps away from the mirror.

Darnell has been keeping Bart company. And the waiter has been busy. Bart's fingers rest on the tumbler's rim, just above a fresh refill. A jaunty glass of wine stands next to her gelling alfredo.

"She has a delicate stomach," Bart explains, freeing one hand to pull her hips against his arm. "But it sure keeps her sexy looking."

She lifts his hand and sits down, sliding the wine to the empty edge of the table. The more muddled he gets, the clearer she needs to be.

Bart notices and smiles as he swallows another mouthful. He sets his heavy glass on their table with extreme gentleness. "Can you believe, Darnell, my baby's gonna be forty in a coupla months?"

Nik stares at the drywall paste on her plate. She picks up her fork and fills it and fits it between her teeth. Chews.

"Begging your pardon, ma'am, if you're still part of the eternal youth cult," Darnell waves his steak knife at her, "but I'd definitely say yes, I can believe it. No sense lying to ourselves and each other, is there? I happen to think there's no twenty-year-old as good-looking as a good-living forty-year-old."

She looks up, finds the waiter near the fluorescent shock of the kitchen door. She signals him over. "Water please. No, wait, can you make it a ginger ale?"

He looks at her plate, concerned. "Is there something wr—?"

She shakes her head, hard, cutting him off. Darnell still seems to be interested in her response, though he continues to carve bits of flesh between his knife and fork. Bart can't bear the silence.

His hand trails down her backbone. "I do make sure she lives good."

She is embarrassed by Bart's gusto, by the anxiousness she hears in it. From Pacific orcas to lemurs of Madagascar, elephants of the Serengeti to Kalahari meerkats, matriarchal societies are widespread. Bart's need to be The Manly Man is tiring.

Maybe they can walk around town after dinner. The stars will be out, and with a lot of places closed for the winter, lights won't obstruct their view too much. Fresh air—it's just what any marriage needs.

In her coat pocket, from the back of the chair, comes the anonymous tune of "Home on the Range." Bart looks at her, his fingers tapping on the tumbler. "Might be Finn," she says in a tight hiss. He looks away, and she can't tell if he knows she's lying.

"Oh, hello. Yes, this is." She glances at the back of Bart's head, not a single white hair showing. "Of course." She reaches deeper into the coat's pocket and retrieves a spiral-bound notebook, the two-by-three-inch variety, and a pen. "Hang on a sec." She scratches the unwilling pen back and forth across the page until cold ink stutters out. "Okay, ready." She jots down the GPS coordinates, then reads them out again to confirm she has it right. "I'm actually in Sprucedale tonight, so maybe I'll be there fast enough to make a difference this time." She is stuffing the notebook back in the pocket, capping the pen. "Oh, no, Russell, you don't have to wait. Well, if you're sure. That's super helpful."

Bart glares at her openly now. The rum and Coke is gone. "Russell is it this time?"

"A snowplow driver I met. He just saw Zolo, and he's waiting for me where the dog crossed a road in front of him. Still out past Yahanna." She waves vaguely west.

"These sightings have never produced a dog. You can't blame me for wondering if there's any truth out here at all."

Her voice is tight and low. Her back is to Darnell, but his presence behind her is a lurking knowledge. This argument isn't private. "First you're jealous of Jaye, then Finn of all people, and now Russell? Can you blame me for wondering if your suspicions come from certain behaviors of your own?"

Bart's face creases into a smile she knows well. He's facing Darnell, of course. He moves in slow motion, a careful containment. Reaches for the champagne bottle. Pours his glass full. Gestures at her glass, the bubbles long done with their cheerful dance. "That dog"—he lifts the glass and takes a gulp—"that dog has been missing over two weeks by now, in dead winter. It isn't even alive anymore, you know, despite the handy alibi it offers." He wipes the back of his hand across his mouth.

He never has been able to keep his volume low, and Nik's eyes flit toward Darnell. He doesn't pretend not to be listening.

Bart pushes his chair back, making room to cross his arms over his chest. "A wolf killed that dog long ago, or a big ole bear crunched its head between those big ole teeth."

She stands up, not as slow but just as careful. She pulls her coat up one arm. Though she can be vicious, normally she tries not to embarrass him in public. She wonders if his statement is meant to test her. Does he make himself vulnerable like this because he expects his wife to support him always, no matter what? Maybe she taught him to expect that. She slips her other arm into a coat sleeve. She leans over as if to kiss him goodbye but just reaches to slide her full glass of wine in his direction. "A bear, really?" She pitches her voice loud enough for both Darnell and the waiter to hear her. "In the dead of winter, as you say?" She pauses, but despite having grown up in Wyoming, his obliviousness is clear. "The word *hibernation* mean anything to you?"

"I'm not going after a damn dog."

"Who asked you to go?" She could cry now, but she won't.

Too late, he recognizes his logistical mistake. A different tack, then. "If you leave now, I won't be here when you get back."

Though grim, her face still wears a smile as she passes Darnell and walks out the door.

Zolo

A few days, resting, restless, his limp improves. What doesn't heal: shock. Alone, he longs to be with a pack. Now strange fear unhinges him, dreading his own kind. He can no longer eat beside brothers, sisters; he can't learn by watching seasoned ones who know.

He knows he needs to learn. He knows he needs to be with . . . someone. Dog is never separate being. Dog is always part of something greater. In daylight, he rests. Day-warmed air catches in tangled tree roots, exposed on dry creek bed overhang, water's journey paused. He turns and turns, curved backbone leaning into roots. Motionless, Zolo's leg pain throbs. Motionless heart leans, longs.

Cold ears listen, sunset playing taut strings of mountain ridgeline. Yearning songs help hearts open, stay strong. Sunset wails, night breaking open. Morning never certain. Cold nose remembers. Mushrooms, soup. Someone who needs him.

He emerges stiff, stretches, trots on wind-crusted layers, breaks through, pain slashing torn muscle. He learns: bitterbrush swirls wind, piles snow. Where crust collapses under him. Where snow gathers, too soft and deep, under sad notes of fiddle's curves. In blue night, he trots, seeking a way westward.

Nikki

STU-pid, STU-pid. Her feet speak the words as she steps out, crunching through many inches of crystallized snow, sometimes a foot. She used to love walking in the winter, at night, with her mother, listening to stories about escapades she and her father had enjoyed, or survived. But tonight the walking carries only guilt.

FAIL-ure. FAIL-ure. Double disasters crawl beside her, dragging at each ankle. She totally screwed up Zolo's adoption, and now she's screwing up his rescue as well. Then, the marriage. She drags that one behind her, an empty sled. She stomps through a deep spot, ice breaking under her boot. He tries, right? Can she say the same about herself? What wife would turn away on a night like this to traipse around after dog tracks? Not even a dog. Not even her dog.

She shivers. She isn't dressed up, but neither is she dressed for a night ramble. She strides faster, swings her arms harder. Her mother taught her this much, how to gauge her body heat so she generates as much warmth as she can without sweating, because to sweat in these kinds of temperatures can be deadly. Her mother's tradition of always packing matches gives her a measure of safety but only if she stops moving to make a fire. She isn't going to stop moving.

She hopes Zolo somehow knows the tricks of snow country hounds. Catahoula dogs come from the Southeast. Choctaw country.

How will he know when to run, when to find somewhere to curl up? As a pup, he must've lived within a toasty pile of littermate limbs and flopping ears. Her hands tingle inside her gloves. The memory of his thin, satin ears under her fingers brings hot tears.

STU-pid. STU-pid. She could have adopted him, made him a place in the barn if that was a compromise Bart could live with. Far better than this.

Air sears through her lungs. FAIL-ure. She can't hang on to her marriage, no matter how sad her mother would have been to see it. FAIL-ure. She can't keep her promise to Robyn. Past is past. But it doesn't always stay there. Lies are lies. And lies might not remain helpful. FAIL-ure. She doesn't have the data to predict whether truth might stay true through time. She can't avoid Finn forever.

Doubt, doubt, doubt, doubt. All she knows is movement. Walking becomes its own mantra, and self-accusations fade behind the sound of her feet in snow. Moonlight shadows Zolo's tracks. Blue snow stretches around her and begins to feel frictionless. The sounds of her passage become something her ears no longer notice. The space between her and her quarry doesn't seem to shrink, but she feels lighter inside this space. She can walk forever.

Jaye

A plume of snow sheds from the plow's huge blade, reflecting the amber strobe of lights. Jaye sees the truck turning up her drive. She hangs up the pitchfork and whistles Polenta out of the way. When the truck stops and the diesel goes quiet, she walks over to the cab's window. Russell leans out to visit.

"You up to anything special tonight?" He turns his music down.

"You asking me on a date?"

"Maybe I'm setting you up for one."

"Well, darn. With who then?" She brushes hay off her face with her glove.

"I just turned your friend Nik loose after a set of dog tracks I'm pretty sure belong to her hound. But we're sitting at only ten degrees of heat, and we won't be sitting here long."

Jaye's lungs freeze, and it has nothing to do with the dropping temperature. "You what?"

"I saw her dog and gave her a call. She was already in Sprucedale so she met me out where he ran by. But last time she got lost on the roads, and now she's wandering cross-country." Polenta stretches up with her paws on his door. "Anyway, the Catahoula wasn't too far ahead of her. But on foot—" He shakes his head.

"Why'd you come here? Why not call Search and Rescue?"

"She's not lost yet. I can show you where I left her. You might want to join her with a coupla horses."

"I, uh, can't." Her words stutter to a halt. Her lungs, remarkably, inflate and deflate as usual.

Russell stares at her.

"I actually just met her the day you found her. We aren't *friends*."

"You do have a hot date tonight then? Is that our problem?"

She steps off his running boards, wraps her fingers in Polenta's hair. "Hardly. But I don't even know if she can ride."

"Jaye, you have dude horses here. Hell, put her on a donkey."

"There's more to it."

"To what? Woman's out on a wild-dog chase. Either you go look for her now while she's still alive or later when you can cart her frozen carcass home."

"To her husband." She meets his eyes in the glow from the cab.

"You're saying he wouldn't want you to help her?"

The Scent of Distant Family

"Her brother tried to blackmail me by sending her down here."

"If that's the kind of men she has in her life, she'll be better off without them."

She can't bring herself to say—out loud anyway—her own life is better without Nik in it.

"Jaye, I can vouch nothing happened the other night. If he's after you. But you can't let him scare you off of doing what's right. This weather is real."

"And all that shit is not. I know." She pushes a warm breath out through her teeth. "Show me the map."

SHE BACKS A HORSE AND A DONKEY OUT OF HER TWO-place trailer, both already saddled. She grabs a bridle from the truck's passenger seat and, in the light of a waxing moon, convinces her gelding to accept the warmed bit. Her always-ready rescue saddlebags are stuffed with extra gear and fire starter, and she added a thermos of microwaved water. Behind the donkey's saddle, she ties a thick wool blanket. The high cantle protects it from frost and helps hold rookies in place, if necessary.

She lays the donkey's lead rope on her horse's rump and mounts up, whistling for Polenta. Once she's settled, Jaye gathers the rope in her free hand. "You two ready?" She nudges Bailey, the gelding, with her heels, and lifts her hand slightly, watching the donkey. Gonzo follows readily enough, considering night rides aren't part of her routine. They ride two short circles around the vehicles, like always, checking their gear in both directions. Then she notices the vanity plate on Nik's car.

"B-I-G-E-Y-E. What the hell is that about?" Bailey doesn't care, and he doesn't wait, striding out. On his own, he would walk straight home to whatever scraps of hay remain from the piles strewn across his field. Polenta lopes ahead, sniffing under sagebrush. She guides her horse in Polenta's direction. Gonzo jogs to keep up, not sure what's going on.

The diffuse moonlight highlights Nik's trail, so they follow with little effort. Jaye will assume Nik is able to see Zolo's tracks, which don't show as well from the back of a horse. The hound might not have the thick hair Polenta's paws do, helping to keep her on top of snow, but he's lighter than a person. Even a skinny one.

She lets her crew slide along in a running walk, hoping to make up the head start Nik has. If she really did say no, Russell would have tried to borrow a snowmobile from someone after he got the plow back to the High Piney road. But he's not a young guy.

"Guy—that's it. Big Guy? Maybe." Better than Big EYE. Bailey twitches one ear in her direction but otherwise does not weigh in. She glances behind her. Gonzo's thin legs are scrambling along in the semidarkness. The snow is icy enough—leg wraps might have been in order. She'll check their ankles when they stop for a break.

The fancy Camaro must be the husband's car.

Bailey's rhythm entrains her ruminations, and she can't turn them off. She and Selina both assumed Phelan's threat was restricted to scaring off clients. But his final comment—painting her as a marriage wrecker. She would have done almost anything to save her marriage. She is not the type to wreck anyone else's. But people change, and Selina's energy belongs with Thomas's boys. Exactly how big is Nik's guy? Someone with the cojones to tell the world how big he is. Physically? That ought to be obvious to anyone who can see, if it's true. So he was broadcasting something else. Maybe.

Her hips shift left and right, mindless with a motion they've known all her life. She couldn't have caught up to Nik without a horse. Even low snow takes it out of a person, step and drop and

The Scent of Distant Family

step and drop. The mountains would be impossible, even for a lightweight dog. Dealing with an angry, jealous husband is impossible too. Even if he isn't your husband. And especially if he is.

She swings off her horse. Running her hands along straight cannon bones and down over fetlocks, she decides they both have enough shagginess to keep the jagged snow at bay. She checks her cinch and strokes Bailey's neck, watching steam rise around him. "Can't be much farther," she murmurs to him. From the ground, she sees the fainter dog prints just to the side of Nik's boots. Gonzo's long ears are pointing forward and alert. She tips her nose up and lets loose with a loud honking bray, repeating herself until, out of air, she winds down. Aw, aw, aww. They all listen, but no response. Not like Nik is going to bray back.

Jaye has never scent-trained her dog, but some things come naturally. "Polenta, follow this." She scratches at the tracks they've been following, until Polenta sticks her nose in the snow to see what she's doing. "Think you can do that?" A wet tongue swipes across her cheek.

She's tempted to turn the donkey loose and follow her, but she could be hearing the little herd of wild horses or even a bunch of antelope, not Nik at all. So she rides on, still leading Gonzo and following Polenta. She checks the ground less often, instead scanning the horizon for telltale movement, anything that looks out of place.

"There—'Lenta, this way." She lifts her hand on the donkey's lead rope to signal a change of pace and urges Bailey into a jog. A person, could only be Nik, struggling up a long swale. The snow is deeper on this side. Nik plows a furrow that will be easy to follow back toward the truck.

She reaches the ridge just ahead of them. She's huffing, hands on her knees, as she scans the country beyond the top. "I just saw him.

He's alive. He was silhouetted on the ridge. I saw him."

"Nik. It's me, Jaye. Are you okay?"

"I am so okay. Zolo's alive." She turns to her. "I saw you coming. Russell didn't think I could do it, did he? He sent you."

It's an accusation. Jaye reminds herself she barely knows this woman. She doesn't know if this testiness is normal or cold induced or what. "Do you need anything? I have some hot water in a thermos."

Nik ignores the offer. "Brought the donkey to pack me in case I was passed out in the snow?"

"She's a great ride, actually. If you'd like her help to catch up with your dog."

"My legs would drag in the snow. But I'll trade you. From up there, I'll be able to see better across all these little rises."

"It's easier to follow the tracks closer to the ground."

"You follow the tracks, then, and I'll look for Zolo. I know what he looks like, after all."

Jaye wonders how many loose dogs Nik thinks they're likely to see. But she isn't going to argue, if agreeing means heading home sooner. "I think Polenta's got his scent now anyway. Does he get along with dogs?" She jumps off and hands Nik her reins.

"He loves other dogs. She might help bring him close enough to recognize me."

Nik mounts like an old hand, answering that question. Jaye unclips Gonzo's lead rope, ties it to either side of her halter, and steps up. "Let's go." The donkey strikes off in a rocking lope behind Polenta, not deterred by the added weight.

Nik arrives beside her, sitting Bailey's long trot well enough. Her eyes scan forward, her mouth a straight line. Jaye senses a strangely layered intensity of effort around this lost-dog rescue. After all, Zolo isn't her dog.

Her own attraction to Nik, however, seems equally dubious. A pretty face just a ready distraction from a tougher dilemma. An immediate something to do in the face of a long-term problem, with wider ramifications. She drops a hand on Gonzo's shoulder, feeling the motion, the bone and muscle and willingness. So many creatures rely on her to maintain focus. Their mutual future hinges on it.

A license plate publicizes a threat, boasts a self-importance she's not ready to buy. A resort developer, scheming, seems not so interested in the future of the ranch she's not willing to sell. In her head, she still argues with him. In the snow, she keeps watch on his sister. Jaye knows she is doing the right thing. Doing enough, nothing more. They've gone less than a quarter of a mile when both of them see the dog at the same time. "There—" Jaye whispers, loud.

"Zolo!" Nik calls out, but her voice is choked and doesn't carry. "Can you whistle him up?"

She manages the whistle a little better. The dog stops. She whistles again, then calls, her voice stronger. He takes a step and stops.

"Maybe he likes horses no better than cattle." Jaye wonders if Zolo counts a burro as a horse. To a hound, they must all have distinct smells. But he might have bad memories from a ranch with all kinds of livestock. "Bring the dog, then."

Nik slides off and tosses her reins at Jaye. "Polenta, come on. Help me out here." Her hand, in its thin glove, slaps dully against her thigh.

Jaye dismounts, too, and watches, the world a blue wash of midnight dusk, the smell of warm animals comforting, hinting of success. Bailey hangs his head on her shoulder, and she scratches behind Gonzo's damp ears.

The Catahoula circles, though, around Nik and Polenta. In the frigid air, she can hear his low whine. He wants to approach, but he stays in the wide circle. Then his movement halts, though the whine continues. Nik hangs on to Polenta with both hands, begging Zolo to come to her. Polenta stretches her belly to the snow, shrinking any possible threat. She looks away from the hound, presenting no challenge. But he can't be convinced. He spins and races to the next ridge. He stops a black cutout in the moonlight, and sends a piercing, desolate howl across the empty miles. Before the reverberations have dropped into the snow, he is gone.

Jaye walks out to where Nik has sunk onto her knees next to Polenta, crying. Jaye stands and waits, feeling an equal share in their lack of success. Holding back the horses hadn't helped. Offering Polenta hadn't helped either; Zolo's recent experiences are unknown to them. She hasn't been as effective as she hoped.

Nik rubs snow over her face, then wipes it off quickly. "I need to follow him alone."

"Not tonight. You need to get back to some heat." Jaye couldn't help the dog, but she still has a chance to keep Nik safe.

"I need to get Zolo back to some heat. He doesn't even have a coat."

"Your coat isn't sufficient for these temperatures either. Neither are your boots. And you can't catch up to a dog on foot. You can look again later. It's supposed to warm up."

"I was just about caught up with him when you got here."

"And you were just about out of wind. Not to mention energy. When did you eat last? You can't keep up that pace in this cold." City women, Jaye thinks. Skinny women with no reserves. And no sense.

Nik glares, eyelashes heavy with ice. "I'm going after him."

"You are not. Because I am not, as Russell so delicately put it, coming back out again after your frozen carcass in the morning." If her own confidence remains precarious, Jaye can call on someone else's. Nik's obstinance seems like cold stress talking. Just minutes

The Scent of Distant Family

away from early hypothermia. "Come on. I want to get these horses home."

"I want to get Zolo home." The sobbing is unstoppable.

Jaye slides the reins over Bailey's neck and, with her hands on shaking shoulders, steers Nik to his side. She laces her fingers together, thick in their warm gloves, and Nik, inconsolable but—thankfully—obedient, steps a foot into them for a leg up. A whistle sends Polenta dancing ahead, ready to follow the long track back to the truck. Bailey follows the dog without any guidance, and Jaye rides Gonzo in the back, keeping an eye on Nik's balance. The wind is coming up, just a breeze really, but it takes so little to turn killer. Jaye is trained to keep people safe in the backcountry. She can be hypervigilant. She tries to narrow her thoughts into one immediate goal, getting to the truck and the heater. She can't imagine Nik's thoughts. A scattered chaos. Suspecting that Zolo blames her for whatever bad luck has been coming his way. Jaye wonders what the BigEye might think about them out here, on this mission. Focus on the truck. She trains her eyes on Polenta, already opening a gap between herself and her followers. She wonders if Phelan will appreciate this rescue or if Nik is a pain in his ass too.

The sky blurs with ice fog, and the world reduces to the repetitive sounds of their passage—blowing breaths, hooves crackling crust. So Nik's sudden voice, almost a laugh, breaks through the delicate space.

"He can't leave. I have his car."

7

Finn

Watching Charlie sleep on the cat room couch is a kick. He's buried under a wealth of touch. His cats consider *George* a term of endearment rather than a sign of memory loss, and they pile on top of him, vying for space. Surely, the warm gathering of small bodies and soft fur serves as a mutual comfort for him, unaccustomed to sleeping alone after the marriage of a lifetime. Finn pulls off his gloves and ski hat, ruffles his hair back to life. He longs for Kiran, who likes to tug the plastered-down waves between her fingers, scratch his hat-head itch with her decorated nails. A blue cat pokes at his attention, pulling fleece from his jacket. One poke at a time.

"Agnes, no need to be jealous. She's not even here." He rubs between her ears, and she lifts her head to meet his hand. His throat closes. He needs Kiran. Already his lover seems to be on a distant continent. But this isn't the Stone Age.

He settles onto a boneless beanbag chair, with its old brown-and-gold wool knit blanket bunching up under his jeans. Agnes moves too fast for him to make adjustments, though, and curls into his lap before he's even pulled his phone out of its pocket. She rides the surf as he tugs it free and taps his number one favorite. Her purr is loud enough to cover the conversation, he's sure. Charlie always says he sleeps better with noise around him anyway.

Kiran sounds happy to hear from him. "Sweet-tart, how are ya?"

Her voice melts him deeper into the chair. He listens while she shares the latest, testing his volume and Charlie's sleep depth with his short responses. "So, then what?" He encourages her stories, but whether happy or sad, the stories matter less than the melody of her voice. He continues stroking Agnes, and she purrs without stop, front paws flexing open and closed. The only animal friends he'd ever had in the townhouse were a series of hidden spiders he caught flies for and protected from the cleaners.

Then she asks about his trip. "What's new with Charlie? When are Nik and Bart getting back?"

His eyes flick toward the couch. Soft snores from Charlie's tipped-back head, a silent cat warming his neck. "New angle on an old story, actually. Intriguing."

"Seriously? Out with it then, you tease."

He licks his winter-dry lips. He has waited, wanting to watch her body language, but he needs to hear her thoughts. Words slow and low, he tells her. Pauses.

"Oh Finn. That *is* different. But probably just wishful thinking on your part to believe Phelan's not your dad? Don't most kids get that way at some point—figuring they must be adopted because their parents seem to be from a different planet?"

He lets his breath out, a surely audible slow swoosh into the phone's speaker.

But she continues. "You know Charlie's memory is unreliable. That's such a common story—it would be easy for him to transpose it over the one he's known for two decades."

He lifts Agnes with one hand and stalks to the cat room door. He sets her down inside before he slips his hips through the door and closes it in her whiskered face. "Or it's such a common story that it actually happened. And Charlie forgot to lie this time."

The Scent of Distant Family

Nikki

Jaye has friends. She called someone to get her truck and trailer and bring Gonzo and Bailey back to the ranch. That would take two people. And someone else to meet her in Sprucedale after she drops the stupid Camaro, with its super-chilled passenger, at the hotel. A friend willing to drive Jaye back to her ranch for the price of a good story about a damn dog hunt. Maybe an early breakfast.

Nik has no friends, and if she thought Jaye might become one, she just blew that option. She can't stop shivering, even as the lights of Sprucedale color the frost hanging in the air. The Camaro is not famous for its heater. She clamps her teeth together because she has no conversation to offer. No matter whether her eyes are closed or open, Zolo disappears over the ridge, again and again. She focuses on the Cattle Baron's blinking vacancy sign as it grows, and when it plants itself in front of the Camaro's grille, she blinks back. She blinks back tears.

Jaye didn't call ahead to the hotel, but the friend who was here to collect her has apparently alerted the overnight staff. Someone holds open the door so someone else can wrap an arm around the blanket that's already wrapped around Nik and make sure her legs still function. Damn them all. She wants to shrug them off of her, like an abominable snow monster shaking off her would-be captors, but the best she can do is collapse on the leather settee, pulling the blanket tighter, out of their unknown hands. In the lobby's soft night-time lights, she registers people's faces. Damn again. Not unknown.

"Mrs. Delaney, I'm so glad you're okay." Miller hovers but no longer touches her. "After you found Cygnus for us, I'm sure happy there was a way I could return the favor."

The kid who must be the night auditor gives Miller an odd look and sets Bart's vase of crimson roses on the low coffee table, using a rodeo magazine to protect the varnished wood. "Here you are, Mrs. Fogarty. Your husband wanted to be sure you got them if"—he hesitates—"I mean, when you returned."

Nik sneaks a glance at Jaye, who is staring at her now, her mouth open. She pulls the blanket higher—can't be losing heat out the top of her head. But then she forgets about the constant shivering. "Where's Bart?"

Without a vase to hang onto, the kid doesn't know what to do with his hands. He pushes stringy hair behind his ears. "He did pay for the room, ma'am, so the bed is yours for the night. I'll get the heat turned up." He spins on soft soles and makes his escape.

As Bart must have done. Nik sees the embroidered pocket in her mind, but all the letters don't come clear. Did he offer the trucker something to haul? Did the post and pole place finish up the order? Darnell. Darn. Anything is possible.

"Is it possible to get something hot to drink?" She turns her head toward the front desk, but no one is there.

"You can make tea up in the room if you want." Jaye looks at Miller, at the empty desk, at the far side of the room. "Or we can move you over by the fireplace and stick another log on if you'd rather."

Miller looks at Jaye, at the desk, at the fireplace. "There's an elevator, if that will get you upstairs easy enough."

"No." Nik has no interest in the bedroom upstairs, despite its heat, despite her chill. She untangles her legs from the blanket and stands. Miller holds her elbow through the dense wool and lets her lean on him, even though her legs work fine. But the night auditor is back and apprehensive about their direction.

"The elevator is this way. You won't be able to sleep there."

Able to? She would take bets on that one.

"Miller, can you help her upstairs? And Angus, how about you go along and nuke a cup of tea for her? I'll go park the car." Jaye directs the others but sounds more anxious than the kid.

Anxious to get away from her. Like Zolo was. "Tea sounds good." Three words choke out, all she can manage. White dog disappears into white night.

"That'll help you sleep until things warm up some and you can go home." Miller tugs on her elbow.

Manners. "Thanks for helping Jaye get home." She wonders who is with Emory. Her guard rabbit, Cygnus. She can't judge Miller's choices. She wonders who is with Zolo.

Phelan

He refuses to rush, chooses to enjoy the airport layover as a continuation of his Melbourne break. Not until he's seated at a solo table with a menu—all organic—in front of him does he check his phone.

The restaurant is quiet enough for him to hear the whole saga, even in Finn's soft voice. Of course Nik would be gone when Charlie has an accident. Of course Bart would have thought Finn's visit a perfect excuse to get out of Moon Valley. But remarkably, Finn has it all handled. Charlie is fine, Finn is cool. He didn't even disturb the Valentine's date to report out. Whenever Nik and Bart get home, Charlie will show off his stitches. Phelan smiles as the message clicks off.

"Good news?" The waiter's crisp navy shirt shows off a clean white cloth draped over his forearm.

"My son is growing up." Phelan hears the pride, smiles wider. Lifts his water goblet.

"To adulting, then." The order tablet is raised to tap the edge of the glass. They share a grin, parent to parent.

Phelan laughs out loud. "Miracles do happen. You have kids, I take it?"

"Three teenagers, Lord save me. What would you like to celebrate this occasion? Today's special is highly recommended." He nods at the small table tent with its plexiglass-covered description.

"Turmeric tahini dressing? Sounds different. I'll try it."

While his meal is prepared, he tests out a New Zealand Cabernet Sauvignon and leaves a quick text for Finn. "Thanks for taking good care of Dad." He contemplates various emojis but scrolls through them without choosing any. Unembellished, the message is at its strongest.

He leans back, sipping, and flips through pamphlets Oliver had pressed into his hand as they waited on the tarmac for the helicopter. "We'll talk about these when I come to Wyoming next week." Different. Yes. An endeavor focused on something besides the singular bottom line. Though Phelan's clients might use their support as greenwashing, the vineyard and winery are the real deal. "Like a classic monastery." Oliver led the tour himself. They provide income through a number of collaborative entrepreneurial ventures, plus intergenerational cohousing options. Phelan pictures Finn across the table from him, earnestly excited about ecovillages, even if he is too busy chasing animals around the globe to land in a consistent community himself. But he'll be surprised, and impressed, if Phelan makes that kind of choice.

The food arrives, with a flourish and the pepper mill grind. The communal endeavor would mean an end to his customary indulgences. He savors his first forkful of exquisitely spiced beans and greens and thinks what it might mean to the taste if he has literal skin in the game, hands dried from digging food out of the dirt. Better? Or bitter? But other benefits surface in his momentary stillness, Melbourne and Teewinot both far from his tiny table. He can let go of two decades of worrying about how his own image reflects on his son. In those earliest discussions with a pregnant Robyn, he'd offered a number of positive financial considerations. But teenage Finn's first bumper sticker on the used car he insisted on choosing—though he let Phelan buy it—declared LESS IS MORE. Monetary success never really won Charlie over either, so the un-cowboy-like idea of what his father will call a commune will be par for the course of their relationship. Phelan sighs. He didn't notice a golf course at the community.

He chews and stares at the dark walls that seem to absorb the sounds of the airport concourse beyond. Abstract art, so you aren't reminded of where you are—or where you aren't yet. The white votive candle across the table flickers its gentle light. Above it, invisible air shudders visibly, despite its unchanging transparency. Because of Bart's drinking problem, Nik will have a problem with the winery. Phelan sips, dismissive. If Charlie is hurt again, he has them living with him, and even Bart has family nearby. No reason they can't be enlisted in a care team if necessary.

Oliver's Australian island vineyard is not an easy place to get ahold of people. And grapes dictate what work needs to get done and when, and how urgent it is. That might seem like stolen volition, hijacked initiative, to people he works with now. The grapes dictate the possibility of leaving to help with family far away. Surrendering responsibility, however, holds its enticements.

Jaye

Horses add movement and color and attitude to the white monochrome of winter on the high plains. Even from this vantage point: a drift she flounders in after her horses tipped over the sledge she stood on.

She is on her third try, two abject failures already under her belt. In possible pairs, she experiments with combinations of horses who might be interested in pulling a hay wagon. She starts with this sledge because it has fewer options for hurting anyone when the inevitable wrecks happen. Her grandparents fed cattle with a draft horse team, and if her grandmother's death hadn't taken the vinegar out of her grandfather, Jaye might have learned to be a decent teamster. Instead, she feels like she's making it all up, and like the horses know that and disapprove. Her coveralls are wet with melted snow, or crusty with unmelted ice. Previous bucking refusals have left her in the snow, but those teams didn't run far. She trudged after them, led them back to the barn, hauled the gear off. She's tired but not willing to give up.

The chunky palomino, Chester, and Malek, a gray Shire cross, seem not entirely disagreeable to wearing the heavy leather pulling collars. After a few false starts, and the one moment Jaye landed in a drift, they get their rhythm and even seem proud of their newfound skill. They prance forward, shedding snow from their legs. The sledge moves smooth as a milkshake, two mismatched horses in old but freshly oiled harnesses easing it forward. "Are we sledding?" Jaye hears success in the affirmative jangle of tug chains. The horses cock their ears back, listening to the sound of runners sliding over crystals. Magpies lift in the willows nearby and offer their own rough observations on progress.

The Scent of Distant Family

She pulls her phone out. From behind, their hocks flex and flash in the midday light, and they toss their heads. They've skidded the stoneboat a hundred yards or so. She has to tell Russell.

He answers right away. "Congratulations. Are you feeding yet?"

"No. Didn't want to waste hay. But I think these two are the ones. Want to come try it out?"

"I just might. My wife's trying to feed me melon today."

"You don't like melon?"

"Not Honey-Do."

She laughs at him. "Well, bring Ana along, too, then she can't say anything about you slacking."

"Oh, no, she's already at the old school baking for the Dora store. 'Handmade by Indian women,' you know."

"Surely she'll bring you something good when she's done, at least."

"You don't know my wife like I do. She's too busy sharing commentary with all the other ladies to remember little ole me. But she also won't know I've snuck off. Be there in a few."

She turns the horses in a big *U*, cautious of another flip, but they pull steadily back toward the barn, three thousand pounds of horsepower at the end of her lines. When they get to the packed yard, a cat stares at their strange apparition, and Polenta chases him up into the hay. Jaye offers both of the horses a few alfalfa pellets from a garbage can lid. The rattle of pellets on metal attracts the rest of the herd at a slow gallop, even those who never heard a thing. They trail in, strung out in a haphazard line, from the farthest reaches of where she'd been dragging the plastic toboggan by hand.

"Only for those willing to work, sorry gang." She tosses snowballs into their field, and they rear and buck and kick, milling around but not leaving. Malek dribbles shamrock-green slobber on her shoulder.

Polenta stands in the field waiting for the next snowball. Laughter bubbles up again, like the relief from an Alka-Seltzer. Something going right, for a change. She ties the team to the hitching rack in the yard and begins hauling bales onto the flatbed. "This is going to be awesome, guys." Chester fusses at the rail, trying to reach around to pull stems loose every time she goes by. She doesn't need investors. The horses will help keep ranch expenses down, just like she counts on them to help bring ranch income up.

Russell arrives in time to help with the end of the loading. "Holy hay bales, Batwoman. How heavy are these things?"

She leans back and uses her knees to heft her bale onto the stack already covering the bottom layer of the wagon. "Supposed to be eighty-pounders, but I think the crew got carried away. A hundred, you think?"

Russell pushes the last bale onto the back of the sled. "Two hundred's what I think. But I'm not as young as I once was." He gives her a crooked grin. "Ready to hook up?"

She walks behind the horses, leather lines in her hands, as they circle to the front of the big sled. With only a couple misaligned mis-tries, they back together into position, and Russell is quick to clip them onto the doubletrees. Jaye climbs up and maneuvers them beside his truck, where he uses the tailgate to climb onto the stacked bales. He flips his knife blade out and pokes it into a bale at the back, then grabs the pitchfork and sticks the tines in another bale. "Ready."

She holds the lines steady in both hands and clucks them forward. "Step up, Chet. Malek, step up." The mare tries to move, but the palomino is trying to get his lips around a piece of hay. Ears back, Malek snaps at him, and he returns to business. They stutter forward.

"So smooth." Russell flashes her a wide smile. "That one Arab?" He nods at the gray.

"The sheiks are terribly disappointed in her. Such labor is beneath her intended glory. The merchants of Leicestershire, however, where her other half comes from, are well pleased."

He jumps off at the gate, waving the rest of the horses out of the way as Jaye pulls through. He climbs the gate like a ladder to get back in position. "You're going to have to train them to go through on their own and wait for you. Or this bunch'll be down the road."

"Don't you think they'll follow the hay?" She still doesn't know what she's doing. Maybe these two horses pulled equipment before she brought them to the ranch, and they're teaching her. She picks the lines up and shakes them a little. Both horses break into a gentle jog, and they sweep across the old snow with its scattering of manure and chaff, heading for the unsullied white beyond. Horses and ponies and donkeys fart and snort around them, and her team fidgets at their task. She's grateful to have Russell's sense of adventure along but worried about having someone else in the mix who could get hurt.

When they get out far enough, he slices through baling twine, ties the two strands into a loop, and hangs it from the front post. Then he starts pitching tightly packed flakes over the side.

Jaye watches from her wide-legged stance on the front bales. "You've done this before." The grateful part of her leans heavy on the scales.

"Muscle memory. So far back in time, my mind has no recollection." He spreads the bale out so more horses will stop and eat. "Next." He waves her forward.

"Is that why you knew someone who knew someone who used to have a team?"

"Uh-huh. The team belonged to a family my wife's family hasn't spoken to in a few years. Had to go through a different channel."

"Well, now you can get word back to that someone. Their gear is appreciated."

He motions her to another halt. She experiments with helping to throw flakes, leaving the lines looped on the other front post, hoping the horses don't notice no one's driving. "Seen our wild herd lately?"

"I have, in fact. Your Tess is apparently doing a good job keeping them out of trouble."

"They came by earlier when I was trying out my first driving duo. Can you say fiasco?"

Russell laughs. "Probably convinced the mustangs to keep running too."

She moves the team to a fresh spot. "I wouldn't mind if the young sorrel wanted to stay, though. She's a firecracker."

"The one you call Razzle? I've told Ana about her too. Cute little bugger. Always seems to be plaguing one of the other ones. Ana says I like her because she's like me."

"I thought you'd have to be the herd stallion."

He grunts, pulling the strings out from under a heavy bale. "The big black, he's getting on in years. *Too* much like me, I think. His wives might want to trade him in for a younger model."

"Like Ana will, when she finds out your list isn't done." Jaye chucks hay toward the donkeys.

"Newer model'd want new babies. I'm pretty sure she's done with that, no matter how much she laments the lack of Shoshone around for our current supply to marry."

Jaye shakes her head. "Unfair, since she married you."

"Maybe that's why she's so adamant. Anishinabe-Cree from the Shoshone-Bannock reservation over by Blackfoot: a hell of a mouthful every time she has to introduce me."

The Scent of Distant Family

"I thought the reservation's at Fort Hall?"

"She won't say that name. No recognition for colonizers."

Jaye cringes. Despite their banter, she recognizes she is one of those people. Her drama around keeping this ranch pales in comparison to losing the whole landscape and its human cultures. She is on a roll—pissing off as many people as she can, without even trying. When she returned Nik to her roses, she'd gotten only one hell of a baleful glare. She'd even been short with Selina. A handy way to ruin a nascent business. She swings the team wide for the return trip, but when she tries to help feed, the horses start trotting toward the barn. Russell, off-balance, sits abruptly on a bale. She lunges for the lines. "Whoa down, knuckleheads. Wait. Stand here." She scolds them, light on their bits but firm with her voice. "Sorry about that." She glances at Russell, glad he didn't nose-dive off the sled.

"How about you hang on to them this direction? I'll finish with the hay." He pushes himself upright again, knees bent for balance as the horses stomp a little forward, a little back.

Her earlier euphoria evaporates. "Sheez. Gonna have to do it alone the rest of the time." Of course, even if Selina had stayed with her, she wouldn't be out here helping. Jaye doesn't know of anyone who would, present company excepted.

"More training's all they need. Let's finish up, but keep driving past the barn. That'll learn 'em there's no guarantee the barn means they're done." Russell remains patient, focused on problem-solving. Disregarding her screwups.

They pull through the gate again, Polenta on the ground prancing around Russell. He climbs back up and sits, legs swinging from the empty edge of the sled. The dog runs ahead along their training track, and Jaye tries to read the horses' body language. They get near the barn, and she shakes the lines over their hesitating backs. Chester can't understand why they aren't unhooking, and he's doing his best to alert her to the mistake. He lifts off his front hooves, then drops and kicks his back hooves toward the sled. She picks up her training stick, but before she can touch his hindquarters, Malek reaches over and snaps at his neck. The gray steps forward, and since he's hitched to her, he's dragged along. He gives the mare a disbelieving look, but she keeps walking. A heavy sigh drags out of his big lungs.

"Ha, did you hear that?" Russell has moved to the front of the sled, and he nods with approval.

"Not sure which one is more disgusted with the other down there." She shakes the lines again, and Chester resigns himself to a slow jog through the snow. She, too, breathes out a sigh but a relieved one. "Thanks for your help. They recognize a rookie."

As river-frothed clouds slide past, Russell spreads his arms wide. "Doesn't get much sweeter than this. You might have discovered your newest way to entice visitors to our world."

"You think?" She considers the idea as the horses settle into steadier forward movement. Mountains in the near, middle, and far distance on three sides and the expansive eastern horizon. Clear air here, away from the hazy oil field. And the historic, rhythmic sounds of traveling. Russell might be right. This could appeal to others like them, preferring to stay away from gaudy attractions like Old Faithful, places almost polluted by people snapping selfies and running off without making any kind of connection. Tallying up something worthless. Learning nothing.

She points at a broken-down old cabin, with a bunch of outbuildings in even worse shape. "A Pony Express station back in the day. People like that kind of thing."

The Scent of Distant Family

"Right—even though it operated less than two years. But it's 'historic.'"

"And we're traveling on a shortcut for the Oregon Trail. It lasted longer."

"Humph—twenty-five years or so. Bringing over 400,000 settlers into lands that only looked uninhabited because smart people stayed out of sight."

"Ah, yes, the Manifest Destiny of white people's handy God." Living here brings a gut-clenching acknowledgment of how history continues in the present. "Can you imagine having all this hanging over my head?"

"Nope, I can't imagine. I'm guilt free. Not debt free, of course. There's the truck and all."

"But you're right. I never see anything about Native history or perspectives on Oregon Trail signs." She treads carefully. "We could offer wagon rides sharing history from a more . . . comprehensive perspective."

"You are so free with your use of the imperial *we.*" He wraps one hand on the front post, his eyes scanning the long ridges around them. "I only do wildlife interpretation. Won't touch history with a twenty-foot teepee pole. People pay oodles to go bungee jumping, but disabusing them of their superior mythology scares them shitless."

She can tell he's teasing, even if he's completely serious. "Surely you know someone who likes to tell these kinds of stories. Someone who doesn't mind making people a little uncomfortable." Like she is, right now.

He turns to her with a wide grin. "Ana loves that, in fact."

"Perfect. Ana will appreciate the irony of teaching from the bed of an imported horse-drawn hay sled." Jaye waves a hand at the horses. "I think they've learned their lesson. Time for you to get back to your melons." She swings the team again, and though their ears prick up, they don't increase their tempo. Much. "Good beasts. Easy on home."

Russell continues to build out the new plan. "If that's how you're going to play this, how about I have some of the boys build you a little ghost town? People love a ghost town."

"We can say Indians chased everyone away, reclaiming what was theirs since time immemorial." She's only been at the ranch for the quick blink of a sparrow's eye.

"Or Ana might say the spirits of Injuns killed by the army's smallpox blankets scared the settlers off. Gnashing their noisy teeth in the wind." He cuffs her shoulder.

"Dang, you're good." She rubs her chin with exaggerated thoughtfulness. "If you ever decide to work with her, I'll try to find wages for both of you." She's warming up to the possibilities and intensely thankful to have Russell's friendship. Despite the ever-present past, he wants her ranch efforts to succeed.

"Maybe I'll just do the moonlight tours. Cover the local history of making moonshine."

"With a little hootch included in the price?" Another story the area's religious elite tend to erase as they go. But her family was never opposed to a hot whiskey on a winter night.

He stops joking around and points at the snow in front of the old Pony Express station. "How long those dog tracks been there?"

Jaye calls to the horses, and they stop, heads tossing with dissatisfaction, bits jangling in the silence. She hadn't noticed tracks before.

He slides off for a closer look, making sure they belong to a dog and not some other kind of canine. He whistles a low, dog-calling kind of sound. Polenta lopes up from the far side of the corrals.

She smells what Russell sees, and her nose goes to the ground. She circles the cabin and then stops in the empty doorway. She turns to look at the wagon and then catches a whiff in the air. Her nose swivels westward.

"There." Russell points at a disappearing line of tracks. "Nik's dog ain't dead yet."

Zolo

Through night's pulsing panic of unknown dog, smell of noodles. Someone needs him. But: dog. He could not pass through fear. Now his legs know only jog on. Jog on, uneven. Longing. Go where heart song lives. North Star shimmers on snow frost, pulling, invisible west-flowing river carving through mountains.

He stops, scratches at surface of drift. Lifting from snow ahead, blood-warm smell, someone. He doesn't know. He whines, sound diluting into distance. Digs. Almost dog but not-dog. Not panic. Alone. He smells someone lonely. Womanish, blood scent, unsalted. Wild.

Cautious, he follows his nose. Blood thickens in air, until he follows air instead of snow. Until blood is dark on glowing snow, and abruptly, he stops. These smells he knows. Lanolin, wool, milk, ewe, lamb. In the distance, sounds of more sheep, more sheep, and smell of dogs. He lifts his nose, searching again. Lonely one left this place.

Zolo leaves too. Sniffing for not-dog. Lonely.

He trots, wind in face, fresh sun bleaching horizon behind. Her woman blood upwind, and lamb blood. Scent thickens, and he knows he's found the one he doesn't know. He drops to hesitant walk, pausing, listening. Tongue licks paw. There, under spruce, under spreading limbs, where snow is thin as daylight and shadow thick.

Her ears stand upright. Not-hound. Her coat matches shadow, thick, dark. Eyes match yellow midwinter moon. She watches him. She neither welcomes nor dissuades. She licks paw, and scents rise from moistness. Not-dog, and fresh blood.

Carcass gone to bone, Zolo belly-crawls near. She growls, low, but doesn't move. He waits, saliva pooling under tongue. She licks her other paw, then stands. Collar around her neck, half-hidden by thick hair. Hanging from collar, long rope. She walks stiff-legged, toward him, frayed line following. He stays on the ground, half–rolled over, legs and belly toward her. At her mercy. Not his nature to remain alone.

She growls and sniffs and stands tall, ears mountainous above her, moonrise eyes watching.

"There he is!" A man's voice, and gunshot ringing.

Zolo rolls, scrambles out other side of the spruce, stands. He smells dogs and people, and gunpowder, and he smells fear and anger.

"I thought you said it was a wolf?"

Another shot careens into the tree trunk next to him. In one leap at full run, instinctively arching around trees. Pain flying with him. Keeping predators off-balance. Fleeing people. Their fear, his fear, doubling.

"At least two of 'em, then. A pack." A shot. "Better kill 'em all, or we're hosed."

Tall-eared one stretches out, legs flashing over snow, to one side of him. Long line slides beside her, lifting and turning as she lifts and turns. A volley of shots, stinking, now spins her away, out of sight. He breaks in the other direction, deep into trees, dodging. Voices, dogs, gunpowder, fade behind.

Warm woman smell fades behind him. Lonely. Alone.

The Scent of Distant Family

8

Nikki

The romantic getaway dissolves in another day's gray freeze, and she's finally home to the dense fir and open-armed fruit shrubs, to mountain chickadees announcing themselves at Charlie's feeders. She slept late enough this morning in Sprucedale that she had to pay extra for missing checkout time, but her exhaustion feels as endless as the sagebrush where Zolo wanders. She pushes through the old familiar door, arranging her face to greet Finn.

"Welcome home," he says, holding up one arm to give her a hug, while the other arm hovers over the stove, big spoon dripping red sauce into a pan.

She sees him looking past her at the closed door.

"Where's Bart?" He lets her go and angles back toward the cutting board. A knife swipe of diced garlic slides into the tomatoes.

"He ran into a trucker at the Cattle Baron and decided to strike out to see some country." Her response is well practiced, over long miles.

"That's rich. Just happened to have a friend show up over there on your Valentine's date?"

Without looking at him, she slips out of her coat and hangs it over the peg next to the door. "Bart's been needing a break. Call it my Valentine's gift to him." She sets the well-wrapped and already wrinkling roses on the kitchen counter and opens a cabinet, looking for a suitable vase. "Where's your gramps? Didn't your dad come down?"

"Grampa's feeding cats. Like we've been feeding your moose all weekend. She's had a heck of a dessert bar to choose from."

Her smile this time isn't faked. "Excellent. I hope it's just dessert though. With luck, her mom taught her enough to feed herself."

"She seems to be figuring it out." Finn balances the lid over the pot's rim so a small amount of steam can escape. "Like I need to do." He waves her into a chair and pulls a second chair over to face her. He perches on it backward, hands gripping the edges. "Aunt Nik, can we talk? I need your advice. Internship deadlines are looming. Kiran's all settled, but I can't decide."

"Honey. Can I eat first? Can I rest a few minutes? I'm not as young as you are." Her backbone softens into the wooden slats behind her. Isn't this what she wants? For him to value her experience? For her experience to have some usefulness still? But her throat is tight with unaccustomed indecision. All those solitary sagebrush miles, and she's still unwilling to break her promise.

Nik remembers her college days, how every experience was new, how that newness imprinted a friendship on her, as if tattooed across her pale skin. Robyn was the first Australian she'd ever met. The first Black woman she'd ever gotten to know—even though, now, the things she knew about her seem so inadequate to understanding. How she liked to drink a can of diet cola before their mutual morning run and have a cigarette when they got back, waiting for the water on the hot pot to boil for instant oatmeal. Her penchant for laughing until she got hiccups, usually about some quirk of Nik's behavior or some version of reality Nik had never questioned.

Finn waits only moments but then jumps up again, faces the stove. In profile, his cheeks tighten. He takes a visible breath, narrow chest filling. "I'm sorry. I assumed coming home without your husband would free you to think about other things."

The Scent of Distant Family

"Finn." Her breath catches, but she pushes through. "I know I've not been very available for you lately. Charlie's doctor visits take a lot of time."

"Speaking of." He pauses but turns in her direction.

The sauce sends wavering steam up behind him, and the scent of it suddenly makes Nik queasy.

"We had a quick trip to the ER. He'll tell you all about it, I'm sure."

"What? Why? He must be okay, if he's with the cats?"

"Of course he's okay, or I would have interrupted your non-date."

She isn't used to hearing sarcasm in his voice. It bolsters the side of her that *is* relieved to have Bart gone for a while. "Give me the short version, then, before he comes in?"

"Slipped on ice. Eight stitches in forehead. Tried to find Dad while we were in Teewinot, but he's apparently out of town."

"And he didn't let you know? Eight stitches, yikes." She has trouble moving her mind from one statement to another. Then, "Teewinot? Why didn't you go to the ER in Callisto?"

Now the muscle along his jawline jumps. "Because you weren't here to provide instructions? Because he didn't complain? Because I know my way around the Teewinot clinic better and, really, the distance is the same either way?"

She raises her palms toward him. "Not complaining, sorry. I'm just super-tired. Spent the night looking for Zolo."

"You what?" Now his facial muscles ease off entirely as his jaw drops.

"Had a sighting from a guy I met over there recently. And someone else brought out horses."

"Oh. But no luck, obviously?"

Her words don't work, so she just shakes her head, eyes on her slippers.

"I'm sorry, Aunt Nik. He's lucky to have you. I'm glad you haven't given up on him." His voice changes, softens.

Stomping boots on the front porch relieve her from thinking about how lucky Zolo isn't. And Charlie's entrance shifts the gears, with him wanting to show off his stitches and boast about the first-aid skill of his grandson. He is concerned, however, about Bart's sudden vacation. "He what?" He steadies himself on the edge of the table as he lowers into a chair.

This movement breaks Nik's heart. Age—or whatever the docs decide his syndrome might be—shakes up more than memory. She fears he has become a "fall risk" now. Clinic lingo.

He puts his hands over hers on the table. "Your husband thinks I'm his prison warden, doesn't he?"

She wonders if he avoids Bart's name because he can't quite put together all the pieces he likes to refer to him with or if he's feeling guilty about the perpetual teasing. "Oh, Dad, Bart's feelings are complicated, I'm sure. But a road trip—you know how inviting that can sound this time of year. He's in a Peterbilt. You would've gone if you got the offer."

"Especially if going somewhere warm. But not without you." He pats her hands, though he still looks worried behind the smile.

Finn distracts them with descriptions of his internship possibilities. "Africa's prestigious, for sure. All that charismatic megafauna, right? Even if the big beasts, in this case, are in the ocean. Twenty different species of whales and dolphins. Marine work's not something I'll get a taste of around here." He pauses. "And Australia's the other option."

The Scent of Distant Family

What Nik has avoided. Only if she can keep him away from Australia can she risk keeping her promise. "Just lizards, though, just more desert, nothing you can't find here in the Great Basin." Where what water exists dwindles into anonymous dusty drains or into the shrinking Salt Lake, next to its expanding city.

"You always liked reptiles." Charlie checks out the window. "No mooseling yet. How long would you be in Arizona?"

Finn unfolds his legs and jiggles one foot where it now rests on his knee. "For a year. But Down Under, Grampa." He leans forward.

Nik sees Charlie's frown. "South to Arizona, you mean? That's a long time."

Finn is gentle with his correction. "Way in the south—Bundey Bore, Australia. Not Arizona. I can't believe this is maybe even possible."

"You still have to interview, right?" Nik can't imagine him doing poorly on an interview.

Finn's fork hangs empty from his fingers. "This study's like nothing done anywhere else. They've documented complex social networks among these lizards. And they're monogamous, and they grieve. All things people assume is way beyond a reptile."

"Grieving is not beyond cats." Charlie twirls up spaghetti. "What kind of lizard is it?"

"Kind of a skink, actually. Goanna, they're called."

"And what would you do?" She phrases it with the uneasy certainty that if he chooses it, he'll get it.

"Anything they put in my way." He tips the milk jug against his mouth, oblivious to her turmoil. "Mostly a thermodynamics study comparing microclimates and offspring success. Modeling climate change effects."

Charlie sticks out his tongue and drops a grape on it. "Are you going to be near Phoenix? I have a friend in Phoenix."

Nik swallows. "Australia, Dad. Or Africa." She keeps both options on the table. "A lot farther away, either one. We won't see him for a whole year." Time enough for anything to happen.

"When I'm not in the field, they want me to help sort through reams of old data points. Only the two guys who started the study knew how things were filed." Zucchini marinara slides off his over-full fork. "But they died within weeks of each other."

"How'd they die?" Charlie's head lifts.

"Lizards aren't bison. It wasn't a goanna goring." Finn grins. "No horns, first off, and they only weigh like a pound, max. One heart attack, one aneurysm. Boom, boom. The guy running the study now is freaked out how much he doesn't know about how data was organized."

"Who wouldn't be?" Nik thinks about all the questions no one ever thinks to ask until it's too late. Where Robyn's parents lived. Is there a reevaluate clause in our agreement? "Won't you miss being with your friends here?"

"You mean the kids who're always asking why I don't *sound* Black? And when I say because I'm Australian, they tell me I don't *look* Australian?" He's already finished his meal. He bounces up and turns away to put his dish by the sink. "Because, you know, Australians look like Crocodile Dundee."

Nik is ready for this argument. "Indigenous people only make up about one percent of Australia's population these days. According to news accounts, it's as racist a place as here. No one in Gabon will take notice of your skin color."

He shakes his head and watches the chickadees at the feeder. "Grampa, what's this thick-billed bird? With the orange on it?"

Charlie looks outside, but his eyes are unfocused. He's had a busy day and now he has to digest Finn's potential changes.

Nik looks too. "Pine grosbeak, isn't it, Dad?"

He nods. "Female or immature male. One or the other."

Same dusky orange as a summer robin's breast. Nik stacks dishes for washing up and thinks about Robyn. Who knew what it might have been like for her to arrive home from her scholarship year with a half-white baby and no husband. In some places, girls are killed for less. And she thinks about her brother. Phelan the Virgin Father—like some angel miraculously dropped a baby in his pocket. He never mentions Robyn.

Nik has remembered her for twenty silent years. She knows she hasn't convinced Finn yet and knows not to act like she's trying. "Speaking of protecting wildlife, why don't you stay the night? You know how many animals struggle in this snow. They'll use the roadways if they can, especially after dark."

He needs little persuasion on that point and retires to the living room and a fire with Charlie. He agrees to a proposed card game, too, though she begs off, slumps by the flames. With her eyes closed, she listens to their bantering voices. Neither of them sound that relaxed with her these days. She drives everyone away, makes everyone irritable, starting with herself.

This is how she got back in college, after she bought the pregnancy test. Robyn hadn't been eating much—Nik had to remind her, had to bring her soup or toast or fruit. Not having a period when she was so skinny didn't surprise either of them at first. When they saw the lines on the paper, though, the world became a different place. Robyn faded even more. Nik became an angry person.

All dreams for Robyn's future, stolen. Nik's allegiance was to her, without quandary. Sisterhood. That has faded, but the pulse beats on, like the erratic breath of heated air against the stove's iron sides. Her promise is the entirety of their friendship now. If she breaks it, the guilt would be stronger than what's left of Robyn's memory. Even if breaking it might be the best way to protect her. She will convince him, in the morning. He wants her blessing, but she'll give him the advice he needs.

Finn

Lonely for a sleepy head on his shoulder, he rises early to check on the moose calf and finds Nik up, too, rocking in Maggie's heirloom chair, cupping her coffee mug between both hands. She sits in the dark, rocker pulled close to the window. She was asleep in the easy chair when he and Charlie called it a night. Maybe she never left this room, empty bed not appealing.

"Any action out there?" He stands off to the edge of the window, where he can see but not be seen.

"Not yet. But the birds are just starting to rouse themselves."

"Are you feeling recovered?" He needs to start slow. But there's more to his decision than they talked about last night.

"A little livelier, yes." She doesn't elaborate, however, just leans her cheek into the heat of the mug.

"You cold? Should I start a fire?"

"If you'd like. She must be used to woodsmoke."

"True enough. I'll be quiet about it." He places the iron cleanout trowel in the hopper to soften the sound of adding pellets. "I still don't want Dad to know about the internships yet."

"Oh?" She leans toward the window, looking up the hill at the dark forest.

His fingers touch the start button. "I don't want the decision to hinge on money, but Africa costs more than Australia."

The Scent of Distant Family

"He'll be happy to help with either one, I'm sure." She settles back against the chair and resumes rocking, as if she held a colicky baby.

"But I don't want his help." Finn keeps his voice low. This is the part he couldn't discuss in front of Charlie.

She runs her tongue over her teeth, then her lips. She taps her finger on the side of her nose. "Because?"

"He doesn't get to take credit for this. He's never wanted me to follow your career path. And these are supercompetitive. I'm sure the volunteering I did on your projects helped my application stand out." He crouches down so he's at the same level as her chair. "And his money, you know. Nothing socially or environmentally responsible about it, no matter his little charitable image-cleansing efforts."

Unsteady, Nik rises from the chair and uses his shoulder for balance. "Let me get a refill, okay?"

He tells her how much he needs for Africa, how much for Australia. So far, as expected, she's pushed him toward Gabon. He pushes her now, angling her toward the more affordable option, the one that could bring him closer to a heritage he longs to explore.

She moves to the side of the window, and this time a smile flickers across her face. She waves him over.

They watch as the young moose picks up a branch and chews. Chooses another.

"I'd like to look for my mother's family. Though I don't know how much free time I might get." To look for people about whom he knows almost nothing. Even a slim chance tips the scales for him, but he needs her to acknowledge this possibility.

She leans into the wall. Her fingers stroke up and down on the rough curtain fabric. Her gaze stays on the calf. "We're all motherless together, aren't we?"

Finn misses Maggie, too, but this is the first time he's thought about Nik missing her in that way. She doesn't talk about her mother any more than his.

She remains motionless, not disturbing the calf, not turning to meet his eyes. "Think about it, though. Africa is Mother continent to us all. Whales and dolphins, Finn. What intelligences to be among. Your mother was a smart woman, and you carry her mind forward. Wherever you go." Finally, she reaches out to him. Wraps one arm around him. At his side, watches the lonely moose.

Charlie

He hears voices out in the living room. The kids must be waiting for their Sunday tradition. He tugs a sweatshirt over his head. The only Bible phrase he's ever remembered: *Make a joyful noise unto the Lord, all ye lands.* He opens his fiddle case. For a moment, the wood's red-tinged greenish brown reminds him sharply of rhubarb sauce, and he tastes it, sour-sweet over the smooth of chocolate ice cream. He is hungry, but his belly can wait.

His thick socks slide over the hall floor until he reaches the living room carpet and sees them. He recalibrates. Kids grow up, grow away. Finn is here, he remembers now. They don't know where Phelan is. Finn is angry with Phelan. Sons and fathers. Fathers and sons. Anger slips out the gap between generations, though. When Phelan made him a grandfather, his own anger left.

Charlie points at Finn with his bow. "Got your harp?" Maggie wrapped this bow with horse hair. Phelan's old harmonica is one thing Finn loves about his father.

"Turkey in the Straw" is a fun way to salute the new week. He fiddles without thinking, watches Finn play. The kid shakes his shoulders, his legs keep the beat, his hips rock forward and side to

The Scent of Distant Family

side. As the music builds, he leans back, eyes closed. The harmonica between his hands points at the ceiling, and its notes climb too. The family that plays together, stays together. He grins, remembering Nikki's version when she studied Canadian wolves. *The pair that sprays together, stays together.* She must not have tried that with Bartlett Beecher Fogarty the Third.

The song reaches its end, and Nikki's applause fills the room. Charlie taps her with his bow. "What next?"

She settles at the piano and flips through loose sheets of music. "'Landslide' a possibility?"

He stands at her shoulder, reading her choice. "Sure, we can do that."

Their trio is anything but tight. Her mother's voice, in her mouth, pours around the notes of their instruments. *Oh, mirror in the sky, what is love?* Charlie's eyes fall on a framed, slightly fuzzy photo on the mantel. Maggie stands with her arm around his waist, her look of triumph daring her parents to deny her the man of her choice. Nikki's song is a good choice.

The last note falls off his fiddle. He shakes his head, surprised at the daylight already around them.

Nikki repeats again, softly, *If you see my reflection in the snow-covered hills*—without finishing the phrase. Finn sticks his arm through the crook of Charlie's elbow. "Fine-looking Gramma you picked out for me." They stand together at the mantel, admiring the photo. "Anyone hungry yet?"

Charlie strokes his fiddle, wood soft as a cat. "Do we have rhubarb sauce?"

"Got a ways until spring yet, Dad," Nikki chides him. "Pancakes and chokecherry syrup work instead?"

Finn seems jazzed up by the playing. "Sounds good to me."

"All food sounds good to you." Charlie pokes at Finn's skinny belly. "If Nikki's cooking, we can play for our food."

She's singing again. *But time makes you bolder....* She shakes her head, touches Finn on the shoulder. "I just had an idea. You cook."

Finn's chin shoots up, his brown eyes shimmering.

Charlie is getting used to not knowing what people are talking about. He tucks the fiddle under his chin as if it is Maggie's shoulder, touches her bow to the strings, and plays solo, a melancholy sound that still manages to soothe his unsettled chest.

Nikki

The magic of the internet marketplace. She posts the Camaro first, with a starting price low enough to sell fast. Then she scrolls around area vehicles old enough that no one need consult a computer before changing the oil. She finds a lovely little option that will continue to give her a grin matching the one she wears right now.

Who would imagine this solution could happen even faster than a three-person pile of pancakes? On the difference between the two cars, Finn can go to Africa.

Jaye

Onions and spuds grow readily at the top of the continent and store into February. Jaye lets the onions sizzle a few minutes, filling the empty lodge with sound and smell while she slices up some potatoes she baked yesterday. Or was it two days ago already? Three? The hours extend and compress in odd ways, what with the awkwardness of a night working that not-quite-a-rescue and a long day searching for the right team to eliminate daily tractor use. She slides thin rounds of Yukon golds into the hot pan. Her body aches but not in a bad way.

The Scent of Distant Family

Feeding horses centers her world, and she loves the fresh way to accomplish that task. What still uncenters her world, however, is everything else. She stands in front of her computer and clicks it on while she waits for breakfast to cook. Seven years, say the small business experts—seven years of stress before you can expect your fruit trees to bear in sufficient quantity for making jam. Humankind's evolutionary forebears only soaked their cells in brief bursts of adrenaline. Extended bouts of it get toxic. She could use more help, as Selina points out, like a cook. She used to love cooking. Her stomach gurgles, and she uses the spatula to flip the potatoes, covers the pan again. Her meals now are positively prosaic.

On the computer screen, the green of her spreadsheet mocks the red direction of monetary flow. She never did like cleaning much, nor laundry, and definitely not bookkeeping. Not marketing, the need to find appropriate angles to sell other people on experiences that she finds indisputably desirable. Even in winter. Sometimes being different is difficult.

She drops a last handful of rainbow chard in the frying pan for the final few minutes. A piece of plywood set on sawhorses in an unused bedroom holds two long window boxes of winter greens, but the most recent planting hasn't caught up to harvest readiness yet. With luck, the lengthening days will give the little sprouts more growth.

Distracted, she clicks into her email, hoping for better distractions. There it is. Her body revs up. Her thighs tighten along with her throat; her fingers itch. After seeing Nik in action, she can't imagine that first trip to Sage Winds was a premeditated part of Phelan's blackmail attempt. This woman wants to rescue the dog. She chose hound over husband, over the crimson roses the BigEye presented her for their lovers' holiday. Jaye isn't sure what reason she has for hesitating, but she does, fingers hot like they get after freezing, in those painful red moments of thaw. Even her cheeks are hot, the back of her ears. The fire can be overwhelming when she's also got food cooking. At her feet, Polenta sprawls, paws rubbing her nose, back of her head scratching against the floor, tail sweeping what Jaye too seldom cleans.

She doesn't open that message from Nik Delaney. Yet. Fortification, all these grounded root crops, that's what she needs first. She turns the heat off on the stove and forks her meal directly out of the pan, hanging onto it with a handmade potholder while her eyes scan the other messages. Nothing of interest, which doesn't stop her from clicking on them. She doesn't get through the new stuff until her last bite is thoroughly chewed and the pan returns to the stack of dirty dishes that it came from. She's close enough to a door that she opens it and steps out on a porch that needs to be shoveled. Polenta crowds out, too, pushing against the back of her knees.

A few horses have returned to sniff through the remains of yesterday's hay, and they look up at her emergence. Her heart fills with seeing them. Polenta sniffs off around the corner, checking for coyote sign. Like a grandmother, the cold kisses Jaye's cheeks, and her ears pick out magpies quibbling in the pasture. One sits on a donkey's butt, proud of the perspective from this perch. If Phelan had any idea how rich she was, he would never have agreed to approach her.

She returns inside, braced. She hasn't told Nik about the tracks Russell found. Seems that tracks won't be sufficient for finding Zolo or at least not for retrieving him. Not up to her to recommend live traps.

She doesn't recall choosing to open Nik's email. But here it is, words arranged in their orderly lines, creating sense out of random appearances by individual letters, some stretched high or low, others

The Scent of Distant Family

rounded or sporting double curves. She stares at the letters for a moment until words sort themselves out of the current, and she realizes Nik wants to thank her for helping out. She wants to thank her, in the old-timey way, by offering something she has. *I'm on the computer all the time anyway*, her offer explains. *I'd love to help spruce up your web presence, if that is something you'd appreciate. I'm sure you'd rather be working outside.*

Nik's already been looking at the Sage Winds web page, and she's already copied a potential improvement into the email. An example, only. She treads cautiously, with almost exaggerated humility. As if Jaye would be insulted. As if Jaye might turn her down.

Her fingers are poised over the keys. A response clicks out. She shares the Zolo news first. Adds a map with a blue *X* drawn over an approximate location. Followed by a *Yes, Please.*

Tess

Snow gathers deeper. For days it falls and blows. The herd moves little, stays in the shelter of a wide creek. Cottonwood trees, willows—and open water on the edge of a curve where they can drink. But today, constant cloud cover sheds no snow. Day stretches an interminable dusk, a pause uncertain of its sun's presence. Tess stands near the Sentinel, who rests heavy cheekbones across her back. She feels his hunger and the need the others have to move away from these sheltered but icy cobbles. They need to find a place where grass might lift above snow. Tess lowers her neck to sniff the ground, and Sentinel stands taller, watching. More snow hangs in low clouds, but she will go.

Razzle, gnawing on tree bark, sees her move first, and a soft whinny alerts her dozing mother. Sentinel hangs back until everyone is moving. They flow downstream like dry leaves. Eventually, the canyon opens, cliffs dropping to the ground. Low hills without trees are buffeted by winds, and winds sweep snow back to clouds. Beyond the cobbles, they can move quickly, and they follow Tess, following her nose.

The hunger behind her is a force. She knows the returning storm isn't patient. She smells an option she's passed before. She smells sun-cured grass, and she smells elk. Elk in a winter crowd of musk and unshed antlers and rounded pellets of spent grass. The horses step through small hills, then between many tawny, bedded-down bodies with lifted heads. Elk smell wild, like wind and river, though they rest unmoving, saving energy, as the horses step past. They have no fight with Tess's herd.

She feels the bones in the horses behind her, and their hungry muscles. She chooses.

She stands aside as the mares smell a hay barn ahead. It is high, just a roof perched above a long series of spruce-tall posts. A broken fence around it and no walls. Sentinel pauses where Tess waits. Together they tune their senses to danger. Eating is necessary. No one owns the grass. Tess knows her herd belongs to earth, and they belong to earth's grass. All one family. She nudges their Sentinel forward. They need him strong.

Finally, all the others are eating, and Tess trots in to join them as the first snowflakes drift down, light in lowering darkness. The golden green softens under her teeth, flows into her muscles. She feels it softening into everyone. Cold spirits lift like rising heat. Grass—preserved sunshine, dried rain—drips deep, into beating hearts, down legs. Their teeth and dreams connect to a warm season that is not here but coming, to the green this snow hides and prepares. They connect to their own energy, jaws grinding dried stems and

The Scent of Distant Family

leaves, loud under their ears. They are one energy, one drumming movement celebrating hunger and its satisfaction.

Razzle steps toward Tess. The snow flies thicker, flakes swirling away in the vortex of a tossing head. The evening's dark protection gathers. Razzle likes this choice. She likes alfalfa harvested at its purple-blossomed peak. She blows out a curled leaf caught up her curved nostril. Tess hears the Sentinel snort too. She is happy when her herd is well. Teasing, she pulls a long stem from Razzle's lips.

A gunshot cracks. Razzle's eyes roll back, and the whites shine in swirling dark. Her knees buckle, and the smell of iron lifts hot into Tess's nose. Sentinel screams, a harsh defiance, and he charges the other mares, driving them ahead, away. More shots in deeper dark and more snow swirls as bullets and horses race. The small herd, drumming fast, storms toward deep draw and the creek.

Razzle is on the ground. Tess circles back to her and hears voices of men, hears another shot, and its wind scatters snowflakes by her cheek. She chooses. Toward the men, she charges.

"I can't get a bead on it, not running at us."

The snow is almost solid now, dense and thickening, and Tess is at their truck, looming over the windshield, rearing up. Then her front hooves fall like summer hail, like lightning, like thunder, striking the hood. One hoof pounds through metal, but she hits something solid underneath and pushes back off again.

She wheels, and her tail blinds the man leaning out the door, whipping his eyes. He pulls his trigger, but his bullet flies only through snowflakes. All adrenaline now, she angles away from the truck, hearing tires spin. Lights aim after Sentinel's bunch, and she stops, knowing he'll have pushed them well away by now. Her breath heaves against her lungs and her lungs against her ribs. Pain. Razzle.

She circles, limping, wary, back to the filly. The snow-filled night burns, blackens around them. Razzle lays on her side. Her legs flail, but they find no purchase in slipping air. Tess leans to her, muzzle to muzzle. With her lips, she touches Razzle's eyes. The filly's breath shakes in, shudders out. Tess stands by her, head down. She breathes in Razzle's out-breath. She holds it next to her drumming heart, for a moment, for two. Her head goes up, and she sees the truck's dim headlights swimming through snow, pointing back now toward them.

Tess shakes her head, whinnies low, then louder. She sinks her teeth into one of the filly's ears and pulls. Razzle lunges, front legs up, haunches following. Tess, in pain, stands solid to steady her. The Sentinel's scream guides them, and night carries them, legs erratic as blowing snow but moving.

The Scent of Distant Family

9

Nikki

The tree trimmings the little calf didn't eat disappear below yet more snow. These mountains are one of the few places in the West where precipitation models show increases instead of decreases—warmer air now allowing for snow where, historically, extreme cold kept dry clouds rolling past. Nik hasn't seen moose sign or tracks of any non-feathered creature for days. Her updates for the Forest Service webpage include backcountry avalanches, some started by snowmobilers, some by skiers, and daily hazard ratings. On internal web announcements, radio towers needing repairs from the wind. February is a tough place.

When her phone rings, even though the number isn't identified, she shakes herself loose to answer it. She could use a real voice at least, not just squiggles across the ether, even if the voice remains disembodied. "This is Nik." Cautious.

"Hi, Nik, Woody here, from Rim Station?"

She sits in silence a beat too long.

"Do you remember me? The guy with the snake."

"Of course, sorry. Took me by surprise." Still she hesitates.

"I wanted to check in with you, see how the dog search is going. See how you are holding up in this weather. Not letting up this year, is it?"

A long breath slides out. Sociable. Be sociable. "I got an email from Jaye a couple days ago. She and Russell found some dog tracks on her ranch. Zolo still seems to be running up and down the east side of the Deheya."

"Ah, I'm glad she called. Good for him to stay off the highway. A lot of snow if he were to take a snowmobile trail over the top."

"I don't trust snowmobilers either." Great. He probably is one. What else is there to do if you live alone at the Rim? She knows people around here who are proud of chasing down coyotes in deep powder and running them over rather than wasting a bullet.

"Some of 'em are fine, but sure, rotten oranges in any barrel of folks. I'd rather take out the old skis myself. Living alone, I guess I'm used to things being quiet. Snow machines are louder'n I like."

She hasn't skied since Zolo got adopted. Got lost.

He pushes through her silence. "So, I heard of a possible sighting too. Still up on this side."

"What did you hear?"

"Some sheep ranchers have been lambing, out there all hours. And they thought they had a wolf steal a new lamb."

"You think Zolo is killing lambs?" Her heart thuds. Her hand clenches.

"Hard to say, and they thought they were shooting at wolves. It can be hard for a dog to learn to hunt, though. And they're less afraid of humans than wolves or coyotes would be."

Fear makes her curt. "I'm a wildlife biologist, Woody, you don't need to tell me these things."

"Oh." He pauses. "That explains the snake sexing expertise."

"Did they see what they thought was a white wolf? Or is everyone simply making assumptions?" She hears snippiness. She doesn't intend to be snippy. She isn't protecting Zolo by getting defensive.

"They saw a black one and a white one. Though yeah, there was disagreement about what they saw. Beyond the colors, that is."

The Scent of Distant Family

"So much for eyewitness accounts." Less snippy but still dry.

"Notoriously inaccurate." Woody is, however, in full agreement. "'We don't see things as they are, we see them as we are.'"

Nik's turn to be surprised. "Anaïs Nin? You are well-read."

"I do like to read. And I like to keep my ears to the ground. We'll keep trying to get your dog."

"I sure appreciate it. It isn't easy to leave here. Dad's not exactly homebound, but he doesn't drive anymore." She leaves it at that.

For someone who prefers the quiet, Woody manages to lure her into conversation. She lets her computer screen time out, lets her eyes close, lets him talk about Guthrie. When he finally says goodbye and she thanks him for calling, she is not just being polite. Grateful to have a friend, even if he's more upbeat than a gas station owner in the middle of nowhere has any reason to be. More content in the face of this abominable winter than she can muster on the balmiest day. Isn't there something he should be doing? She imagines springtime, imagines all her plans for the garden, her ambitions for the mountain bikes, getting Charlie out on the logging roads with her. Contentment seems like laziness. But Woody's contentment has cleared the gray from her mind.

Before she gets back to work, she stretches her legs with a trip to the kitchen. She pulls one arm overhead, then the other, while her tea water boils. Like clearing sludge from her arteries. She hopes he'll call again. She hopes she'll see more emails from Jaye.

She pulls one leg under her on the computer chair. The phone rings again. But this is Finn's ringtone. She snatches it up.

"Hey Aunt Nik—the check arrived today, and I wanted to call and say Thank You. So much. I already ran down to the Careers Office and paid up. I'm smilin' like a dolphin."

"Things do work out, then, don't they? I'm learning that bad luck—isn't always." She is a slow learner, but in this case, she's got it down. Finn is going to Africa. And Bart has yet to come home for his car. Or anything else. "Tell me when you leave so I can put it in my calendar." Of course, he won't commit to a return date. The project could hire him following the internship.

He shares the details that make her heart soar and her stomach sink. Not her work anymore, but she is passing the torch. She plays her part in his excitement. She keeps her word to his mother, without the risk that he'll learn about their deception.

"And Aunt Nik, one last thing before I gotta run to my next class. Kiran and I have a bet on this. We need you to tell us who wins."

"What's the prize?" She hasn't heard him sound this lighthearted since he first found out he had two internship offers, before he had to work through the powerful lure of mysterious bloodline versus potential career bounty.

"One of us will need to make the other's favorite ice cream sundae."

"Okay, I'll see what I can do to help." Her turn for a dolphin smile.

Then he drops his cannonball. She's grateful to be sitting down, grateful to have hot tea to ease her throat open enough to answer. Wrong story, or correction of the wrong story? Nik gauges how far to open the door. This much seems safe. "Charlie was telling the right story, for the first time."

"Dad's not my real dad?"

All levity disappears. An act. He manipulated her, so she couldn't find an excuse to flee. He's as good at pretending as they've apparently taught him to be.

The Scent of Distant Family

"Biological father," she corrects him. "No. He isn't. But real means someone who has fathered you. Not just donated sperm."

"Then why couldn't someone clue me in about this earlier? *Real* sorta means 'truthful,' in my book."

Nik flinches. He's right, sorta. "Your father loved you from the moment he saw you. He held you as much as he could; he wrapped you in a blanket and kept you on his lap while he worked the stock market online." On the other hand, Nik gagged at the smell of baby powder. Phelan's interest was a shock and a contrast to Robyn's postpartum depression.

"Even my name is a lie? Was the boyfriend who ditched my mother even Irish?"

Such strange things a person will focus on when their assumptions crash apart. "The sperm donor is unimportant. The man who's put twenty years into you is your father."

"All this evasion about my mother's side of the family." He breathes into the phone. "Smokescreen. You didn't want me to know I was actually an orphan. If I'd gone to Australia, maybe I'd have found a real aunt. Someone who trusts me enough to tell the truth. But don't worry. I'm off to Africa. Thanks again for the money."

She turns her computer off early. The porch is slick with packed snow, but she walks down the stairs in her slippers without falling. The cat room where her father is napping calls her name. The fresh snow is clean enough to pour syrup over. She should make Charlie a chokecherry sundae.

Jaye

Everyone's energy swings, and even with the team and the big sledge, days of snow without a break suck blood from Jaye's marrow. She wonders what makes her think she can grow a business here, when even spinach and rhubarb have a tough time. A person can't eat the view. Empty space is less pleasing when it's between the ribs. The emptiness inside the lodge's living room cracks open with a knock on the door.

"Jaye—¿Qué tal?¿Cómo pasa?" Selina doesn't wait for her to open up. She knows she doesn't need to.

"Amiga. Why aren't you in Disneyland?" Jaye wraps her well-bundled ex in a bear hug.

"I am headed for our fair capital city. But I've been hard at work on a new story in Casper and Sprucedale."

Jaye wishes *she* was hard at work with something useful. Growing cattle to feed the growing country seemed so laudable in her parents' generation. Positive purpose much more elusive now. "What, pray tell, is the story under investigation this time?" She waves her in to the heat.

"Hidden subsidiaries, corporate malfeasance, creeping environmental catastrophe. The usual." Selina tosses her coat over the arm of a chair and plops down.

Jaye isn't capable of being interested at the moment. "How are the boys? Did they win their last game?"

"Nope, lost, so the season's over. They don't seem too sad. Until baseball practice starts, more time to be kids now. And more time for me to sniff around."

"Hound dog." Jaye says it with affection. "Can I get you a beverage? A snack?"

Selina shakes her head. "Just sit." She leans forward as Jaye settles back on the couch. "Dirty dogs do leave stinking scat along their trails. Present company excepted, of course." She lets Polenta sniff her extended hand. "I'm finding some interesting connections around Delaney's clients."

Delaney has become more of a puzzle than Selina knows. "I've moved on. I'm sure you can too." Jaye brushes her hand over Polenta's coat.

"What I can do and what I want to do: two different things. I want to let his threats backfire in his face." Her face glows with the sweet anticipation of victory.

Jaye notices a collection of cobwebs on the ceiling that needs to be brought down. "He stopped in here a couple days ago."

"See! I will not stand by and let him plague you."

"Calm down. He swung in to apologize."

"Say what?"

"You know, 'Sorry my client was so insistent. Not really me,' kind of defense." Polenta's long nose drops on Jaye's hip bone. Between her fingers, fluffy ears ease remembered tension.

"He's trying to manipulate you. Hollywood hero, trying to get his own way, didn't film well the first time. Take two." Selina leans back, sure of herself. Her fingers drum on the armrest.

Jaye thinks—hopes—not. "He brought a friend. Maybe to witness his effort at reconciliation." The friend, anyway, seemed to have a real heart.

"More like: to scout your ranch for whenever they finally manage to steal it out from under you."

Jaye's breaths shudder into the silence.

Selina doesn't like silence. "All right, I'll bite. Who was this friend?"

"A guy here to work with a new permaculture nonprofit near Rock Springs. Had an accent. Kiwi, maybe?"

"Definitely a spy then. Permaculture near Rocket City? I can't imagine a less believable alibi for 'stopping in.'"

Rock Springs is cold and a desert and way too conservative for something like permaculture. Jaye gets it. And she also gets defensive. "That's how little you exercise your imagination. I've been talking with this group about partnering options. They'll do visitor workshops here, and I'll buy their produce, at least until I get enough cash to build my own greenhouse."

"So the group is real." Selina concedes with the briefest of nods. "But what makes you think Delaney's friend is really involved with them?"

"I didn't know this guy, but the group had told him about our little exchange, so I was already on his agenda, though Delaney didn't know that ahead of time."

"Go on, then."

"My theory? By way of explaining why stopping in might be inadvisable, Delaney confesses his earlier tactics. The Kiwi tells him he needs to apologize. Get it off his chest? Turn a new leaf? I don't know. For whatever reason, the guy has Delaney eating out of his hands." A charismatic sort of guy, even to a dyke.

From Selina's side of the conversation, silence reigns for a moment or two. An expensive fingernail taps at her lips. "I pretty much stick by my first instinct. Unbelievable." Her breath pushes out with a loud popping sound. "But maybe in a whole different way." She hops back up, always the Energizer Bunny, always thinking steps ahead of Jaye.

"Now what are you talking about? *No entiendo.*" Polenta shifts, spooning up against Jaye's side. She drapes an arm over her back.

"You said he'd done enough research to know all about my family? So he knows where I work? And what issues I cover, yes?" She paces in front of the picture window, though she never looks at the view.

Jaye wonders what records she might have looked through in Sprucedale. At least she's driving across the state while there's a break in the weather. "You can be sure of it."

"By George, woman. You standing up to him might have caused ole Delaney a serious change of heart." She whistles. "This could explain the anonymous tipper who left a box of papers at the office and requested me for this assignment."

"How so?"

"A subsidiary hierarchy leading backward to Hayden Gustavus Cook, or Gus, and his sister, Nora. Neither ever married—probably too nervous about sharing any of their precious dollars." Selina stops in front of the couch, her hands punctuating her statements.

Jaye strokes Polenta's ears. "And they're in the business of . . . ?" The endless gray outside seems to have filled the space between her ears because she can't make any connection.

"Power companies hiding overseas, pipelines, minerals, dams, household cleaning supplies—the more toxic, the better, as far as I can tell. Neither of them have kids, and there's no evidence of thinking about future generations. They probably invest in immortality schemes, hoping their money will always be all theirs." Her hands rub together in front of her. "Unless this story sends the tax collectors in their direction."

Jaye squirms lower in the couch, hugging Polenta to her side. "I don't have any kids."

"That's different." Her pacing halts. "Some people don't have kids precisely because they intend to save some of the planet for future others, including other-than-human others. I know someone who's kinda like that, in fact."

Jaye sighs and rolls over, displacing her dog. She pushes herself upright with a groan. "I'm too young to feel this damn old." The radio stations here get country or religious music only. She knows which side she lands on. "But I took your comments to heart."

"Quit stealing musical lines without giving due credit. The lawyers will come after you. What comments?"

"Trained Malek and Chester to pull a hay sled. Or they trained me. They don't like being called prima donnas."

"Ha—you know me. That's hardly a denouncement, or I'd be in trouble."

That gets a smile. "Well, the whole episode is giving me new options for the business plan."

"Business, right, back to business. You lured me off topic. The Cook's business plan, as I've tracked this anonymous tip around, includes buying up faltering ranches around Yahanna to broaden their natural gas holdings. You know, the supposedly green fossil fuel that's largely methane? Delaney's investors interested in supporting your progressive ideas—a farce, entirely."

It is only well after Selina says goodbye that Jaye hears the click in her snow-softened brain. No wonder he thought his threat would be so frightening. Phelan having a son—was another kind of farce, entirely.

Phelan

He's arranged his day for a midmorning connection with Charlie and Nik, since they have a clinic appointment. Nik insists on a Teewinot elk refuge walk, rather than a coffee shop, saying they need to stretch their legs before heading back down the canyon. But as he slips in to the plowed pull-out at the refuge sign, he doesn't see her rental. He sighs. She never prioritizes his timelines. He digs out his phone and slides his thumbs across the screen, but someone taps his passenger side window.

"Charlie?" His father wears his hood over a fuzzy hat, and yes, his glove points toward the plowed dirt road stretching north along the base of the buttes.

Phelan steps out and pulls his long cashmere pea coat over his day clothes, grabs his gloves, and slides a rabbit fur–lined aviator hat on his head. This wide meadow is as famous for its frigid nature as for the elk. "What're you driving?"

Nik looks at him upside down, her mittens on the ground, stretching her legs—sporting nothing but thick leggings—behind her. "Like the new Bug? New to us, that is. Vintage." She smiles like the whale that swallowed Jonah and waves her arm over the powder-blue vw next to her.

At least the flower power daisy decal is small and stuck on the back of the rearview mirror. "What is it, 1972?"

"So close." She returns to upright. "A '74, but the fresh paint job makes us time travelers, don't you think? Traded Bart's Camaro for it."

Phelan peers at the interior, also pretty fresh looking. "Such a usable choice for winter in Wyoming." He imagines she picked it primarily to piss Bart off but doesn't ask if her husband even knows.

Charlie pipes up. "Engine in back gives you weight where you need it. And the bench back seat is perfect for when we find Nik's dog."

Phelan shakes his head. He's not sure if he should admire their persistence or decry their fantasies. "Shall we?" He gestures up the road. No opinion is necessary—that's their lives, not his. So freeing.

Charlie walks ahead, always on the lookout for elk. Nik gives him a little space, leaning a hip on the Bug's grille, one arm stretched, curving, over her head. "So, you needed to talk about something?"

"Coyote!" Charlie calls out, looking back at them and pointing.

"Nice pounce," Nik hollers back. She steps after him, running a little in place, knees high.

Even Phelan can tell she's anxious about something, and they haven't read each other's minds for years. "How'd Dad's appointment go?"

"More of the usual. The trajectory continues." She flicks her hand, dismissing doctors in general.

"Nothing specific to worry about, then?"

"Nope. What's up with you?" She bounces on the balls of her feet but keeps her stride short so they won't catch up with Charlie. Without waiting for him to answer, she waves toward the mountains. "These clouds make the valley look like Nebraska. Maybe if there's no peaks, the tourists will go away too. Traffic's kinda ridiculous here these days."

He hadn't noticed, but the mountains are completely obscured. That happens. His mind just compensates by picturing what he knows is there. "Tourists can spend the day in the photography galleries instead. Better for the economy if they aren't taking all their own pictures."

"Of course. An angle I would expect you to come up with." Her stride lengthens.

He steps faster to keep up with her. "Well, here's something you won't expect, then."

Her head whips around.

"Beautiful bird, isn't he?" Charlie calls out, pointing at a boulder along the road between them. "Like a long-tailed penguin."

She mutters under her breath. "Oh my hell. He can't even remember the word *magpie*?" Nik arranges her face into a smile to respond. "Gorgeous, Dad. Fun to be out of the car, isn't it?"

Phelan argues with her, as usual. "But he can come up with *penguin*? Just because he didn't say *magpie* doesn't mean he doesn't know it. *Bird* is perfectly correct." His sister can be so condescending.

"Your surprise?" Her voice has replaced anxiety with disdain. Also typical.

"Let's catch up with Charlie first." Not that he's far ahead. But let her wait.

When they reach him, Phelan stretches an arm around Charlie's shoulders and faces Nik.

"There they are," Charlie says, pointing. "Can you hear them?"

Elk spread across the frozen slough, cows with big calves curled at their feet, an occasional bull carrying only one antler, most still with two.

"Little birdcalls." Nik smiles. "I hear them." She is turned away, watching them too.

"Ah, look over there. Where the warm water comes in. Swans." Phelan can't wait. "There's *black* swans where I'm going. Who can guess?"

"How long are you going this time?" Charlie is used to his frequent business trips.

"Two-year commitment." Phelan is used to commitments. Two years is nothing compared to twenty.

"Australia? You're kidding?" Nik's attention is all on him now.

Unsurprisingly, she knows where black swans live. "Quit my job." He squeezes Charlie's shoulders a little. "Our jaunt across Moon Valley that day got me thinking. Dad got me to feeling, actually, and I realized how my job makes me feel. Not so great. Lots of changes around the valley, yes, and time for me to make some too." He's practiced this speech for days. His chin is high, regardless of what responses come next.

Her face fades to the color of the overcast. She turns to continue walking, then pauses. "I'm sorry, Dad. Is that far enough for you? We have our elk sighting."

"We do, we do. I can't hear them, but I'm glad you can. Sure, we could turn around. Not warm out here, is it?" Charlie switches direction. "Where are the black swans, again?"

Phelan turns with him and walks close so he can hear. "Australia. The other side of the world, basically. Working at an organic vineyard and winery on an island in the Pacific."

"Still sounds pretty posh. As one would expect." Nik studies the headless hill as they walk back.

"I found the place through my clients, yes, but it operates on completely different principles. Finn won't believe it. Communal."

She stops but keeps her eyes on the snowy outcrops. "As in, commune? Is that why there's a two-year commitment?"

She'll catch up. He and Charlie keep walking, and he lets the wind carry his words over his shoulder. "It takes a year to get to know the vineyard's annual cycle, so a second year when people help new arrivals get the hang of things. But a lot of people who stay through two years don't ever want to leave."

"You were right about one thing. I'm having trouble picturing you at a commune."

He corrects her. "Collaborative cohousing, and worker-owned business collective."

Charlie puts his hand on Phelan's arm, stopping him. "Australia, you said?"

"Down by Melbourne. No snow." Phelan checks his watch. He needs to get back to work. He gave them their two-week notice.

Nik takes Charlie's arm, as if he might need help on the ice. But he stays focused on Phelan's news.

"That'll be a change. And you could look for Finn's cousins. Remember, we talked about him needing cousins." Charlie's forearm and Nik's swing together.

The Scent of Distant Family

"We did, didn't we? And you know what, you're right. I probably could." Phelan hasn't considered this. His son is old enough that his work associates will be more important than family. And cousins might come with additional responsibilities no one needs.

He starts his rig with the keys in his pocket so it will be comfortably warm when he climbs in. Nik shakes her head, lips tight.

When she's got Charlie into the Bug's low-slung seat, she walks over to the Rover. Phelan doesn't need to read minds for his guard to go up.

"What'll you do with the townhouse?" Her opening engagement.

"Might as well sell it. Finn's pretty much on his own these days." Parry. Phelan slips off the peacoat and folds it onto the back seat.

"Your contribution to the worker-owned commune, I suppose?" She doesn't wait for a reaction to that charge before moving to her main point. "You aren't serious about looking for Robyn's family, are you?"

He feints. "Twenty years is a long time, Nik. They'd be proud of Finn if they got to meet him."

"We made a promise."

Always so righteous. "Robyn was a kid herself. What could she imagine of twenty years later?" He's arguing with her again. He doesn't need her permission. Maybe cousins would be good for his son.

"She didn't want Finn to think she'd abandoned him. That pain would still hurt. He's the same age she was. A kid." Nik's earnestness is practically a lunge now.

Phelan opens his door, heat on his face. "And you wouldn't want him to know he might have someone to turn to besides yourself?"

She stomps away from him and drops into the car that's from an older generation, a more restricted world. It's only got rear-wheel drive, and the tires spin in the snow before it finally catches some gravel and lurches away.

Finn

Butcher paper unrolls from the thawed antelope meat. Kiran's brother-in-law, a real Wyoming kind of guy, always kills more than his family will use. Finn drops the cut chunks into the cast-iron pan and turns the heat down. Pepper shakes out over the top, a little salt.

"No sage needed, right?" He looks at Kiran, studious still at the kitchen table.

"Yeah, hardly. They come field seasoned. Thanks for doing that. No matter how much I review this stuff, I don't feel ready for midterms."

"Your dream job awaits only successful completion of your internship. You probably don't need to worry much about grades." He runs water over his fingers, diluting the cold blood that wants to stick to his skin.

She puts her pencil down and shakes her hands out as she stands up. Circling behind him, she lays her head on his shoulder and sticks her hands in his front pockets.

He twists and ducks under her arms, pulls her hands into his. "Way too early for that. Dinner will go up in smoke." Their fingers fit together so well. "We don't want an antelope to have died in vain."

He nuzzles along her collarbone. "Listen to the sizzle." His voice muffles against her neck, his tongue toys with the thin silver chain she wears. He wonders whether his mother had a favorite necklace or a favorite meal or a perfume that identified her as soon as she walked in a room.

Kiran's fingers play in his hair, but soothingly. She could be one of Charlie's cats. "You've had a few distractions lately. But you don't have to worry either. With Gabon under your belt, you'll be well

*

launched. People will see right away what you can do."

"Do you think it was inherited misogyny that made me assume my mother was the diabolical half of my lineage? All the stories I thought up that could explain why no one would talk about her. When all along, I had some asshole of a father."

"Nik and Phelan sure didn't give you any clues to go on. But consider this. You were raised in a white family. Internalized racism? You blamed the brown."

"Shit. Either way. My poor mother. Dead *and* defamed. See, I inherited asshole genes. You aren't ever gonna want to get back together." She is in his arms and gone, gone.

She taps on his breastbone. "No wait—there's still an assumption we're making about Phelan. What if he is your bio dad *and* the cause of your mother's actual beloved leaving her? Those were the days when drinks were spiked. She could have had a brown boyfriend, and some white guy used to getting whatever he wanted, no names here, slipped her something and had his way."

"Whoa." Finn holds her forearms and pushes space between them. "We've put our energy into painting Phelan into the bad-guy corner because he's a privileged capitalist. That version steps over the line."

"You think this story is just my antiwhite, anti-male, womanly genetics? Or that my parents taught me to be so suspicious?" She leans back against his hold, like a dancer might. Then she spins toward him, her arms pretzeled in front of her but her butt snuggled close. "He did nurture you, or at least made sure you had nannies who would, no arguing there."

"Is nurture stronger than an accidental sperm donor's asshole nature? Whoever he might be?" Finn lets go of her arms and fits her hands into his again.

She spins back out to face him, as if they are dancing a western swing. "If your dad was drinking maybe he took a wager, you can't rule out that he was both the asshole and the later nurturer. Out of guilt, and obligation. How else did he end up with you?"

He is struck silent, brooding. Maybe other people find it necessary to live a lie, but he needs truth. He is tired of conjecture. "If I ask him straight up, how will I know his answer is even real?" He drops into a chair and pulls her down with him.

"You won't. So why bother?" She wriggles deeper into his lap, slips a cool hand under his shirt. "Look at you cooking me dinner. That's not asshole behavior." A single light finger traces his belly button. "You're cuddling, not just carrying me off to the bedroom."

"Only because I know you need sustenance before the midterm. Or while we burn in the bedroom, dinner would burn out here." His fingers travel up her arms, down the knobs of her spine.

"We have time, sweet-tart, for both dinner and delight." Her slow kiss lingers on his lips. "You're right. I probably don't have to worry about grades so much."

Tigers won't be the only ones eating out of her hands. He slides his fingers along the ribbed corduroy of her thrift-store pants and scoops her into his arms as he stands up. He fakes a step toward the bedroom but then settles her back at the table.

He needs to talk to Phelan. He needs to add the antelope to the onions and cabbage. "Smells close to done. Better finish up with that." He nods toward her notes.

10

Nikki

She hasn't deleted Bart's email yet, but he hasn't written back since she replied that his Camaro was sold. She lifts her gaze out the gray windows to the gray-and-white nuthatches at Charlie's feeder. His cats still live in the barn, even if she has no idea where her husband is living. Separation leaves everyone in limbo, except the wild birds. For people, change causes such disruption and distress, but the birds carry on, so chipper. Some now experiment with winters farther north than usual, shorter migrations. Nik needs their resilience.

She switches back to the Forest Service web page, but her attention continues to wander. She sighs, then decides to check on Charlie out in the barn. Fresh air, a little movement to remind her heart to keep on pumping.

He's carving intricate crown molding for Zolo's new doghouse. Wood shavings surround the table and chair in the center of the room, and cats have chased random blond curls around the space so cleaning will be even more of a challenge. Since wooden toys didn't sell so well at the craft fair, he's shifted to a new project. Equally doomed, in all likelihood. She shivers despite the electric radiator. "Lookin' good, Dad."

He holds it up for her inspection. "Cats are good company. Think he'll like it?"

The pattern is a repeating line of curled cat bodies, eyes closed. Charlie does not believe in opposition between canines and felines. Of course Zolo would enjoy being surrounded by cats. Would be warmer than the scratchy branches of snow-covered bitterbrush, for sure. She doesn't trust her voice, so she just nods and drops a hand on his shoulder.

But her phone rings, that unknown caller "Home on the Range" tune that still opens her to painful, weakening hope. She clears her throat, answers. "Oh, Woody, hi." She hasn't added him to her contacts, nor Jaye. The far side of the mountains. A single-purpose acquaintance. Her eyes flick to the continued motion of Charlie's carving knife, and Woody's next words slice the soft muscle of her heart. "You're sure? Three days you've been watching the tracks?" Her father looks up at her, hand still.

When she hangs up, a plan continues painting itself in front of her eyes. "My friend at Rim Rendezvous saw Zolo this morning. Woody's got a camper parked in back of the gas station, and we can grab live traps at the shelter on our way over there. Let's pack for a few days—there's a big storm coming in. I'll put extra food out for the cats while you get your coat and boots—and your meds."

"And scarves. Better bring scarves. Windy over there." Charlie's all in.

The drive begins dry enough, and the Bug plays Charlie's old cassettes from Grateful Dead shows he and Maggie had been at together. The low fidelity doesn't bother him a bit, but Nik's mind slides away from the faded music. All her careful maneuvering, to get Finn to Gabon instead of landing on the same continent with Robyn's family. And here goes Phelan, blithely off to see if he can find Finn some cousins. Their age group won't have any connection to Robyn's catastrophic year in Wyoming.

Or? An exchange student to the United States was undoubtedly a family story. Nik has no idea how that story might play out in

The Scent of Distant Family

an Australian context. How the gum trees might hear it. How the black swans might murmur disapproval along the reeds. How the red desert dirt might absorb unwanted memory or how memory might erode out in unexpected floods.

She needs to warn Phelan off his Charlie-inspired mission. And Phelan isn't wrong. Finn is a young man to be proud of. Culture in both their countries changed over the last twenty years. But they both made a promise. And she made two. In a world where some people have more limited options, Nik wants to respect Robyn's choices.

Phelan is right as well. Robyn was just a kid. Finn is a young man, but the motherless kid inside does not go away. He can still be hurt. And if Phelan helps Finn find her family, he will learn just enough to blame them all. The little car closes in around her, claustrophobic in the steep canyon.

By the final valley, snow falls in fat flakes and thick waves. The roofs of buildings carry three, four, feet of packed snow. Charlie rides shotgun, keeping a lookout for drivers on the wrong side of the road or thick-limbed elk crossing the highway. Nik grips the steering wheel as they wind up the last long switchbacks through open, blowing slopes. Her dad doesn't ask if she has tire chains. Probably because he knows she doesn't.

They pull in past the pumps, and she spots the camp trailer. Woody must have shoveled it out not long ago, though the steps are covered again already. "Come on in to the store. Let's find out what he knows before we try to go set the traps."

Woody holds the door open when they approach. "Glad you made it. Not going to have any more traffic from your direction. The canyon must have closed right behind you. Everything's avalanching out there."

"We weren't even listening to the radio. This is my dad, Charlie."

"Woody, sir." He reaches out his hand. "Good you could come along. Hope the trailer serves you well. Plenty of propane anyway."

Nik appreciates his respectfulness and how genuine it seems. She looks toward a closed door. "Guthrie still with you?"

"Good and sleepy in this weather but still eating a bit." His smile is warm. "Thanks for asking. Charlie, I tell you what. All this hot food in the deli is going to waste. Whatever you want, it's on the house."

"You don't have to do that. You're losing business with the storm. We can buy our food." Nik pulls her wallet from the back pocket of her wool pants.

"Consider it my contribution toward the dog rescue. Charlie, you like pepperoni calzones?" Woody grabs a pair of tongs to deposit a calzone in a folded cardboard bowl.

While he's busy, she slips some bills under the order pad by his phone. "So where's the culvert you've been watching? Close, I hope?"

"Just shy of a quarter-mile east. Two mornings in a row, just the one set of tracks. Thought it must be coyote. So this morning I took my run extra early, before the snow got any thicker, and voilà. White dog, with patches. And those eyes. In my little binoculars, spooky blue."

Nik rubs a hand up and down her arm. Her breath whistles as she watches the snow pouring down. "This supposed to let up any?"

"Slow down, yeah. Why don't you two get settled in the camper? Still a few hours' daylight left. Weather might change before dark."

The camper is just a cab-over and old. Little curtains with cowboys riding their bowed-up broncs on stiff fabric. The heat is on, and Nik climbs to spread her sleeping bag on the mattress over the missing cab. She fluffs Charlie's bag out over what would otherwise be the table. He perches on the edge of his bed, licking pepperoni grease off his fingers.

"Here, use this." Nik pulls a paper towel off the roll by the tiny sink.

Slowly the storm breaks into smaller flakes, windier but not as heavy. She can almost see light behind the cloud cover in thin spots and then a shot of blue. Sucker hole. They climb back into the Bug, and Nik twists around to consider the traps in the back seat. She slams her palm on the steering wheel.

"Forgot bait, didn't we?" Charlie pats her knee. "Bet your friend will have something."

Woody looks up from his paperback when the doorbells clamor. "Ready to get 'em out there?"

"I didn't bring bait." She mimes hitting herself in the head. "Stupid."

"You got excited. Understandable."

"Do you have any mice, for Ms. Guthrie?" She runs a hand up and down her hip, hard.

Woody shakes his head. "Since they're frozen, you might have better luck with people food. Not like he's a wolf." He waves a hand across the shriveling options under the heat lamps. "Anything here you know he likes?"

Charlie makes the selections, and well supplied, they strike off for the culvert. The fresh snow is a blank canvas, even deep inside the corrugated pipe, wind scouring and depositing. He helps her carry a trap down the embankment and decides how to display the goods. A couple hot dogs outside, to establish a sense of safety and whet the appetite. Barbecued beef soaked into a bun on the way in. Then chicken tenders at the back, in a decent mound—some consolation, then, after the clang of the door shuts off his escape. Her hands clench.

Charlie huffs hard when they climb back up to the highway, and she urges him in to the car to rest. She wrestles the second trap past her bent seat and onto the ground. "I shouldn't have made you sing all the way here."

"That's hard work at this elevation. Takes a guy's wind."

"Well, this side won't be so bad. I can slide this down to where I want it."

He's half-asleep when she returns. "How about you nap for a few minutes? Now it's stopped snowing, I'd like to look around a sec."

"Sounds good. I'm plenty warm." He pats the arms of his thick jacket. "Be careful out there."

Zolo

His lungs fill and empty. Each inhalation bursts with confusion and fresh pain. Reek of gun and threat—people's essence now. All people. Each exhalation pushes away one he tried to trust, to treasure. Mushroom-scented woman, joy of being needed, fades from under his ribs. Even this not-dog who might have been friend, packmate, is tainted. Experience that did not bind but separated them. He runs, runs, pain of loss tearing through him, every stride, confusion refusing to dissipate in wind. Threat lingers, into canyons dead-ending in deep snow as mountains rise.

Alone, he doesn't know how to be dog. He doesn't know how not to be dog, how to disconnect from parts of him that need to share—running, resting, rolling in snow or dust. He runs, afraid. He runs. Alone.

He tires, he hungers, he thirsts, and still he runs. No memory of sleep. Pain isn't in his muscles but saturates bones and breath. Breath pours through him, out-breath of lonely pain, in-breath of snow and mountain, creek and mesa and deer and sandy outcrop of rock. Small drops of confusion fall from his tongue.

The Scent of Distant Family

He finds open water, falling snow sizzling onto surface. Water becomes his pulsing blood. He walks, and rustling wakes his nose. Without thought, he pounces. Warm vole swallows his pain, becomes part of connecting, part of him. He can't be alone. He isn't alone. He rolls. Snow cools his back, air soothes tired paws. World has not abandoned him. That's something people do.

In trees upstream, movement. From belly and elbows, he watches, listens, smells, for danger. Smells horses—who always come with dogs and people. But. No dogs, no people. He waits, wind drifting snow around him, around his stillness. Horses, different shades, different ways of moving. One moves crooked, as if in shock. One, though, isn't moving. On the ground, hovering smell of sick. Sick just starting, but she knows it's there, on her foreleg. She rests.

He walks, hesitant, respectful, toward small herd. Black stud steps in his direction, head up. Horse whuffs, sifting smell of dog through nose and memory. Zolo waits, not bear, not lion. Not people with guns and greed. Big horse, too, is tired. Twitching shoulder. Black steps closer, between dog and mare on the ground.

Zolo is near. He smells infection, sees swollen cut. He lays on his belly, watching. Mare nickers, hollow sound, creek rolling under curved rock. Her voice calls him. Big horse stands in falling snow, watching.

It happens slowly, but it happens, a mutual agreement among the three. Zolo licks her dark leg. She blows warm breath over his ears. He licks as snow builds around them, and stallion guards against danger. Three others sleep, standing nose to tail to nose under cottonwoods, sheltered by arched willows. Zolo licks, rhythm speaking of movement, of possibility. Possibility for movement, free and bound together. All things possible in movement, landscapes opening secrets, grass and vole together, fed by sun, together moving horse and dog.

Phelan

He fiddles with his favorite tie, a green-and-blue paisley with Yoda hidden in the design. So much he'll need to unlearn. The videoconference doesn't require attention, but a lack of attendance would be noticed. His hands, not visible, tip the vibrating phone toward him so he can see the name. Damn, his son. An actual call. He clicks his computer video off, mutes the mic, and leaves the volume on so he can hear if anyone asks him a direct question.

Finn is excited, he couldn't wait, hopefully he isn't interrupting anything? The text he sent earlier?

Phelan missed that.

A picture of the congratulations letter admitting him to Gabon's Marine Protected Area internship program? That is exciting. What will it cost? Need to send money, where? People on his computer screen, ties in basic stripes or medallions, look uncomfortable but try not to look at each other. Phelan would probably think it was funny if he knew what they were all stressing over.

Finn's got it covered. Already sent the money.

Wow. Excellent. Phelan still doesn't see anyone's mouth moving on-screen. This team doesn't tolerate silence much. Curious.

Distracted? Yeah, still working.

Something else—sure. Undivided attention? Hold on. Can I call you back? Sorry, sorry. We can talk. I can listen.

Phelan clicks the red button to leave the meeting. Best to close the computer all the way down. Maybe he can claim electrical outage—though he knows someone will call the power company

The Scent of Distant Family

to double-check. Worry about it later. Not like they can fire him. Something else to unlearn.

"I'm all yours. What else is going on besides this big news?" He loosens the tie, tips back, and puts his heels on the desk.

"Charlie said something odd the other day while I was there, and I tried to just ignore it. You know how he gets sometimes now." Finn pauses, as if gathering his thoughts.

"He really values your time together, though. Thanks for your patience with him."

"Well, I couldn't put it out of my mind, so I called Nik to see if she'd say he was just confused. But that's not what she said."

Phelan tries to stay as relaxed as his posture would indicate. Finn's tone has flipped from enthusiasm and confidence to something bordering on belligerence. Apparently afraid to take that last step. "I can't wait to hear what Nik had to say." He slides the tie all the way off, focusing on the smooth silk in his hand while Finn's words stumble.

So *that* is the wrenching question his son is trying so hard to spit out. He feels himself hovering in space, watching his body tense, holding its secrets. He would have told Finn this part someday. Soon. But too, he hovers in time, Robyn with her face turned to the wall, away from the baby. Not an image to share.

He rubs the back of a hand over his closed eyes. "You're the biologist. If asking me was going to be so difficult, you could've just gotten one of those genetics tests, couldn't you?"

Finn doesn't answer right away. Maybe he actually hadn't thought about that. Maybe he's wishing now he had.

Phelan doesn't wait out the silence. "Well, then, news flash. I never slept with your mother, before or after her boyfriend bailed.

You were always the one I loved. I hope that's enough to count as your real father." He presses the patterned silk, its repeating Yoda figures, to his forehead.

Charlie

The pressure on his bladder must have woken him. He steps out into the deserted highway, and wet splashes mark the car tires. The blowing snow has hidden all their earlier tracks, and he doesn't know which way Nikki went.

His empty bladder, though, lifts him like a helium balloon. He remembers a view of the Neaippeh mountains. Always those jagged peaks a surprise beyond the treeless swells of this foreground. He won't have to hike far to see them.

Charlie loves moving into a landscape, leaving cars and trucks behind. Hunting, whether for food or, with Nikki, for photos. Knowing to move so his scent doesn't run ahead of him to his quarry. His heavy coat was once the wool of sheep who could have sampled this pungent sagebrush that keeps tangling his feet whenever he breaks through the crust. The clouds catch some gleam of an early rising but hidden moon. Snow clouds, more snow moving onto the land, slathering the ground so hills and horizon are indistinguishable. But enough light for walking. Maggie is such a walker. Starlight or pouring summer rain, any kind of weather is right for Maggie. He pulls his scarf tighter around his neck and brushes snow out of his hair. As he walks, he digs in his pocket for the hat.

The wide hills give away little. Distance and time, both meaningless. Charlie huffs. The hill climbs more than it lets on. Slow going. But a person doesn't hunt fast. Maggie always gets ahead of him. He'll find her, even though the falling snow hides all shine now. He stops to breathe and tries to listen. He can hear motion over where the trees grow. Trees are friendly. They break this endless wind.

At the base of a Douglas fir, he slides to the ground, resting his back on its thick trunk. He smells the soft green of the needles. The cold spell, at least, has quit. The forest will coat the snow with its scent now that things have warmed up. He stretches his legs out and leans back. He loves a warm forest. The sound of wind in the needles, snow falling on tree bark, is so different than out on the open hills. The forest purrs like a cat. The cats are in the house again, and they help him sleep.

The wind and the storm grow, until their song holds lyrics. *Before I knew Mariah's name, I heard her wail and whining . . . .* He wakes, shivering, and listens. The snow can't hold its crystal form, and it slashes down in a cold rain, much colder than the warm snow was, stirring wind with its movement. He crawls back, away from the forest's edge, into a sprawl of piss fir that makes a holey umbrella. The ground is half-dry; maybe the duff could burn. He reaches into his coat pocket. Every coat in their closet has a small plastic bag with matches and shredded tinder. Maggie insists on it.

He pulls off a glove to get at the matches, and his fingers tremble white. He drops his first match. He breaks the second one. The third one sparks against the striker and blows out. A wailing lifts through the black branches and through the green smell and lifts the hair on the back of his neck. He blows on his hand. He sticks it inside his coat, rocking back and forth under the tree. He can't get warm. He drags the glove back over his fingers. Better than nothing. With his teeth, he zips the plastic bag. Maybe when the wind settles down.

A whine tugs at his attention. Closer. He is still rocking, can't stop rocking. But a different kind of movement catches his glance.

Snakelike, it stretches and slackens, but unlike a snake, it doesn't move away. He stares and listens. Whining slashes cold in his ears. The snake becomes a rope, caught around the shattered end of a broken tree. Charlie reaches for it. Around tractor trailers, untangling ropes becomes second nature. Even with his fumbling gloves, he threads the loop through the splintered wood of the stump.

Then he feels the rope tense in his hands. His eyes follow the far end to a dog with bright-yellow eyes, peering out from the dark.

He holds on to the frayed pieces and remembers. He is hunting a dog, Nikki's dog. A dog with bright eyes, he remembers. He feels his heart beating strong in his chest. He feels the warmth of a successful hunt, knowing he is taking care of his family. On his hands and knees, he approaches the dog. The whine hardens to a growl.

He stops. Lifting the rope, he tests whether it is caught anywhere else. It moves with his movement. He doesn't need to go to the dog. The dog can just come with him. He climbs upright with the help of a damp tree trunk and turns his back on those gold-dust eyes. He pulls and then leaves the line slack and pulls again and holds for a few beats. The line goes slack on its own, and he smiles. The dog slinks behind him, rustling branches Rain still sings through the woods, so he moves slowly under what cover the woven needles overhead can provide. He is bringing Nikki's dog home.

Nikki

She bursts into the store, greeted by jangling bells and a strong smell of snake. The door to Woody's living quarters is open, and she calls out. "Woody, you have to help—" She hasn't got enough air to finish her sentence. She gasps. "Please." She pushes the word past her clenched teeth.

In two strides, he is around the counter, holding her shoulders.

"What's going on?"

"Dad's gone. He got out of the car, and he's gone." She left him alone. She can't believe she left him alone. "I tried every direction. I can't believe he got so far so fast. I left the car out there, but I know he won't be able to find his way back."

"Nik, it's already dark."

"I know, I couldn't bear to leave." She can't believe Woody needs to tell her it's dark. She can't believe she's been so stupid. "I kept thinking I must've missed him in all the snow. It's dumping."

"Again. Yes. Hard to see anyone, much less track anyone. Is he wearing warm clothes at least?"

Woody saw what he was wearing. Why does he even have to ask? "Not nearly warm enough. He's an old man."

"It's a lot warmer than it has been, so good news."

"There is no good news, Woody. My father is missing. He can't even remember the names of his cats." She sobs now, and air refuses to fill her lungs. "He loves his cats."

"He gets confused? Is that what you're saying?" He grips one shoulder firmly still, but his other hand presses the center of her chest, just below her collarbone.

Of course she hasn't told him this. Her father is not necessarily the capable man he might appear. She sobs harder, but Woody's steadiness holds her, like a dog in a thunder shirt. She nods, sucking for a breath, swiping at the meltwaters flooding her face.

He guides her to a chair and presses her into it, then pours a cup of hot coffee. "Cream, sugar?"

Her coat sleeve is drenched, and still she presses it against her cheeks. She shakes her head. Someone as stupid as her does not deserve cream or sugar. He shouldn't even ask.

Handing the mug over, he picks up the phone. "We'll have a plan in no time. Like you said, he probably isn't far at all."

This is what she wants to hear. "People go in circles, right? That's why I waited. Why I left the car there, but we haven't had it long. He won't remember it's our car." Her breath hiccups out again. But Woody isn't putting on coveralls and boots, he's staring into space, listening to the phone ring.

"Jaye, Woody. Can you mobilize a search? Your friend Nik's dad. Yeah, Charlie." A long pause, his inward gaze stuck on the counter. "Sure, that's a start. They were just up the road from here, setting live traps for her dog. Yeah, I saw him early this morning. Her car's still out there, in case Charlie makes it back." He pauses, but this time looks at Nik, holding the phone away from his mouth. "How long has he been gone?"

"Too lo—, two hours. I can't believe he left." She can't believe she left him. STU-pid. STU-pid.

He repeats the information, looks out the front windows. "Right. Will do. See you soon. Drive safe."

The empty coffee mug sits on the counter, but Nik is pacing, swinging her arms to get heat into them, shake guilt out of them.

"Jaye's really good at this kind of thing." He says that first but then pauses.

Nik stops pacing. "But what?"

"Two local Search and Rescue teams are already out tonight. And roads are closed in every direction. One tractor trailer blown over on the interstate, avalanche in the canyon, and the plows haven't cleared out the drifts over the pass yet. Jaye's calling some other people, though, who live inside those boundaries, people she trusts to be helpful and not get lost themselves. They'll head this way as soon as they can."

The Scent of Distant Family

Her fingers grab the closest thing. Her used mug flies across the counter and crashes against the back wall in a shower of ceramic shards. "I'm going back out there."

Woody grabs both her arms and pins them against her sides. "Not yet."

Her eyes fill, and she glares her hopelessness at him. He releases her but stands between her and the door. "We need to get his sleeping bag, okay? And we'll drive it out to your car, in case he does get back there and in case he does recognize it and decides to climb in to get out of the weather. That's step one."

When his headlights strike her car's reflectors, Nik's door is already opening. Woody puts a hand on the top of her knee, just until he gets stopped. Then she is out, calling, looking. Woody bundles up the sleeping bag in his arms and transfers it to the Bug. He lays the passenger seat back and spreads the bag out, unzipped and folded open. Enough to give anyone the right idea.

"Looks great, thanks." She knows Charlie won't make it back to the car.

"Any sign anywhere?" He flicks on his headlamp and skids down the low side of the culvert.

She careens down next to him. "I keep thinking he might check the traps. He could hurt himself. Break an ankle, or worse." She needs to stay out here and see if he stumbles back this way.

"If he does, he'd be able to stay dry in the culvert. It's plenty big."

The negative possibilities race through her mind, but Woody seems to know not to voice any of them. Nik knows it takes a conscious effort to focus on what could go well. She's grudgingly beginning to welcome what she found frustrating about him earlier.

"Okay." Woody swallows. "Now we go back for step two."

We, my ass. "I'll stay here."

"I need your help. Searchers are assembling. We have to get supplies organized."

"You think I'll go after him." She doesn't care what he thinks. She needs to go after her father.

"I know it's hard not to." His shoulders lift, then fall. "And I know we don't have enough of a search party to split it in two before we have a plan."

She is about to argue more, and her mouth opens but then closes. "I might be able to ask someone else to come. My phone got cold though. I'll need to use yours."

"The roads are all closed, remember? Someone from near here?"

"Come on, let's get this show rolling." She bangs on the hood of his Jeep and climbs in the passenger side.

True to his story, Woody begins gathering first aid supplies and trail food. He leaves her alone with the phone.

"Phelan, it's Nik."

"Hey Nik, what's up?"

"It's Dad. We're at Rim Rendezvous, and he's gone missing."

A dish crashes in Phelan's sink. "How'd that happen?"

She needs to sweep up Woody's broken coffee mug. "And rescue crews are already all out elsewhere in this weather."

"What were you doing?"

English is a forgiving language. She can pretend his *you* is meant in the plural. "The canyon's closed, but the storm's on its way out. Can you get here?" She means it in the plural too. He has connections.

"Jeezus, Nik. We're talking about Dad. I'll be there." The phone clicks off.

Pilots fly through storms in the dark all the time. They know when it isn't safe. She finds a broom and dustpan, and the sound of

The Scent of Distant Family

stoneware clatters into a wastebasket. The brewing coffee mutters its constant accusations. STU-pid. She can't un-hear it.

Woody measures fresh coffee into brand new thermoses. "Nik, can you go in back and grab spare blankets? They're in a linen closet straight ahead of the door, against the back wall."

The closet is next to Guthrie's pen. The snake hides from her, like so much wisdom, like so many correct choices. In front of Guthrie, she stands exposed, like Charlie, like Zolo. Her failures gather around her for everyone to see. She wants to ask Charlie for advice—about the very things she's never been able to share with him. She wants to crawl into the snake pen, under a rock, hibernate like Guthrie can't seem to do. Maybe a rubber boa can feel the slight tremor of Charlie's feet over the snow, know which direction to look. Nik wishes she knew how to ask, how to listen for the answer.

Tess

Small filly darts into her dreams, berry bright, one who will always attract attention. Waxwings perch on alligator juniper nearby, and their voices float through scaly leaves, naming the still dog-sized horse after their favorite fruits. Tess watches her, the herd's only remaining descendant. Mother mare, making milk, needs to graze, needs to rest. Tess can watch. She likes to play, growing the filly strong and swift.

Snow has played in the mountains for months, and now in the sun it grows the river, stronger and swifter, life's language noisy along the cliff's lower edge, loud under the canyon's crumble. Dirt jumps, slides in, rides away, a cradle for cottonwood seeds somewhere else, life for catbirds perched among the curve of leaves, in a distant valley along a swerve of river.

Tess's ear twitches in her dreams, her memories. An exposed root twitches, too, catching the waves' unsteady rhythms. The root wriggles over the water, a cat toy, an enticement. Tess watches the filly watch the water, watch the root. Water brown with moving dirt, loud with warnings not always heard, or heeded. Danger, yes, life is danger too. Life is learning. Imagination draws the filly forward, dream of playmates, dream of dancing on the river's fluid dirt.

She darts toward the waggling root. Dog-sized horse makes no sound in the wild water.

Tess's dreaming legs leap, timelessness suspending her in dream-time air, over the wet filly, splashing past the root, past the tangle, past the crumbling bank. Grass-strong teeth grab, dreaming head twitches. Darkened filly damp and defiant, splashing on mud, descending the canyon, drops from Tess's teeth. But she's the one to carry the herd through time, and Tess won't stop at a single try. Again she flies into the river, wings folded, legs flailing, finding purchase where the smaller horse cannot. She bends her head to the filly's raised neck and grasps; she stands in the chaotic current and lifts the river-dancer to land.

Whickering over the river's raucous race, Tess rejoins dry land. She licks water from the filly's drenched coat. In the sun now, small horse stretches horizontal, warm on the river's old rocks, rhythm of warm tongue drifting her into dreams, into learning.

With his rhythmic licking, the filly-sized dog dreams Tess toward the future. She sleeps, and she heals. The dog's rhythm forms the bass line for a clicking song of running together. She imagines she learns new ways to sing.

The Scent of Distant Family

11

Jaye

She brought a whiteboard and dry-erase markers, things she uses to post daily options and schedules for summer guests at the ranch. They don't seem much use against a classic Wyoming winter. She focuses on the blizzard of white space in front of her trembling breath. She thinks about her grandmother's strength. She thinks about the grulla and her leadership. She hopes she can summon the same resources.

She outlines who is already committed and what their promises include. Making the work visible. Russell will show up with a number of handheld radios. On the way over, he'll collect enchilada casseroles Ana always keeps stocked in her freezer. He's already been by the Dora store, and Miller is, at this moment, hooking on to a second camp trailer to bring over for a sleeping option if needed. She puts Bailey and Barney's names on the board—she brought them with her, knowing in the dark it would be better to ride horses than snowmobiles. Nik can call out, and they can listen for Charlie's response.

Jaye's left hand runs through Polenta's tangles while she writes. Two sleds will arrive by daylight with Selina's husband and the two boys. They were out riding at Sprucedale yesterday, which means, unlike Selina, they can reach Woody's place despite the road closures. Though noisy, sleds will allow some of the team to cover more territory and if the snow stops, maybe see Charlie's trail.

A row of gear is lined up by the door. On top of each stack is a brightly colored safety vest. Fluorescent pink, brilliant green, hunter orange. The door jangles open, and Russell sheds snow as he enters. With a quiet word, Jaye sends her dog behind the counter, where she waits, chin on her paws, out of the way.

He hands over a small box of radios. "These are all programmed already. Here's the channel you'll be using—Tac 2. Nik, come see how these work. Woody? You going out too?"

Woody takes the wood-handled bag of glass casserole dishes so Russell can pass around radios, explain the squelch, low- and high-power options, how to replace batteries. Jaye sketches a quick map of their search areas and makes assignments. "Russell, can you wait up the road by Nik's car until Miller shows up? Once he's got the trailer off, you two can take this section on the south side of the road. Be careful, it's steep. Woody has some snowshoes and ski poles you can use for extra balance or to test cornices. Nik and I will take the horses and head out opposite your area. When the sleds arrive, the Jenkinses can take this quadrant past you two, in case he's got farther than we think." Russell gives her a thumbs-up and a nod. Nik's eyes are glazed. Woody rubs her neck, though his attention is on the whiteboard.

"Probably best to have you stay at base, here." She makes eye contact with Woody. "You call Russell and Miller in if Thomas and the boys show up. If Charlie misses the car and ends up here, you can call us all in. If you hear anything by phone or if we get crazier weather predictions, keep us posted. Periodically, check on the Bug. If the roads clear and any S&R crews become available, they'll need a briefing."

"Can do." He turns toward the counter.

She needs Nik to loosen her grip on guilt, make herself useful. "Nik, what's Charlie wearing?"

The Scent of Distant Family

She swallows, rubs her eyes. The silence stretches for long seconds. "Quilted wool coat," she finally pushes out. "Black . . . and red."

Not the most auspicious for a night search. Jaye can feel the skin on her own face cooling to some shade of snow.

Phelan

He meets his friend Beryl at her place, not far from town. A place with space enough for her helicopter. A woman with money enough for a helicopter and for the high-dollar space to keep it just outside her overly spacious house. But Hollywood is about entertaining people, so the house covers that requirement. She uses the house to help her career, but she uses the helicopter to help with area Search and Rescue operations. In the mountains, that's a frequently useful thing.

She is bundled up beyond recognition, but Phelan knows that voice. He hears it in some of his favorite movies. As in so many of them, she berates the man in the heavy coat on the other side of her. "No-no-no. Not like that. Bart, let me get it."

Phelan's head snaps toward her helper. He squints. For shit's sake. "Bart?"

"I tried to tell her you wouldn't want my help." His face is in the shadows.

Beryl snaps the half-folded tarp as it slides down. "Grab that end. Personal agendas have no place here."

Phelan wants to agree with her. He steps up to snatch the flapping ends of the tarp, hold them together in the wind.

Bart's shoulders are hunched, and he doesn't seem to understand her instructions. But he apparently feels obliged to explain himself. "I'm doing maintenance here for a while."

Phelan shakes his head. Doesn't look like it. Whatever. He eyes the helicopter. "How many people can that carry?"

She stands in the light, where her eyes study him. "Depends. You have someone else you need to pick up?"

"He's driving now. But he won't be able to get through."

"We can probably make something work. You'll have to help find a landing spot while we're in the air. Plenty of maps on board." She waves him into the back.

Once seated next to her, Bart is quick to pull his headset on over his black beanie.

Charlie

They walk, but not fast enough to stay warm. He keeps breaking through, stopping to catch his breath. Charlie isn't sure he's going in the right direction. He doesn't remember where he started from. He started in snow, woke up in rain. Now, though, the air is drying up. He still can't see stars, but he can feel the clouds thinning. The temperature descends, and his feet choose the direction that also feels downward. Always a river in the bottoms, and a river always goes somewhere.

The wind blows the clouds apart. Charlie sees a star. He forgets how to make a wish. He knows there's a right way the words have to go. He knows what he's wishing for—besides food, that is. He grabs a handful of snow, and it's cold on his teeth, but at least it crunches. Song fragments creep up from the slow rhythm of his footsteps. *And now I'm lost, so cold and lost . . . .*

But he's not alone. He looks behind him. The wind covers any sounds the dog's passage makes, until he forgets she's even there. *Mariah makes the mountains sound like folks're up there dying.* Wind tugs on his heart, and he hears the pain everyone knows, everyone hides from. Loneliness sounds like that. He wants to reach out and wrap his arms around the scared dog, but she stays at the

The Scent of Distant Family

farthest reach of her rope. They keep walking. Under the wool, Charlie is cold.

He sighs, tired again, even though they aren't walking fast. Shivering takes a lot of energy. He isn't sure how far they've traveled. He can't say how long either, except it's still dark. Enough stars appear now, he can see his breath shimmer in front of him. The trees shake overhead. He stumbles on a snow-covered stump and barely catches himself on the wide horizontal trunk that used to stand above it. In his weariness, he recognizes the small shelter below. Tall grasses took advantage of its protection last summer and now make a fine nest, surprisingly dry.

Bending low, he rustles into place, turning in a slow circle until his bones find the best rest. For Nikki, he ties the frayed end of the rope around his waist. Her dog sits out in the snow, facing him, ears alert and upright, on guard. From his bed, Charlie looks into those sulfur-yellow eyes. "Your shift, my friend." He is so tired.

The wind rises louder in the branches, old needles and spent cones dropping onto the snow outside his hole. His eyes close. Wind wants to fly free over the wide desert, but it tangles in the forest. Its longing becomes a long howl, starting high and descending, deep into beautiful sorrow. His fiddle knows how this goes. So does his heart.

The grasses aren't enough padding to get comfortable. Waiting makes him too anxious to sleep. Maggie tells him worrying wastes energy, and he has too many things to do to be wasting energy. He gets their camp ready, the tent set up, firewood stacked by the rock-lined pit, and waits near her favorite waterfall. The air pushed around by the dropping water makes him shiver. He hears her horse approach at a thumping lope and looks up. The stirrups are flapping;

one rein is broken off short. The saddle is empty. Emptier even than Charlie's heaving stomach.

Nikki

Bailey carries her through the snow, again. Again Nik scans the slopes for motion. Sometimes stars light the snow into a pewter gleam, and she imagines she sees Charlie in his old plaid coat. Contrast is a thing of utility as well as beauty. The clouds hang around, though, and sometimes even the open hills darken like the forest. Her imagination sees Zolo then, a white hound appearing through the dark. A hound's nose worth far more than her night vision.

Beside her, Jaye rides another stout horse, a deep-brown gelding. He matches Bailey's long strides well, and their saddles creak together in the night, murmured voices praying in a high-ceilinged cathedral.

Jaye wears a radio harness strapped over a thick sweater and under her oilskin duster. Woody's voice crackles. "Miller's here. No action near the Bug. He and Russell will have snowshoes on soon to hit this south section."

"Copy that." Jaye meets Nik's eyes and nods. "Thanks for the update. Quiet out here so far too."

"Sure wish Zolo could be helping." Nik sticks a hand under her warm thigh, while Jaye zips her coat back up. "He liked Dad. A lot." She hears the past tense in her statement, but her throat tightens before she can try to correct it. *Change* it? She doesn't know what might be correct. Change happens. What might have been correct—not wrong—once might need to be corrected now. She swipes a glove at her eyes before ice tracks her cheeks.

"Polenta's not trained for it, but I'm sure she'd alert to Charlie's scent." Jaye pulls her horse up for a moment, while her dog chews at snow packed between her toes.

The Scent of Distant Family

If Charlie dies, Nik will be an orphan, like his mooseling. Like Finn believes he is. Maybe she's been wrong. Maybe she needs to let go of her promise, her lies. Finn needs to know he has a mother. She might tell him that much.

The horses step and drop through the snow, step and drop. Her backbone is shaken. She could tell him the rest too. The part even Phelan doesn't know. She can still protect Robyn. Like she has failed to do for Charlie. Failed to do for Zolo. Protecting Robyn, she'll lay more pain on Finn.

Nik pounds her gloved hand on the saddle horn, leather against leather, and pushes Bailey forward. "I've made such a mess of everything." The night amplifies every sound they make. Every mistake expands into the endless dark, growing instead of dissolving. Jaye doesn't contradict her.

The clouds defy the wind and consolidate again, leaving the stars and their thin light on the far side of nowhere. Saddles creak. The wind fights back, sending cold swirls of snow across the darkened plains. Nik shudders. She sticks one hand under a thigh.

"Does Charlie know to hunker down, not waste energy?" Jaye's voice is muffled through the shearling of her turned-up collar.

"He knows plenty. What he'll remember from one minute to the next, though, I can't say. Half the time, he thinks I'm my mother."

"Probably better than thinking you're *his* mother." Jaye cracks a grin at her, then turns her head into the wind and sticks her tongue out to catch a snowflake. "You thirsty yet? Woody made us coffee."

Nik wants to be offended at Jaye's joke. But involuntarily, her own lips curve up. Maybe a laugh will release the roaring in her ears so she can listen better. So she can hear Charlie when he calls out. Shaky, she exhales. "I can't believe how incredible everyone is being. Especially you. Thank you so much."

"Is that a yes?" Jaye twists to her saddlebag and extracts a thermos. She hands over the full cap. "Black okay?"

"Oh, you mean you brought cream? How about whiskey?" Nik sips, hands it back.

"No cream. You caught me there." Jaye takes the cup and tips a healthy swallow down before the heat blows away.

"I suppose Polenta's the only one with whiskey." She has her eyes on the dog, hoping she'll start digging at buried footprints.

"She's Bernese, not St. Bernard. And no booze. Totally a myth that whiskey's helpful against hypothermia."

Nik no longer has the energy to be offended by this needless lesson. She no longer has the confidence to be anything at all. She wants to disappear. "No, no, I know. It's just, I just, I don't know what to do. I don't know how to guess where he might go or where he might be."

"Can't know everything or even much of anything. But we can keep moving. Sometimes that's enough."

The horses stride forward, snow swinging down around them, beginning to mix with rain. Warmer isn't safer, not in a winter storm. All these changes in climate make everything so much harder to predict—the feedback loops more complex than people imagine. She should have predicted Charlie would forget to stay in the car. She should have known Zolo's adopter was a fraud. Making a promise to a frightened girl can't predictably protect her curious son twenty years later. The world holds so many kinds of danger. A howl rises from the dark firs lining the sharp drop to the west.

Nik doesn't think she's ever heard a coyote sound so sad. But then. "Is that a coyote?" Reintroduced wolves are thriving in the ecosystem, though she's not seen any yet.

Jaye cocks her head. The howl stretches out across the wide space. "I don't think it is."

The Scent of Distant Family

Charlie

His own shivering wakes him, but he feels Maggie's strong backbone against his spine. Her soft snores match his own pulsing lungs, steady as the seasons. Steady as their comforting love.

Finn

From this height, daylight colors the clouds, still covering the sky but no longer in one undifferentiated mass. Their curves and edges catch the far sun in sad blue shadows. On the land below, Finn sees two horses, saddled, tied to a porch railing, their noses buried in feed bags. A dog sprawls on the porch nearby.

As Beryl angles the helicopter toward a far corner of the parking lot, a truck and trailer with two snowmobiles on it also arrive. The tires make trenches in the drifted accumulation, but the truck has clearance enough and power enough. Finn spots Nik's humped little car a half-mile or so away, snow heaped around it.

Spinning blades crack the helicopter's sound into a broken vinyl record. No runway is needed. The people just arrived jog toward the porch, where others gather to watch the ship settle to the ground. Beryl pulls off her headset. The three men unbuckle their belts, and Bart pulls the door open. Finn is the first one out. He can't believe Nik lost Charlie. Out in the storm, overnight.

Everyone is surprised at their arrival, except Nik. But seeing Bart will shock the snot out of her. All hands on deck. And of course, people stare at Finn. He's used to it. He spots Nik but he's not about to make reassuring noises to ease her guilt. He joins the general flow into the gas station, where people collect in a half-circle in front of a whiteboard and a warmly dressed woman with a handful of markers.

"My name's Jaye. Thomas and crew—welcome aboard. And Phelan." She nods, her chin high. She knows his father but seems ambivalent about his assistance. "Introduce your team, if you will."

He starts at the top, of course. "Beryl Raye, our pilot, a friend." Then "Bart," who moves toward Nik but stops after a single step. A few people exchange glances as if they might have heard Bart's name before. "And my son, Finn."

The marker scratches along the whiteboard. Jaye chews on one end, her head moving back and forth between the list and the lightening window. Finn catches sight of a young girl perched on a stool by the counter, a small rabbit in her lap. She waves at him.

"Hi Finn. I'm Emory, and this is Cygnus. We aren't on the board. Miller's my dad." She points at a skinny man leaning against the wall, who gives him a nod and a tired smile.

"Russell." A hand lifts in a welcoming gesture that starts in Finn's direction, then turns toward the rest of the newcomers. He could be close to Charlie's age himself, but the melted snow beaded up on his wool pants show he's been out searching during the night.

Jaye nods toward Emory. "No school today?"

Miller shrugs. "She'll learn more here anyway."

Jaye faces a wiry guy at a computer. "Woody, road report?"

"Not much moving. Search and Rescue's off the rollover, but then South Pass avalanched too. They're still recovering bodies from the first one—a minivan got caught under it." His voice manages the newscaster's stoic but concerned tone.

Finn feels his guts clench. No one better refer to their efforts as a recovery. Charlie is tough.

Woody steps over to Nik, carrying a fresh coffee. "Unless you'd rather have tea and soy milk?"

He must have entertained her before. Finn wonders if any of these strangers know Charlie or if he's just some anonymous old guy to them. The search may be perfunctory. It took a family member to rustle up the helicopter. He's surprised and grateful Beryl hadn't already been enlisted elsewhere. Now that he's here, no one will be able to call him off until Charlie is safe. He fights off other words that might be possible outcomes of their search.

Nik shakes her head at Woody, folds the warm mug between her palms, and holds it up to her cheeks.

Woody looks at Russell. "If you could stay here by the phone with Emory, I'll go ride. I have a sled here."

Jaye nods first. "You're fresher." She pushes Russell's argument away before it starts. She turns briskly to face them all. "Here's what I'm seeing, then, for the next two hours. Beryl, your ship okay to go back up for an overhead look?" A nod. "The youngest eyes will go with you. Two from the Jenkins clan and Emory. Up for a helicopter ride?"

Finn sees two teenage boys straighten their backs and give each other a fist bump. This is just plain fun for them. They don't have any connection to Charlie.

Emory has only one hesitation. "Can Cyggie stay with Russell?"

"Of course he can." Russell strokes Cygnus's long ears between the cracked skin of his hands. "I won't let him get eaten by the snake." He winks at her.

Finn catches Jaye's cringe. She casts a glance toward a closed door at the side of the deli. He can't believe the leader of their search is scared of snakes. And other than the kids, she's probably the youngest one here. He doesn't find that reassuring.

She takes a deep breath before she continues. "Polenta needs to stay too. She's got a limp from last night." She nods at Russell. "You're in charge of base. If the roads get cleared, we might have more people showing up. Woody and Bart with Thomas, take the sleds this way." She draws a loop on the map to the northeast. "Miller, can you keep an eye on the Bug? Take your truck to see if he's turned up along the road? You have chains on, right?"

A quick nod. "I'll look where I can."

"Phelan and Finn, you take the snowshoes. You'll check back over where we rode the horses last night and either see what we couldn't see in the dark or maybe find Charlie making his way toward the gas station." Her face stays neutral as she faces them, but a muscle twitches in her jaw.

With no challenge to her instructions, his father agrees. She waits for Finn's assent.

He doesn't believe she's as confident as she tries to look. "We'll be able to follow the horse tracks? Not too much fresh snow?" He pushes for clarity. They have to get this right.

"We only got back a little over an hour ago." Jaye glances at Nik, whose eyes remain closed, her head leaning on the wall. He will be glad for the exertion. He gives Jaye a nod. Hopefully his father can keep up. And hopefully, yes, Charlie will be making his way back, once he has the daylight to sort out where he is.

She points at the map. "Nik and I will take the horses a little farther west this time, and if we see a decent game trail, we might dip into the forest off toward the valley."

Nik rouses herself to watch the marker trailing across the board. She hasn't even acknowledged his presence.

Jaye looks everyone over. "If that makes sense to you all, Woody has piles of gear on the floor. Enough for all the newcomers?" She gets a thumbs-up. "We won't have enough radios to include the ship, Beryl, but yours can stay in touch with Russell. He'll show you the frequency. Charlie can't have gotten far. Could you cover all this territory we'll be checking on the ground, plus a bit past our edges?" She swings her arm over her drawings.

The Scent of Distant Family

The crews disperse, as directed. Finn straps on snowshoes and watches the storm's renewed energy while he waits for Phelan. Fat flakes in clumps big as a baby's hand swoop down on the porch. They are too heavy for the wind and drop like white rain.

Nik walks past to where Jaye is trying to brush the saddles off. Woody follows behind her. "You better get on while your seat's clear." He has a hand on her back.

She meets Finn's eyes for one second only. Her eyes about to brim over. He grabs the ski poles leaning against the wall and steps away.

Zolo

In fresh storm, Zolo doesn't run through culverts, looking for rabbits. He stays near herd. If a horse kicks up smell of vole, he digs. The Sentinel slips in, nips off any grass scrabbling claws uncover. Razzle's mother moves, awkward, in willows where they take cover. She eats for hours, finding little in each frozen nibble. She bites soft tips off branches.

From Tess's leg, he smells no infection. Jagged edges on long gash grow together. He watches her rest, storm's gift.

The Sentinel rests more too. Zolo helps, sorting scents, checking unfamiliar noises. If either grows concerned, Tess decides. Wait or move. When Zolo paces between bull moose and old matriarch, Tess shows no worry. When coyote pack passes, all three guardians stand, watching.

Tess reads scented air—and chooses. Time to move. Night's ongoing darkness doesn't distract her. She crosses snowed-over, iced-over creek, jogs north. Bruins still sleeping.

Zolo lopes with her until they've climbed above willows, black pines ahead. He pauses, looks back. Other mares across now, picking up pace. As always, the Sentinel guards blind spot, vulnerable rear, for his mares. Once they begin to climb, he works his way over ice.

At the top, wind tosses manes, forelocks whip into eyes. Razzle's mother fills her mouth with grass, in quantity not tasted for days. Though dried blades are wan and faded, she nickers, welcoming green in them, promise. Older mare joins her, head bent to earth. Zolo in rabbit country now, lopes wide circle, sniffing onto erratic paths. Fresh snow gathers s unmelted on Sentinel's insulated back.

New scent reaches him, and his head cocks, trying to remember. Tess smells too. Her head springs up, focused intensity. She stares north but down into dark timber. The Sentinel joins her, whiskers on muzzles touching, ears turning, all directions. Zolo drops his nose, finds lingering touch of scent under fresh snow. He takes a step closer to trees. He whines.

Scent sounds like fiddle song. Smell of one who knows songs heal.

But Zolo's learned from running high plains. He's learned: what he thought he knew isn't whole truth. People can be dangerous. Maybe even: people he once knew.

His whine echoes now.

Not his whine.

He steps closer again, curious, whimper. His head twists, and then—he smells her too. Her warm woman-blood lifts on air with replying huff. She remembers him. He remembers people they ran from, together, then apart. Fear pinions him in place.

Tess stomps and spins. She leads gallop across high white prairie, Sentinel at their heels. Then she bounces, halts, spins again, looking for him.

Zolo turns toward low whine, toward canyon. He steps, careful, around fallen trees, uprooted boulders. They aren't far, warm dark woman with upright ears and the other. Rope stretches away where she stands, watching him approach. Scent, the other scent, turns his nose.

He can't make sense of it. But. Connection tugs, longings swell. River floods in his direction, riding her howl. Man whose fiddle could sing does not move. Zolo steps close, settles. Waits, no sense of waiting. Cold is less cold when small warmth is shared.

Dark finally goes dusky. Distant sun lifts, while snowflakes drop around them. Not-dog rises with slow sun, stretches, tugs long line tight. He stands, too, head back. Pines carry discordant howls, his, hers, to missing fiddle, to horse herd. With their breaths, faraway horses melt frost, ice coating grass blades. But these people—human and not-dog—are also his people.

Oh, to sing together. His lungs fill with sage air, his heart swells. Mariah's eyes close as her voice opens. They belong, to each other, to winter world, singing.

Then horse hooves echo through mountain bones, not his horses, sound of saddle leather, smell of coffee.

12

Nikki

They're still riding along the ridge, the dividing line between high desert and the mountain slopes and narrow valley bottoms that alternate westward for miles, when the chorus begins. Both women rein up at the same moment, listening, their eyes meeting. Nik, without thinking, swings her right leg over and slides off Bailey. She tosses the reins at Jaye as she starts running.

The howls reach out, low and rough, then higher and throaty. She knows two coyotes can sound like a large pack, but this sounds . . . like no coyotes.

Gravity pulls her sharply downhill. She falls on one knee, hard, but stumbles upright and struggles forward. Bare branches slap her and scratch, loud, against her jacket, tearing the wind pants that cover her warmer layers below. She crashes through brush into darker timber, bouncing off snow-hidden obstacles, setting loose from the branches cascades of crystal showers that wet her face. In the swirl of falling white, a white dog, frightened by her rampaging rush, bolts through the woods toward the top of the rim. Nik stops, breath ragged, unable to call his name. Her eyes fill with tears, then tears spill down her freezing cheeks, melting snowflakes as they drift in below her hat.

Jaye catches up with her and stops at her shoulder, squinting up the hill they've just descended, following Nik's wet eyes. "Is that him?"

Nik nods, swiping at her running nose.

But another quiet whine pulls Jaye's head around. She touches Nik's forearm. "There. Wolf."

Nik turns, just her head first, but then, slowly, her body follows. "If it's a wolf," she whispers, "why is there a rope on it?" The rope is taut.

Jaye stares, then shakes her head. "Must be caught up. Better see what we can do." Her voice is low, and the wolf's ears flicker, forward and back.

Nik sees a dull glow, like dried rosehips hiding in their bramble. Slowly, out of the tangle of bare branches, the red-and-black plaid of her father's coat resolves. "Dad? Dad—" She glances at Jaye. "Dad, it's me. Wake up." Her voice rings out, harsh and harried. The wolf flinches backward.

"That rope is under him." Jaye has a hand on her arm, but both of them are still moving forward, tacitly not so fast that the wolf might think they're a threat. Jaye has already pulled off her glove by the time they reach Charlie, and she reaches for his wrist.

"Dad, please." Nik's hands are on Charlie's forehead, then they stroke his cheeks. So cold.

"He has a pulse." Jaye leans over his chest, her ear to his lips. "Shallow but breathing. Shake his shoulders a little." She shrugs off the pack she'd pulled from the back of her saddle and tugs out a silver space blanket.

"Dad. We're here to take you home now. You have to wake up." Nik's words tremble, start to choke in her tight, tight throat.

His eyes open, unfocused. Nik throws her arms around his shoulders and hugs him half-upright.

He finds his voice. "You're here. You aren't dead." He wraps his arms around her back, and they rock together.

Nik gulps and sobs, sobs and gulps. Almost a laugh. Rocking.

Jaye flips the blanket around behind him and pulls it up to his neck. "Hi Charlie. It's Jaye. From over to Yahanna. Nik and I have been helping each other out a bit."

The Scent of Distant Family

His eyes find her and begin to focus.

"Charlie, who's this you have tied to your waist?" Jaye touches the rope and, with just a small motion, waves toward its far end. She doesn't look toward the yellow eyes.

Nik steps away from her father and digs into Jaye's pack. She pulls out the mini thermos. "You must be really thirsty. Take a sip of this. It's hot, though. Careful." She holds her hand around his hand as he tips the cup to his lips.

He swallows and looks back and forth between the two of them. Then he reaches a hand down and feels the rope's tension. He takes another swallow, the drink unsteady but for Nik's hand under his. His face breaks into a wide smile. "I wished on a star. And I got to bring your dog back."

Nik feels Jaye's boot press onto the top of her foot. She hears a crash through the trees above them.

"Grampa? You all right?"

Jaye's voice cuts across the noise of Finn's passage. "Finn. Go slow."

He stops. "What's wrong?"

"Where's your father?"

"Right behind me. What's going on?" He is still walking toward them, his head swiveling.

Jaye gives more instruction. "Take off your snowshoes. It'll be easier in here. But go slow so you don't sink in somewhere and break a leg."

"Is that all you're worried about? How's Grampa?" He stands on one foot to unfasten a binding, then switches.

"Right here. I can speak for myself. And I'm cold." His voice slurs, unsteady.

Jaye turns her attention back to him. "Nik, he's shivering."

Phelan makes the ridge above them and hollers down. "What's happening? We saw your horses."

"We've got your father. Stay up there and radio out to Russell." Jaye manages to project her voice without adding volume. "Have him try to round up the snowmobiles. If Woody has some kind of pull-behind kids' sled, that would be great."

"Is he hurt?"

"Just cold, it looks like."

"Hallelujah. Thank you, thank you." His final words muffle, as if he's already turned away.

Nik rubs Charlie's arms under the blanket. Phelan's thanks seem specific to a singular 'you' that doesn't include her. "Got to get you warmed up somehow. All this snow. Just won't stop." Clouds cover the sun. Gray is suspended in the forest, danger that just won't blow away.

Finn gives her a look, exactly like Charlie might, then reaches into his grandfather's coat pocket. He pulls out the plastic bag with the matches, but before he turns away, he notices the rope. "What the—?"

Charlie beams at him. "I found Nikki's dog."

Finn looks at Nik. "That's not Zolo."

For a second, Charlie frowns. But only for a second. "I've gotten so bad with names."

Nik grabs the plastic bag from Finn. "Why didn't I remember that? I put it there."

"Well, he sure isn't George." Finn laughs. "Let me help. Here's a bunch of dried grass. Grampa, did you sleep under here?"

"Not George. Mariah." Charlie is almost pouting, frustrated with them.

Jaye looks at Nik. She lifts her shoulders and shakes her head.

"I brought Mariah home for Nikki. She's too lonely without her dog."

The Scent of Distant Family

"Dad, I'm right here. I can speak for myself." She smiles at him. "I would love her company. Did you see her name on her collar?"

"Never got close enough."

Finn pulls off his fleece-lined choppers and pulls them over Charlie's gloves. Then he flicks a flame into life. Nik feeds it bits of the grass Charlie slept on. Jaye unwraps a soft energy bar from the pack.

"Mariah doesn't like the fire."

Everyone looks up at Charlie's words. The wolf is flat to the ground, pushing herself back against the rope, the bones of her feet raised with effort.

Nik eases upright. She unties the rope and slides it away from her dad. He smiles at her, still shivering. She makes room for Jaye at Charlie's side. "You got him for a minute?" She doesn't look for Jaye's answer, though, her eyes on Mariah. She murmurs reassurances as she approaches, looping rope into her hand as she goes. The wolf crawls backward as much as she's allowed, eyes unwavering, on her. Once Nik is several body lengths away from the fire and all the people trying to warm Charlie at its tiny flames, she folds herself down, balancing on the balls of her feet, knees close to her chest, making herself small. With Jaye and Finn taking care of her father, she feels very small. The mistake she made leaving Charlie in the car, so large. She faces away from Mariah, and only peripheral vision gives her clues to any movement she makes.

Her smallness must be enough. Mariah stills. Nik lets the arm with the rope stretch out and puts slack in the line. This isn't going to be as easy as loading her onto a snowmobile seat or even leading her out with the horses.

Phelan calls down. "Woody comes through. Sled's on the way."

Jaye checks with her first, gives a wordless thumbs-up, before calling back. "ETA?"

"Within fifteen, Russell says. I gave him our coordinates."

"Okay, you stay up there to flag them in. We've got a fire started, so give us a few minutes to absorb some warmth. Then we'll come your way."

Nik hums under her breath, hoping to gentle the clamor of people's voices in the wolf's ears. Their words cut painfully through the cold air. Their competence cuts painfully. Mariah flat on the forest floor. Even the trusty Bailey is unlikely to go along with a wolf dragging behind him. They need a plan.

Jaye leaves Finn with Charlie and eases nearby. "Finn and I can carry your dad out between us. Will she follow you up?"

"I can tie her here. She's going to freak out at the snowmobiles, I think." Nik throws a couple half-hitches around a staub. She needs to help with Charlie.

Jaye keeps an eye on the wolf, who hasn't warmed up to their presence at all. "Looks likely." She double-checks the knot before heading back toward the fire. "Think she's a hybrid? Or full wolf?"

"Doesn't much matter. Illegal to turn either option loose." Nik hears contempt in her voice. Sleeplessness, adrenaline dump. Plenty of excuses for being short-tempered. "People are so stupid."

"Looks like she made her own escape, to me." Jaye glances back at Mariah.

Nik relents. "Point taken." Not Mariah's fault she wound up in someone's household, and really, to her credit if she didn't want to stay there. What a mess people can make of things. A long out-breath whistles through her lips. She should know.

They sit with Charlie for a few more minutes, assessing his limbs and taking his vitals. As he stops shivering, his words get stronger, and he chats with Finn, sharing his adventure. Nik marvels at the way Finn applauds Charlie's hardiness without making him feel guilty about wandering off in the first place. How he seems to cheer for the childlike Charlie, who mostly drives her crazy. Finn doesn't talk to her. Jaye taps her watch and nods toward the top of the slope.

Phelan

Morning temperatures must be moving upward, despite the hovering gray. Phelan unzips his down jacket, pulls off his gloves, runs a hand across his forehead. From the open meadow at the top, he watches Finn and Jaye cross their arms for a four-handed carry through the trees. They tilt and slide over the slick, uneven slope, Charlie's arms around their shoulders.

"I'll bring up the packs, then." Nik sounds half-relieved, half-deserted.

They are less than practiced, an awkward team, and Charlie's legs are long enough to knock into piled deadfall along the way. Jaye can't push aside branches in front of him, and can only give verbal warnings. Phelan sees how Charlie watches Finn more than he watches out for what's about to poke him in the eye. One final stumble at the top lands him in Finn's lap, collapsed in a wind-thrown spruce. "I should've just walked up."

Phelan hoists him upright. "We figured you've already reached your quota of walking for the week." He holds his father by the forearms a moment. Then they are hugging. He doesn't care who sees the flash of wet on his cheeks.

The snowmobiles, one now pulling an ancient open sleigh with gray metal showing under patchy paint, throw up sprays of fresh powder as they speed toward the rescue party. When the helmets come off, Phelan is surprised to see Miller has replaced Bart.

"Your chariot, I believe." Miller puts an arm under one of Charlie's elbows and helps steady him into position. He sees the question in Phelan's face.

"The helicopter and the kids are back on the ground, once they heard Charlie was located." Miller is gentle with Charlie's leg as he lifts it into the sleigh. "Your legs must be even more tired than mine were after a night's worth of snowmobiling." His voice lowers a notch when he can tell Phelan is not yet satisfied. "Bart thought they might head off to South Pass and see if they can help there."

"I'm sure he did." Finn's voice is loud enough for anyone to hear.

Phelan doesn't know how much of Nik's family life Jaye might be privy to, but she quickly takes command again and points at him first. "Phelan, you jump in there with your dad. Finn, tie your snowshoes on the back. Then you and Nik can both ride out on Woody's sled."

Finn leaps to carry out instructions. Nik makes it up the hill carrying two packs of gear. Phelan doesn't move.

"Woody, can you give Nik your snowmobile helmet and ride Barney back? You can lead Bailey. I've got a dog down the hill to bring out. Phelan, I'll keep your snowshoes."

Nik drops the packs on the floor of the sleigh between Charlie's boots. She pats his shoulder.

"A dog?" Phelan looks at Nik.

Charlie answers. "I found her dog."

"Well, finally. Excellent job." He's speaking to Charlie but looking at Nik.

She shakes her head, puts a finger to her lips.

"Well," he says, as he pulls the blanket around Charlie. "This escapade better teach you to behave in the future. You won't have all of us around to help out." Phelan is glad he had the connections to get here. Maybe having this crisis now is good, if it teaches Nik where her priorities should be. Clearly, it isn't within Charlie's capacity to be learning things at this point.

Charlie isn't warmed all the way up yet. His eyes return to worried. "You'll all be in Australia, right?"

Phelan watches the series of reactions. Jaye glances at Woody. Nik adjusts Charlie's scarf around his neck. "I'm not leaving you, Dad."

"Africa." Finn corrects him but looks at his father, frowning.

"For you." Phelan keeps both his hands on his father's shoulders, steadying himself to talk with his son. "For me, though, Charlie's right. I'm headed for Australia."

The word holds an ocean's worth of surface tension on Finn's face, and Phelan needs to dive into the breakers. He can hear them crash. They'll have time to talk when this is over. He'll have to bring Finn back to his car.

"Both so far away." Charlie looks confused and sad.

Phelan wonders if Nik is to be trusted. He's going to Australia. End of story. "But we're here right now." He reaches out and claps Finn on the shoulder, man to man. "And you can tell Finn about my new venture while you ride back to the gas station." He motions for Finn to climb in the sleigh with Charlie.

Woody hangs his helmet on the snowmobile handlebar for Nik.

She leans close to her dad and brushes his cheek with a kiss. "You are incredible, you know. Finding the dog for me after all this time." She pauses. "Maybe I should be the one to bring Mariah out. What do you think?"

He gives a ready nod. "The boys got me." He stretches an arm around Finn as he folds in next to him. "I'll be warm in no time. Just don't look at her, and she'll follow you."

"Okay. Your boys are good guys." Nik looks across the sleds. "Woody can drive you all back to the station. He'll make sure you get some hot food. "

Jaye grabs her arm and pulls her away. She's muttering, but loudly. "You've been up all night, worrying about your father. Jump on a snowmobile and go back with him."

Nik pulls her arm out of Jaye's grip. "You were up all night directing a rescue operation. A successful one. The adrenaline will power my legs back to the store. Trust me."

Phelan almost laughs.

Jaye's voice tries for firm, but the situation is starting to get beyond her. "Charlie needs to get to a hospital for a check-over, except the road's not open yet."

Woody speaks up. "Helicopter could take two out. Beryl and Bart and whoever should go with Charlie."

Phelan considers this option. Convenient for Bart. No need to face Nik. He'll stay at the gas station so he can pay everyone for their expenses. "Finn can call back here once Dad's been checked. As soon as the roads open, I'll take Nik's car to Teewinot to pick them up." He's more than fine if Nik stays behind with all her locals. She can think about consequences for a change and find her own damn ride home.

Jaye looks around, trying to sort out the change of plans. Nik is smug, leaving their father to the youngest one, as usual favoring some four-legged creature over her own blood.

"I can handle Bart." Finn lifts his chin and stares at his father. "We're set." He slaps the rusted side of the sleigh.

A smile flickers across Nik's face, though she keeps her eyes on the snow fluttering again through the air.

Jaye claps her gloves together. "Let's get this show on the road, then. Charlie's shivering again. Thomas, Phelan can go with you, I suppose." The adrenaline is leaving her voice already, but she soldiers on, keying her mic. "Russell, is the helicopter still there?"

"One sec." Russell forgets that everyone can hear him as he yells. "Bart, don't leave yet." He apparently was not waiting nearby. "What's up?"

"Charlie and Finn need a lift to the Teewinot clinic."

"Copy that. I'll let them know. Everyone else good?"

"Relieved and yes. I'll ride out with the horses. Miller will share our other news."

Phelan hears Emory's voice in the background. Even the kid is hoping they've got Nik's dog. He ignores instructions again and climbs on behind Miller, listening as the sleds chug into life. Jaye undoubtedly wants him to get up close with the man he tried to drag through a gossip mill. He hopes Thomas hasn't pieced together who he is.

Jaye looks at Nik. "I'll wait for you?"

Phelan can hear her waning self-confidence. Or she's just tired.

Nik turns away. "Mariah and the horses won't be a good mix. You go ahead." Without saying any more, she drops into the dark shadows under the trees, obviously too embarrassed to say thank-you before everyone heads in their separate directions. Phelan will have to do that too.

Zolo

Gone, yes, in flash and crash of fear, in scramble back to Tess. Tall-eared one left behind, tied to fiddle man. Breathing. Remembering.

Zolo doesn't doubt. Song comes from beyond him. Singing links times together, and people. His people in different times, singing different ways. High desert's swells are rolling rhythm, pattern. Beyond fear, Mariah's song frees forgetfulness across sage. Memories behind him, he runs toward today.

Thin sun streams song warm into flesh and into bones, song like meltwater dancing through pebbles. He streams whitely across white sage, returning. Black horse snorts, settles. Zolo sleeps in sun, and he twitches. Her back to his back, mouse-colored mare mirrors his movement, flicking ear. Tess mirrors his dreams. Freedom, in bonding.

She flies, wings beating with strange, ancient pattern of sandhill cranes. Dawn horse flying into spring sun. She welcomes rain's softening, its chill. Her nose quivers. Cold rain touches prairie in herds of hoofbeats, drumming awake unseen green. Believing needs no eyes. Her eyes closed, she hears hungers healing.

He yips, soft like a pup in pile of pups dreaming. Snow flies, and he leaps skyward, snapping fat flakes in his mouth. Hunger melts into him, flowing. He flows across desert, chasing gravity, ocean of hot rock below, sea of salt far away, in time, in distance. Piss of sharp-toothed, horse-sized cat smells like juniper. Tracks of cat-sized horses shine in starlight, reflect from long-covered sands. He sniffs at them and follows.

Nikki

Nik slips and skids down the hill to the wolf. She lands near the cold remains of Finn's fire and sees something she missed when he was pulling grass for the flame. Next to the flattened outline of Charlie's body, she makes out prints. Dog prints, not wolf. A white hair snagged to a twig. She looks at Mariah, then back to the ground.

The Scent of Distant Family

Two voices raised the howl that brought them to Charlie. She knows now which one kept him warm, alive. She swallows and pushes her hands against her eyes. A deep breath fills her chest and then loosens, slowly, under the trees.

Crab walking, hunched over and sideways, she eases to where she'd tied the rope. The wolf comes along readily enough now that everyone else is gone. At the top of the hill, Nik stops to strap on snowshoes, adjusting the binding to her smaller feet. In the distance, Jaye's two horses stride steadily after the rescuers. At least the snowmobile trail is packed now, though the top layer is loose as beach sand. The sun should be shining on the day's success, but shards of obstinate cloud hang over its light.

A fog-colored landscape still hides the dog Charlie thinks he's rescued. The one who rescued him.

Nik lurches, and the rope in her hand goes tight. She straightens, doesn't look back. She croons musical reassurance for the wolf. *Mariah blows the stars around and sends the clouds a-flyin'* .... She listens to the sound of snowshoes scrunching. She can't hear Mariah's feet, but a fuzzy shadow glides along, and she watches that, sideways. Maggie taught her to sing count-down songs to outwait a fish at a hole in the ice or to finish a long day's hike up steep mountain slopes. *The ants go marching one by one* ....

Twenty years ago is a long time. She remembers Robyn had siblings. She doesn't remember their names. Australian towns all have such strange names, hard to remember. But in Australia, Brown was almost as common a name as Robyn. She didn't like being named after a bird that never flew over the Australian landscape. Her parents thought it might have advantages. Nik tried to find her, years ago.

A flash of anger—frustration? fear?—drains what little energy she still has. Her legs pause. She wonders what Australian cousins could have taught him, when he was a lonely Teewinot kid. Geeking out because facts wouldn't give him that *look*. Data added value; they didn't subtract self-worth. Would cousins teach him the smell of eucalyptus? The sound of kangaroos moving across grasslands? Her legs move again, across the snow.

Charlie still believes Robyn died on the way to the airport. He doesn't need to know anything different. But she can do this. Tell Finn that they lied.

She listens to her heart, to snowshoes scattering crystals in a tide-like hiss. The minutes spread out across the steppe. Unvarying light offers no sense of time. Years collapse, ice into a flooding river. Robyn liked the name Jannali. A grandmother, maybe. If she changed her name, then she didn't change her mind about Finn not finding out.

They tromp along, breathing. Nik counts her breaths. She remembers holding Robyn's hand, Robyn giving birth. The breathtaking pain of it all. She can't go back on her promise if it will bring back so much pain. A past life Robyn—Jannali?—could have walled off.

Phelan was part of one secret, part of protecting Finn from thinking his mother abandoned him. Her feet stop, heavy in the snowshoes. Phelan finds it easy to believe his lifestyle in Teewinot is better than what Finn might have had in Australia. He found it easy to believe Robyn was dead, once she was gone.

Zolo isn't dead, but he, too, is gone. Nik glances at the wolf. Here. Finn is here, not Robyn, and she's protected him for twenty years. Helped him embrace his potential. Walking, her breath grows heavier now, black night catching her from around the other side of the planet. Years catching her. Her legs step, step, snowshoes scraping audibly over the fresh crust. Movement scraping at memory. Her eyes half-close, her head in the past. She hears Robyn's voice. *Promise me*, from a traumatized nineteen-year-old on a foreign continent, pregnant as hell.

But now, if Phelan finds her, if she agrees to meet her son. In Finn's mind, Nik would become the kind of person who steals someone else's child, who steals someone else's motherhood. Thief of his culture. Someone not to be trusted. The litany of unappetizing risks offers a nervous tempo that's moved her legs across the past months, the past miles. She and Mariah walk, the wolf maintaining just the slightest slack, with the farthest possible separation. Wolves have great endurance. Already Nik must endure Finn's distrust. Zolo's distrust. Though she meant well.

If she sits for a minute, maybe Mariah will come closer. She lowers herself all the way onto the snow, stretched along her side, cradling her head in the crook of an elbow. Her knees feel stronger, pressed against the earth. She can do this one thing right. Bring Mariah out, with a future, a family. Charlie proud of them both. They will be there for each other, in that future.

Air leans heavy against her eyelids. Her weight sinks, depressing snow around her, seeking that buried heat so far inside the earth. Her shoulder blades curl forward, as if seeking to hide from the mistakes collecting around her.

She doesn't look at Mariah but listens to her settle on the snow, not any closer. Her breath is silent. She doesn't pant or wail or whine. The world is too dangerous for her to run wild. She's too familiar with people for her own good. Nik eases down further, her spine resting along forgiving snow. She longs for Zolo's forgiveness. She's hopeful for Mariah's growing trust.

Jaye

The sky holds only the same endless cloud, erasing evidence of the sun's journey. Beryl's helicopter lifts into the overcast, two separated generations of Delaney men strapped in. Jaye loads the horses into their trailer and slings hay nets up for them. By the time she gets inside, Russell reports the highway is clear in two directions. Thomas and the boys tighten the tie-downs on the sleds, ready to head for Cheyenne. Miller takes Phelan out to the Bug, and she's relieved when he's gone. A skeleton crew remains at Rim Rendezvous, eager to see Charlie's wolf.

Russell, with Emory's rabbit draped around the back of his neck, gives Jaye's shoulder a soft punch. "Excellent job today. You can be proud of yourself."

She passes by Guthrie's pen without looking, lets a held breath out, and steadies her hands before filling a mug from the reflective silver carafe. She imagines Nik needs coffee by now too. But Nik sent her away.

Nik let her whole family take off without her, Australia and Africa somewhere on their horizons. Said not a word about her husband showing up, and leaving again, with a Hollywood star. She scared her dog away too. Those were the only tears Jaye saw her shed, right before they discovered Charlie and Mariah.

The search for the missing dog almost killed Nik's father. Jaye thinks it unlikely that she will try again. Much more likely that she'll hole up at the house in Dust, pretending that Charlie found the dog she's been trying to save. Stop answering emails. Be done with her exploits on the high desert. Forget the people she met during her long string of failures and expect that they'll forget about her too.

Jaye still doesn't trust Phelan, despite the newsworthy tips about his shady clients, despite quitting that work to head for whatever's in Australia. Maybe he's just in love. At least Sage Winds no longer has his attention.

Miller stands next to Emory, who brought her telescope and now is learning the names of the Neaippeh peaks as a few slowly become visible from the windows. Woody is her expert instructor. Jaye bends to rub ointment on Polenta's paw pads. The gas station carries an oatmeal and aloe blend for people who like to skijor with their shaggy friends. She sniffs it, then smears some around her own windburned lips.

"Why aren't they moving?" The child's high voice cuts through Jaye's exhaustion.

"What?" She pushes upright, leans over the telescope. Nik and Mariah aren't far, but Emory's right. They aren't moving.

"Just taking a rest?" Russell gauges her concern level.

She isn't one for hysterics. But she knew better than to let Nik talk her into leaving. She keeps the self-disgust out of her thick voice. "Won't hurt if I hike out and join them for the last bit." She doesn't want any more hurt.

She traces her way across the snow. Nik is sprawled on the ground, eyes closed despite the noise Jaye's passage makes. The wolf's muzzle lifts from her front paws as Jaye approaches.

"Nik—what are you doing?" Jaye's voice is too close to panic. Mariah backs away, the rope going tight around Nik's clenched hand. Jaye drops to her knees now, shakes Nik's shoulder. "Wake up, honey."

Nik rolls her head back and forth against the snow and meets Jaye's eyes. Only for a second.

"Can you get up? Can I help you?"

13

Nikki

Her eyes open again, half-focused on someone who might hear her confession, her confusion. "Phelan still believes her boyfriend jilted her when she got pregnant." One gloved hand digs, aimless, in the snow.

Jaye doesn't understand. "Nik, you can't stay in the snow like that."

She can stay like this forever. The snow supports her, like she's supported Robyn. All these years. "She never had a boyfriend." Jaye frowns at her. Nik knows she has said too much. She's known too much. A weight crushes her deeper against the ground, a human weight, inhuman, taking her air away, her innocence. Taking her big-hearted, vulnerable, foreign friend to a helpless place. A hopeless place. Leaving her with a memory that wouldn't fade because it's attached to someone who continues to grow. Her fingers close around the rope wrapped across her palm. A night-dark wall of white snow consumes her.

"Nik, stay with me here. Mariah is with you. We want to get her to Woody's, okay?"

"Phelan's gone, isn't he?" She needs to tell him. Robyn deserves this much, the privacy that revealing her secret might give. "He'll find her, in Australia. I can't keep my promise and still protect her." Silence wraps Nik's fragmented worries.

Then Jaye pieces things together. "Finn's mother was raped?"

Her eyes clench tight. Jaye said it—she did not say it. Her stomach clenches tighter. Phelan might treat his son differently. He might use this information against Finn, against Robyn. She doesn't trust him. Her own brother. But it's the only way she can think of to convince him to respect Robyn's needs.

Jaye speaks, soft as snow drifting. "Australia's a big place. You don't have to tell him anything. Let him look."

Nik hears a belly dragging along snow. Her eyes flick open. Mariah is at her side. The wolf pulls closer without standing up. Phelan has a lot of resources. "I've waited too long already. I have to stop him."

Jaye's voice is tight, curt. "You aren't in charge of him. Come on, let's get you two somewhere dry."

She's unraveling. "I have to do something. Everything's coming out wrong." She can't predict what Phelan will do, or Finn, if Phelan tells him. She can't get Zolo into a trap, to safety, and the winter isn't stopping. She can't stop the divorce from coming or Charlie's mind from leaving.

Jaye's hand at her hip. "Mariah needs to get some food. Are you ready?"

Walking might loosen the hold Nik's mistakes have on her neck. Jaye helps her upright. Their steps crack the crust, again and again, loud in the still air. Like promises, breaking. Like trust.

When they get to Woody's, she sees dry grass under the camper. "Mariah might feel safe there."

"Good idea." Jaye lets go of her elbow and nods. "Tie her up, then we'll go in and get some soup, okay?"

Nik crawls under and Mariah follows. Her collar has no name or phone number or tags. A safe bet—no microchip. "Can you find some food for her?" She eases down into the dead grass, giving the wolf space. Like she gave Robyn the space she wanted. Space to build her own necessary walls. The silence Finn needed for protection—at least for a while. Until he started filling the silence with stories.

The Scent of Distant Family

"Come with me."

"Jaye. Mariah and I need some time. I'm warm under here now." She needs to figure out when to tell Phelan. How to tell Phelan. Going inside feels unbearable.

"You know Robyn made her call, right? It isn't your choice." Jaye's sigh shows her frustration. "I won't be long."

Mariah turns in a circle and settles on the dirt. Nik sees a purpled streak of fresh scab where the hair is gone at the top of her hip. Her whistle is a whisper. "Lucky that bullet just grazed by." Robyn's wound might have scarred up, healed over. Or not.

She closes her eyes. Jaye can't know all the thoughts that have haunted her, the possible ramifications of remaining silent, as promised. She counts her breaths, listens for Mariah's breath, but her ears aren't good enough. She drags her eyes open again. Yellow eyes avoid hers, gaze across hazy horizon. What comes next, unknown. The dark wolf—or wolf hybrid—seems undisturbed by not knowing.

Jaye

Jaye nibbles on a jalapeño popper, cream cheese oozing out its deep-fried sides. She's left Nik outside, again. Nik pushed her away, again. Woody makes up a dish of something for Mariah. Miller leans over his daughter, sprawled on the floor drawing on the back of a postcard. Emory finishes and pushes herself up. She walks over and offers the card to Russell. He gives her a hug before turning the sketched side toward Jaye to see. "Lepus, the hare. A lesser-known constellation. Young lady is well acquainted with the night sky. Might be a future snowplow driver here."

"Ah, hence the telescope. You were smart to alert us."

Emory cradles Cygnus against her chest, rubbing her chin along his ears. "Russell guarded him from Guthrie so I could keep watch."

Jaye's heart races, and her breath gets short. That damn snake. Emory has a reason to fear Guthrie, and doesn't. She has no reason, but does. She hates this. She is stronger than this. Illogical. She is. No—not her, the phobia. She forces herself to stare into the long, open-topped cardboard box with sand and straw, a free-form sculpture of dead sage providing useless hiding cover. Innocuous, Guthrie is. Terrifyingly legless. Almost the same length but only a quarter the width of her own forearm.

Russell nods at her, waves her closer to the little boa. Sweat starts from her pores, right at her hairline. Even behind her knees she can feel it seep out, drip. This is absurd. Jaye pulls her breath in through tight lips. She focuses her gaze on the snake. A gentle convulsion, a curve of motion, catches her by surprise, stops her breath in her throat, lifts bile from her gut. What an unknowable thing, how a snake manages to move, even swim. Unknowable, how other people think. How someone else might want to experience what the ranch is wanting to share. Unknowable, what other people feel. She can't imagine what Finn's mother felt. But she can imagine her choice.

Unmoving, she watches the snake's eyes, which don't seem to notice her at all. What a snake might see: far beyond a single person, or lifetime. Ouroboros, spinning. In a constantly changing world, maybe Guthrie sees the invisible constant. Invisible connection, everywhere. Easy to imagine what Nik is feeling. Disconnected. Severed from the successful self she once thought she owned forever.

Sun pushes through the clouds, finally, pulling her head up. Glazed crust blinds her eyes for a second. The full Neaippeh range sheds the endless gloom. In its spaciousness, Jaye's breaths even out. Her hands unclench, and the skin over her knuckles regains blood flow.

The Scent of Distant Family

Her attention swings toward Guthrie again, testing. Her heart beats only double its usual speed. Better than triple. Improvement.

Russell sticks his phone back in his pocket. "That was the sanctuary in Colorado. We're in luck. One of their oldest wolves died recently. They have room for her."

Woody hands Jaye a plastic container with eggs and potato and hamburger mixed together. He studies her face. "Gonna take some guts to tell Nik that."

Nodding at Guthrie, just a thin width of cardboard away from her, Russell smiles. "Looks like you'll be able to handle it."

Woody, too, registers her success. "Look at you. Not that she's frightening."

Her snort sounds distinctly horselike. "Oh, but she is." The bottom of the plate is warm on her cold, cold palms. She looks around at her friends. She has something she can offer Nik. But every offer stands the risk of being rebuffed. "Get through a storm quicker if you walk into it. Grandma's wisdom." She heads for the door, sending a quick request to her grandmother through the ether. Courage, please.

Nikki

She sets the food down in front of Mariah and eases backward on her hands and knees until she bumps against a frozen tire. Hunger outweighs the wolf's wariness, and large gulps make short work of Woody's concoction.

"She'll sleep now, don't you think? Especially if you leave her be?" Jaye squats in the snow beyond the dry edge, peering into the dark.

Nik hears tension in her voice but balks anyway. "I don't want to leave her."

"She's not your missing hound. Charlie will figure that out, too, once he's more recovered."

"She needs a home. I can give her one." Nik tries to keep the quaver out of her voice. Tries to pass it off as a shiver.

"You need some food. And real heat. Everyone's waiting for you."

All that everyone's already done for her is a burden she can't carry. She can't face them, not all together like that. "You could bring me some food out here. She's been alone so long."

"Nik, she's been hungry too. I don't think you want to eat in front of her."

"Then I'll share my food with her. We'll be good."

"She's a wolf. You know better than that. My knees are starting to lock up. Please. Come back with me, so I don't have to call the troops to drag you in." Jaye's voice hints of a grin, but a larger portion sounds like gritting teeth.

She doesn't want to imagine being manhandled from under the camper. With a last long look at Mariah, Nik crawls out and stands up next to Jaye. They step toward Woody's.

Only a few strides away from the camper, Jaye puts a hand under her elbow as if to ensure her continued progress. "Keeping her isn't her best option, you know."

"She might be a hybrid. Definitely not wild." Nik shakes her elbow free.

"But not domestic either. Clearly. You can't guarantee Charlie won't do something that scares her, sets her off."

Nik's heart lands like a boulder on her feet, and she quits moving. "We can't just click open her collar and pretend we've never seen her."

Jaye touches her back and faces them both toward the station again. "Come on. People want to congratulate you for finding Charlie and for saving Mariah." She takes a deep breath. "Russell's found a place that takes in wolves and hybrids, lets them live more like they were meant to."

Now Nik's teeth grind hard together, her jaw tight, tear ducts loose. She swipes her hand across her face. To lose Mariah too. Damn it. Her chest constricts. The lonely house in Dust will echo with Charlie's confusions. Her remaining role: matriarch of nothing.

Jaye sucks in another deep breath, stands motionless beside her. "Around here, we're used to figuring out who our real family is. You've got one in there, if you want it." Her chin points at the station.

Nik looks at her feet. She's indebted beyond all possibility of repayment. Jaye tugs on her again, firm. She lets herself be propelled into the gas station, guided through the far door into Woody's place. Lets people's gentle cheers and applause blow around her like a spring snowstorm, sure to melt away soon. She stands alone in front of them and manages to choke out her thanks, her glance flitting across the assembled faces.

Woody pries her tight fists open and slips a wide mug of potato soup between them. When she perches on a stool, sipping, he keeps a hand between her shoulder blades. Like she might fall over otherwise. Her hunger gapes like all the empty holes in her life. Soup pours down her throat, and she knows there's no stopping the loneliness flowing her way.

Woody's hand stays steady, though his words interrupt her rush of emotion. "Easy goes it there, friend. You'll burn yourself." He rubs her upper arm with his other hand, friction for warmth, for sanity. A sense of the physical to catch on. She slows down enough to meet his eyes. But she can't tolerate the kindness in his smile.

Emory stands in front of a telescope by the window, and she turns to Nik, then to Jaye. "You gotta see this."

The two accidentally jostle each other, and Emory moves out of their way. Jaye waves her forward, and Nik steps up to the ocular. "The horses." Her words ride a hushed out-breath. Tangled mane blows off an arched neck as the black rears. The big bay glows as if hennaed with liquid sunlight. In the face of their aching enchantment, her hunger vanishes.

Jaye tries to see across the prairie heights unaided. "Tess's herd?"

"That's her stallion, I'd say." She pauses. "And a white—dog. Not wolf. They look like . . . they're playing?" She backs away, needing Jaye's confirmation. Her hands land on Emory's shoulders, as they both gaze outward. Her heart stretches across the snowy distance. For once, Zolo doesn't look scared.

Bending to the scope, Jaye describes the herd. "The Sentinel's our hambone. The bay mare, ahh, bulky with the next generation. There's the old roan—and Tess."

Nik sees the grulla, head high, looking back at Woody's as if she knows she's got their attention. She can't decipher the message in that look, but she knows there is one.

"Your little Razzle?" Russell squints in the sun.

Jaye keeps her eyes on the herd. "Razzle too. Right behind Tess. They're watching us watch them, I think."

Emory, with her young eyes, picks up the narration. "Then that's Zolo, Nik's dog? Playing?"

Jaye turns the telescope back to Nik. "They *are* playing." She faces the others. "By all rights, wild horses should've stomped that dog on sight, but they're playing. He bows down, and the black chases him."

Nik speaks from the scope without taking her eyes off them. "He rolled in the snow, and—get this—now Razzle is rolling."

Woody stands next to her, shoulders not quite touching, for a turn to watch. "Never seen anything like that. Not with a wild herd."

The Scent of Distant Family

She slides onto the floor next to the tripod legs. Jaye squats and takes both of her hands.

Nik stares forward, hands limp. "I can't bear to trap him." Her voice is a whisper.

"Deciding not to do something can be the best decision." Jaye meets her eyes. "He's survived the worst of the winter. And he apparently survived being shot at."

"Which might explain some things." Nik squeezes Jaye's hand. "They look so—"

The whole room seems to pause, take a breath. Jaye doesn't try to finish Nik's sentence. "It'll be a lot easier to keep tabs on Zolo with a herd of horses to watch for. He'll be famous around here." Her voice carries a flavor of admiration. A taste of reassurance.

Woody adds an idea to that thought. "I can start a Zolo sighting page online. Emory can share it with all the kids at school."

"You'll regain his confidence, in time." Emory is all for it. She has faith. "I'll put out a jar for donations too. Gas money for the drive."

Nik's face flames, and she thinks about her cold resting spot on the snow. People just want to help. It's part of being human. They aren't just helping her but Zolo too. And Zolo helped Charlie, in his own way.

Jaye jiggles their still-joined hands, her palms warm. "You and Charlie can stay at the Ranch as much as you want. Lots of room at the lodge. And elk burger, or bones, for sharing."

Nik extracts her hands and pushes hair out of her burning eyes. She feels like she's turning inside out. Polenta lays at her feet and rolls on her back, wriggling, her open mouth a relieved smile. Nik stands up and fills her lungs with air, refills her almost emptied promises. Polenta pushes her nose into her hand. What the universe has in mind for Robyn, or for Finn, is beyond her. She and Charlie can keep trying to win back Zolo's trust. So different from trapping him, thinking he isn't smart enough to have choices. Her fingers burrow in Polenta's hair. She imagines how well the sound of a fiddle will carry across the sage.

Miller rests his chin on Emory's head as they watch the horses, transfixed. Four interlocked arms cradle Cygnus against her chest. "We all have our own journeys," he murmurs.

She still doesn't know the story of how his wife ended up in prison or how long she has to stay. She hopes he'll bring his daughter over to Dust sometimes. Nik knows a pond along the Yotay where they could see overwintering trumpeters. They can talk about birds, and Emory can show her meteor showers. A gentle rabbit has given the girl so much strength. Nik hopes Gabon's whales will sing their ancient songs for Finn. She rubs a hand up and down her forearm. "I guess we can't know where those journeys end."

Russell stands beside her, both of them staring north. "Maybe they don't." He looks at her with his now-familiar cockeyed grin. She gets the feeling he would be perfectly comfortable with Charlie talking about Maggie in present tense. Her dad might get to meet Russell's little owl after all. She pictures them laughing together over a card game at Jaye's.

She thinks of another way she might help Jaye too. "I can write grant applications for projects at the Ranch. While we're hanging around. There's lots of interest right now in funding sustainability experiments." She shakes her hair back. "It isn't begging. It's doing the work someone else wishes they could do. You have the place, and the energy, to make things happen."

Jaye looks surprised, and surprisingly grateful.

Again, Woody directs Nik's attention through the telescope to Zolo's herd. His hand touches her cheek, moving her head to the right angle. Horses snatch at the tallest grasses poking above the crust even as they trot, loose and relaxed, across a low, flat-topped mesa. At the back, Zolo bounds like a pronghorn beside the thick-legged Sentinel. Tess leads them beyond the near horizon and out of view.

In the room's sudden silence, Nik hears her mother's low, sweet hum. She straightens her back, then one elbow crooks through Jaye's elbow, one hand settles on Woody's arm. "Looks like life doesn't read our reference manuals." For the first time in what feels like a glacial epoch, she hears herself laugh. With a sharp blue crackle, a block of aromatic pine shifts in the fireplace, scattering cinders and warmth.

Printed in the USA
CPSIA information can be obtained
at www.ICGtesting.com
CBHW030028170824
13309CB00002B/225